Gary Kemble is ⊔ortlisted
for the Ned Kell〟 ⊔ction. His award-
winning short fi⊔ ⊔n published in magazines
and anthologies in ⊔⊔ralia and abroad. He is a two-time
winner of the 'One Book Many Brisbanes' short story
competition, and several of his stories have been republished
in 'best of' collections including *The Year's Best Australian
Fantasy and Horror*.

His journalistic career has included stints with local
newspapers, national magazines and online publications in
Australia and the UK.

garykemble.com / @garykemble

GARY KEMBLE

BAD
BLOOD

echo

echo

Echo
A division of Bonnier Publishing Australia
534 Church Street, Richmond
Victoria 3121 Australia
www.echopublishing.com.au

First published 2016. This edition published 2017.

Cover design by Alissa Dinallo
Page design and typesetting by Shaun Jury
Image credits: Felicia Simion / Trevillion Images

Typeset in Garamond Premier Pro

Printed in Australia at Griffin Press.
Only wood grown from sustainable regrowth forests is used in the
manufacture of paper found in this book.

National Library of Australia Cataloguing-in-Publication entry
   Creator: Kemble, Gary, author.
   Title: Bad Blood / Gary Kemble
   Edition: 2nd edition
   ISBN: 9781760406974 (paperback)
   ISBN: 9781760402969 (epub)
   ISBN: 9781760402976 (mobi)
   Subjects: Suspense fiction
   Dewey Number: A823.4

🐦 bonnierau
📷 bonnierpublishingau
📘 bonnierpublishingau

for Aurora, Eamon and Amelia

PROLOGUE

He clutched the hammer and stared around the darkened room. His eyes caught the mirror.

'What the fuck are you staring at, motherfucker?'

She was right. The fucker was trying to steal his soul. It looked like him, but it wasn't him.

Smash it!

She always knew what to do. He laid into the mirror before he had time to think about what he was doing. He squinted as the mirror shattered, pieces of broken glass cascading across his feet and the floorboards. He stood there panting as the sweat cooled on his bare chest. He scratched absently at the hairs there, reached around to his back. He could still feel her mark.

'How do you like that, fucker?' he muttered.

It's in the bedroom!

He strode out of the dining room, barely flinching as a shard of glass dug into the sole of his foot. He limped down the hallway but didn't stop to pull it out. With each step he painted the floor with blood. First a dot, then a smear, then a full footprint. He could feel the demon's eyes watching him through the walls. But not for long. Oh no, not for long.

He stopped just inside the doorway of the bedroom and saw the demon sneering back at him on the other side of the room. He looked down, noticing his foot for the first time. Blood on the carpet. *Sienna will kill me.*

He's going to eat your soul.

He let out a low grunt, flinging the hammer across the room. It glanced off the sideboard, missing the mirror entirely but knocking over a bottle of his wife's perfume.

'Fuck!'

Shh...

He closed his eyes and saw her staring back at him, the way she always did before she released him. His breathing slowed. He gained control of himself.

'It's just fucking carpet,' he muttered, limping across the room. He glared for a moment at the thing on the other side of the mirror, smirking as though he was some sort of fucking imbecile.

'Ugh!' He slammed his foot into the mirror. The antique dresser rocked back on its spindly legs, then came forward again. Drawers opened and fell to the floor, spilling his wife's lingerie and jewellery. How much had he spent on that lot, and then she still couldn't do it for him? Not like Mistress. He never knew why. Even Mistress kept the reason from him for a long time. It was the man in the mirror. No, not a man. A demon. Stealing his breath while he was sleeping. Draining him and then fucking his wife.

'Motherfucker!' he cried, voice breaking as he raised his leg a second time, smashing the mirror and cracking the backing. *Don't make them like they used to*, he thought, and hysterical laugher bubbled inside him.

'I'm going to burn you,' he whispered. His bare leg caught on the splintered mirror backing, tearing the flesh above his ankle. He fell back onto the bed, panting. Blood oozed slowly from his wounds. Dark spots danced before his eyes and pain lanced up his legs, but then the black spots became Mistress's eyes again, and the pain went away.

Your daughter's room. Hurry!

He leapt, ignoring the glass splinters that sliced into his feet. A pair of his wife's undies stuck to his bloody left foot and he dragged them down the hallway.

Carrie's Room. The sign was surrounded by flower stickers and topped with a purple unicorn dancing on a rainbow. He paused for a moment, trying to reconcile what he was doing with what it would mean. He'd never see Carrie again. Never read her a bedtime story. Never comfort her after a nightmare.

NIGHTMARE! YOU DON'T KNOW WHAT A NIGHTMARE IS!

He flinched, jamming his hands against his ears, waited for the sting of her crop across his back, the touch of her knives.

Get the fucking mirror and smash it. Do you want that demon reading your daughter bedtime stories?

'No, Mistress.' He pushed the door open, not realising his hand was bloody until he saw the handprint, black in the moonlight. He checked the bedside table. No. Under the bed. No.

Hurry!

'Yes, Mistress!'

He crawled around the room, searching. His bloody feet had dragged pieces of glass into the room, which now stuck in his knees. Splotches of blood dotted the carpet. He found the hand mirror in her wardrobe, picked it up and looked into it. The demon was showing its true self: a pale face smeared with blood.

'You don't scare me.'

He punched the reflection. The handle snapped and the shattered mirror bounced under his daughter's bed. He clawed it out. The thing was laughing at him. Laughing! He raised the small mirror over his head and slammed it against the corner of the white chest of drawers. Glass shards sprayed across Carrie's bed. The mess, the mess. For a moment, sanity pressed forwards.

They won't be back until tomorrow. And it will all be over by then. Now, collect the pieces and put them in the bath.

He nodded, supplicant, imagining himself kneeling before her. It would all be over soon. He scraped the shards of glass off the bed, not noticing the stings as they dug into his hands. He staggered through the house to the bathroom and dropped the bloodied diamonds into the bath.

By the time he'd collected the glass from around the house, the hallway was slick with blood. Little light filtered through the small bathroom window. He dumped the last of the glass into the bath, brushing his gut and driving a shard into his belly button. The exquisite pain drew him out of his stupor for a moment. He stood on the cold, bloody tiles, listening to wind in the trees. Wishing his wife would come home early. *I don't have to do this. I don't have to do any of this.*

Get in the bath.

He stepped in before he could think about what he was doing. When he did, he went to step out but her voice was close in his ear again. So close it tickled his flesh. He could smell her perfume.

Sit.

He sat. A large piece of glass sliced into the fatty underside of his leg. He hissed in pain, but didn't get back up. His wounds pounded.

Eat.

'No, please...'

Every piece of mirror has a piece of your soul in it. You need to reclaim it. You need to eat the glass.

'Please, Mistress... please...'

He stared down at the shards. A thousand eyes stared back at him. A thousand hungry mouths, tainted with his blood. He watched blood ooze from his feet, his hands, his belly. Without realising, he'd picked up a shard of glass. Just a small one. An appetiser. He snorted laughter. It turned to tears and he cried hard. He dropped his head between his knees and watched bloody snot drip from his nose.

EAT IT!

He cried, harder than ever. 'Sienna. Ca-Carrie. I... I...'

He put the first piece of mirror into his mouth and swallowed.

CHAPTER 1

Harry Hendrick saw the fist coming but was too slow to do anything about it. He pivoted, raising his knee in a futile bid to reduce his opponent's reach. His head rocked back and black stars bloomed behind his eyes.

He shook his head then backed off, bare feet dancing on the mat. Harry felt the Afghan tattoo on the back of his neck warm and welcomed the sensation. It was like an old friend visiting.

His eyes fluttered slightly. He shook the sweat from his face as Adrian advanced, looking to maintain momentum. Time slowed. Harry feinted a step-kick, drawing Adrian's hands away from his padded body, then switched his feet and drove into Adrian's ribs with a roundhouse kick, yelling his kat-ra to maximise power. Harry felt the force of the blow all the way up his leg. It would have floored a smaller man. But Harry's heavy-set opponent just winced, grunted, and pressed on with a flurry of punches into thin air; an obvious attempt to divert Harry from what was coming next.

A blur of movement. He felt the sweaty cotton of Adrian's uniform. Harry knew what he was doing, but only after he'd done it. It was instinct now. The ends of

Adrian's red belt flailed, as did his arms and legs, as Harry took him down hard enough to drive the air from Adrian's lungs. Harry rolled to deal the final strike. The flat of his hand sliced through the air, driving towards his opponent's throat. He delivered another bellowing kat-ra, but managed to stay his hand millimetres from Adrian's Adam's apple.

'Break!'

Harry blinked. Jim, his instructor, stood above them, eyes darting from Harry to Adrian and back again, assessing the situation, possible injuries, the intent, the potential for this to flare up. Not for the first time, Jim's handlebar moustache and stocky build reminded Harry of a villain in a spaghetti western.

'Ade! You okay?' Harry asked.

Adrian nodded, offering Harry a wary stare.

Jim turned on him. 'Harry – push-ups. No take-downs, remember?'

'Sorry, Jim.'

After class Harry and Adrian helped pack up the mats while Jim checked forms for new students and packed away his EFTPOS machine. The 'dojo' was transformed back to a state school room. Desks, chairs, whiteboard. Harry offered Adrian another apology as they carried the gear back to Jim's RAV4. Adrian waved it away. In ones and twos the students bowed their way out. Harry pulled on his jacket and went to follow them.

'Harry! Can I see you?' Jim shut his briefcase, gave him a penetrating stare.

'I'm sorry,' Harry said. 'Sometimes I lose...'

'It's not that. I just can't believe that someone who's been doing martial arts less than a year would know those moves. You sure you haven't been training somewhere else?'

Harry shook his head. 'Just a few taekwondo lessons when I was a kid, honest.'

Jim nodded. 'Uh huh. Well, I might see if I can bump you through the gradings a bit faster. You'll have to learn the forms but somehow I can't see that being a problem for you.'

No, Harry couldn't see it being a problem either. It was about a month after he almost died on the water tower that he saw the flyer for karate taped to a telegraph pole outside a school near his place. He'd been looking for something. And this felt right. Harry had arrived at the first class in his shorts and t-shirt, bought his uniform that night, and hadn't looked back. The techniques, the forms, came easily to him.

'Listen,' Jim said, 'don't get me wrong. You're one of the most promising students I've had come through for years. But it's potentially dangerous putting you up against other students like Adrian, who are technically senior to you, when you're pulling things like leg sweeps out of the bag.'

'Yeah. Makes sense.' Harry turned to leave.

'One other thing – are you interested in fighting competitively?'

Harry considered. 'What? Tournaments?'

'Yeah. Mixed martial arts.'

'I'd never thought about it.'

'Well, do.'

'Okay. See you, Jim.'

At the doorway Harry bowed into the dojo, then went out into the cool July night. His breath plumed as he walked back to his car. A single floodlight shone on his battered Corolla. Wind rustled through the trees. Harry always felt good after his training sessions. It was the perfect blend of cardio and strength work, and also gave his brain a workout.

He pulled out his phone, switched it on to check for messages. The screen lit up. One message. He called messagebank and listened.

'Hi… Harry… It's Bec…'

Harry's stomach did a slow roll. He reached for the roof of the car to steady himself, then cursed. It had been almost a year since they split up. In a lot of ways he'd really grown as a person in that time. The martial arts was one aspect of the journey he'd taken. But he still hadn't let her go, not really.

'Just phoning to see how you're going. I'll try again later. Bye.'

Harry tapped the red button and stood staring at the phone's screen, cold wind gusting around him. He got into the car and slammed the door.

Jesus. *Bec?* In a way, it was because of her that he'd almost died. And also because of her that he'd broken the biggest story of his career. Maybe that's why he hadn't got back in touch with her after getting out of hospital.

He turned it all over in his mind. How he'd felt when Bec had told him she didn't love him anymore. All those tears. A mad rush to find somewhere to live, which ended up being a ramshackle old Queenslander in the shadow of the Paddington water tower. And then the tattoos. The first – the only one that still remained – was on the back of his neck. A grid filled with strange symbols. Harry remembered waking with the mother of all hangovers and with that tattoo on his neck, and how he'd passed it off as a drunken misadventure. But that was just the start. Over the next few weeks, tattoos had materialised all over his body, bringing with them vivid nightmares that weren't nightmares at all, but memories sent from beyond the grave. A few years earlier SAS trooper Rob Johnson – a true-blue Australian hero – and his girlfriend had been murdered after discovering a drug-running operation involving a prominent property developer, an outlaw motorcycle gang and Andrew Cardinal, a former army intelligence officer turned politician.

As the tattoos covered Harry's body, Rob's spirit exerted control over his mind, until he found himself hunched over a sniper rifle, peering through the scope at the back of Cardinal's head. Harry managed to regain control, then found Rob's dossier of evidence against Cardinal in the Paddington water tower, and Rob's body under the house. But in the process he'd almost died: first at Cardinal's hands, then from a lightning strike. Cardinal fell to his death and the lightning burnt all the tattoos from Harry's body – all except the first one, the one at the base of his neck.

Harry thought he hadn't been holding it against Bec. But it was worse than that, he realised. He'd been avoiding her because he didn't want to have to relive everything that had happened. A feeling of deep melancholy washed over him. They'd been together six years. If the stuff with Rob and Cardinal hadn't happened, would they have tried to make another go of it? Probably.

Jim slammed the classroom door, drawing Harry from his reverie. He slotted his keys into the ignition and started the engine.

CHAPTER 2

Harry sat at the dining room table, laptop open, heater under the table warming his feet. Outside, wind whistled through the eaves and rattled the loose gutters. At least the landlord hadn't raised the rent. Although, given there had been a body found under the house and Harry had decided to stay on, maybe that wasn't so strange.

His fingers played over the keyboard, stopping every now and then while he referred to his notes. He tried not to think of the growing collection of bills on the fridge, and the growing list of debtors in his invoice spreadsheet. It would work out. He'd lasted this long, and his news blog was growing, the freelance journalism work slowly coming in. He clicked through the tabs on his browser to the link Dave had sent him. A YouTube video of a kitten riding on a dog's back. It had been viewed over twenty-five million times, which was about a lifetime's traffic to his blog, at current rates.

'You're only as good as your last story,' Harry muttered, wondering again whether he should have taken his colleague's advice to go solo.

After he broke the Cardinal story, Harry quickly realised he couldn't stay with the *Chermside Chronicle*.

He tried going back after he'd recovered enough from his injuries. For the first month, the phone barely stopped ringing – fellow journos still chasing the 'inside story' on the scoop of the decade. Many of these had some claim on Harry: they went to uni together; they saw him at the media awards; they always believed in him. Harry refused them all. He wanted to leave the past in the past. When the attention had died out, Harry found himself staring at his screen. He was working on the Community Notices section. He realised he just couldn't do it anymore. It wasn't all to do with the job – he'd changed as a person. He'd *been* changed.

The phone rang.

'Hey, Harry, it's Phil, from Queensland Police Media Unit.'

'Hey, Phil! How's things? It's been ages.'

'Yeah, too long. I'm not bad, not bad. You?'

'Ah, y'know, keeping my head above water… just.'

The line fell silent, and Harry heard the traffic in the background. Phil wasn't calling from the office. Harry imagined him standing outside Police Headquarters on Roma St, trying to shield the phone from noise as cars and buses belted past. When Harry had been at the *Chronicle*, they used to talk every week.

'Erm… I may have some work for you… kinda…'

'Oh yeah? Always keen for some work.' Even though he was sitting in front of the keyboard, Harry reached for his notebook and pen. Old habits die hard. He flipped to a new page and put Phil's name and the date at the top. Despite being known for his investigative journalism, Harry half expected Phil to come out with a pitch for some Queensland Police fundraiser.

'I'm not speaking to you on an official level, if you get me.'

Harry was conflicted. If it wasn't official, that probably meant Queensland Police wouldn't be signing the cheque. But this sounded like it could be interesting.

'That's cool. What's up?'

'I don't really want to talk about it over the phone. Can we meet? I'll buy you a coffee.'

'Sure. Sure thing.' Harry checked his calendar. 'How's Friday for you?'

'Perfect. You right to come into the city?'

Harry laughed. 'Yeah, I can just about afford the bus fare.'

'I'll meet you at Java Coast. How's ten a.m.?'

'Yep, good. I'll see you then.'

'See ya, mate.'

Harry hung up and added the appointment to his calendar.

He checked his emails. Scanned social media. When he'd used up all his standard procrastination techniques, he returned to the story he'd been working on.

Harry had received an email a couple of weeks earlier from someone calling himself 'Johnny'. Every day, emails dropped into Harry's inbox. He checked out the ones he could. Most turned out to be cranks, or scams. Still others just went unread, because Harry didn't have time. But there was something about this one. Harry's hunches weren't always right, but he'd learnt to trust them anyway. Johnny said he'd been molested by the former headmaster of one of Brisbane's most prestigious schools. Multiple times. Johnny said the headmaster was involved in a paedophile ring that included several high-profile identities. He'd been spurred into action after hearing that the ring was still active.

Harry had started collecting notes about the headmaster. Not surprisingly, Johnny wasn't using his full name on his email. He could have been using a fake name, for all Harry knew. Harry cross-referenced what he could – namely that the headmaster was at Johnny's school when he said he was victimised. That all checked out, but that wasn't saying much. He'd sent Johnny an email, but was yet to receive a response. Maybe his instincts were wrong this time. Or maybe it had all got a little bit too real for Johnny when Harry's email arrived.

Harry sighed, opened his paedophilia file again and stared at it for a moment. He pulled up his background notes on the school. St Therese, Brisbane, for years six to twelve. One of the richest schools in Brisbane. He scanned the website. Boys with straw hats and blazers grinning at the camera. Lush playing fields, kept green all year by artesian bore water. World-class IT and science facilities. Drama department headed by an Academy Award nominee. Rowing club, of course, on the river. Shit, they even had a shooting range. Past students included business leaders, world-renowned scientists, politicians at the state and federal level.

Harry pushed the laptop away from him. He felt like a cup of tea. No, he felt like a walk. He switched off the heater, grabbed his keys and phone and headed out the door. The winter wind had a real bite to it. He thrust his hands in his pockets, staring at the ground as he strode up the hill towards the water tower. It loomed above him, fresh white paint against the blue sky. In the wake of his investigation, after the police had finished with it, the government had stepped in and finally granted it heritage listing. Harry's old mate's campaign to save the tower snowballed into a campaign to restore the tower, and now Paddington's old dame stood proud, peering down on the poor plebs below.

At the top of the hill, Harry turned left, away from the main road. He had barely raised a sweat. It was hard to believe that not even a year ago, when Bill had taken him up to the tower that first time, Harry had been gasping for breath at this point. He watched the pavement cracks disappearing under his feet. Weeds in the gutter. An old Coke can. Above him, clouds skated across the sky. He saw the water tower every day, and every day he thought of those last terrifying moments, when the wind howled and his life hung by a thread.

He walked into the park and found the bench that looked over the city. His phone buzzed in his pocket. He pulled it out and tapped the screen without looking at it.

'Harry Hendrick.'

'Oh, hi, Harry. It's Rebecca.'

'Bec?'

'Yeah. How are you? Are you okay to talk?'

'Um... sure. Yeah, getting there. I'm sorry I haven't returned your call. I...'

'That's okay. Really. I know you've... you've been busy.'

For a moment Harry thought that was going to be all it was – a shallow conversation. Two people who'd once travelled together, lived together, ate and slept and fucked together, trying to find common ground.

'Did you hear that I split up with Paul?'

'No. I... No.'

Paul. Paul from Queensland Health. Paul who'd been

the guy good enough to get engaged to, right after she'd told Harry she couldn't see them spending the rest of their lives together. He should have felt angry, but there was no anger left in him.

'Yeah. A couple of months ago. We... I don't know...'

Another pause. Harry didn't know what to say.

'Harry, I miss you.'

Harry felt his heart lurch. He wanted to tell her he missed her too, but worried it would sound shallow, coming right after her declaration. But he did miss her. He rubbed his face. Stared at the ground, where ants moved in sluggish circles in the weak winter sun.

He was lonely. There was the work, but there was little else. His best friend Dave was busy with his final year of med school, Sandy the psychic was taking on clients again. All the people who'd rallied around him in his time of crisis were getting on with their lives. And now here was Bec. Harry had thought it was all over until her message the night before.

'Do you want to go out for a coffee or something sometime?'

Harry nodded, then realised she couldn't see him. 'Yeah. Yeah, I do.'

'Oh... oh, okay,' Bec said. She sounded surprised, like she expected the opposite answer – expected anger. 'Um... are you still at Paddington?'

'Yep. In the shade of the water tower.'

'How about Black Cat? Ten. Saturday morning.'

'Okay.'

'Okay.'

'Okay.'

Bec laughed. Harry smiled. He'd missed that sound.

'I'll see you then, unless you want to keep saying okay to each other?'

'Yep. Okay. See you, Harry.'

CHAPTER 3

Harry sat on the bus, gazing out at the inner-city landscape but not really seeing it. Bec's call on Wednesday had knocked him for six, so much so that he hadn't really thought much about Phil's cryptic request for help. Until now. Phil hadn't wanted to talk about it on the phone. He didn't want Harry to come to Police Headquarters. Harry stared through the dirty glass, watching people pulling coats tight around themselves, beanies over their ears, trying to keep out the westerlies.

He got off the bus at Roma St, right outside the monolithic Police Headquarters, and crossed the road, shivering slightly. George St was crowded with grim faces. Brisbane wasn't a winter city and, although these were hardly arctic conditions, its citizens weren't built for it. Harry was relieved when he could duck out of the path of the icy wind into the alleyway that led to the coffee shop. He couldn't also help noticing that Phil had chosen somewhere off the main road, a place where they could talk without much fear of being overheard.

Brick walls covered in faux antique tin signs and posters for upcoming gigs rose on every side, fencing off the coffee shop's courtyard. Despite being open to the blue sky above, strategically placed heaters made the space almost cosy.

Even though they'd known each other for years, Harry had only met Phil a handful of times – the last time had been at a *Chermside Chronicle* Christmas party the year before last – so he was a little surprised by how much older Phil looked. His hair was greyer, the lines around his eyes deeper. His Queensland Police Media Unit ID was clipped to his belt, barely visible under his middle-aged paunch and charcoal suit jacket.

'Harry Hendrick!' Phil pulled himself from the booth he'd taken over and offered his hand. His grip was ironclad as ever. Harry had once asked if Phil had ever considered joining the police force proper, and Phil had told him he was too much of a coward for that. But hanging around cops all the time had rubbed off on him, because he carried himself like a cop: square-shouldered; direct eye contact.

Harry squeezed into the seat across from Phil. They shook hands and caught up. A waitress came and took their order.

'So, what's up?' Harry said.

There was an iPad on the table. Phil pulled it over and Harry felt butterflies in his stomach, similar to when he'd decided to take on the paedophilia story.

Phil cleared his throat. 'I need to show you some crime scene photos, you'll understand why shortly. Can you handle that?'

Harry nodded. Phil handed him the iPad.

The first picture, mercifully, was just a photo of a piece of paper, with the address of the crime scene, the name of the victim, the date – last week. Harry swiped.

A broken mirror in what looked like a dining room.

The long, black table had been dusted for prints. *Swipe.* A lounge room, covered in footprints the colour of maroon paint. Harry guessed it wasn't paint. Whoever it was, they had a lot of money, or a lot of debt – the lounge room was lorded over by one of the biggest TVs he'd ever seen. *Swipe.* Bathroom mirror, also smashed. Blood all over the counter. Fingerprints, smears. More fingerprint dust. The basin contained so much blood it looked like black marble. *Swipe.* A girl's room, bloody footprints tracking in and out. *Swipe.* A close-up of a girl's hand mirror, smashed. *Swipe.* A king-sized bed, blood smears all over it. More bloody footprints on the floor. Harry's stomach did a slow loop. The dressing table mirror had been smashed. Harry suddenly realised what was wrong with these photos. He swiped back through them to check. The glass from the mirrors – it wasn't in any of the photos. Not a splinter. Plenty of blood, but no glass.

Swipe. The bathroom again, but this time the camera was pointed at the bath. There was a pasty-skinned man in there. Long cuts crisscrossed his feet. His knees were a mess of pulped flesh. The bath itself was black with blood. His lips looked as though someone had put them in a blender.

'Oh Jesus,' Harry said.

Phil nodded. 'He died from massive internal bleeding. The coroner found shards of mirror wedged in his mouth, his throat. You'd be surprised how much he ate before he died.'

Harry handed back the iPad. Shook his head. 'Why?'

'There was a note.' Phil picked up the iPad and swiped through more pictures. Harry thought he was going to hand it back to him, and somehow seeing that handwritten note would have been worse than everything else. But to his relief, Phil just read it out.

'"I have sinned. I give my life for the Goddess." We checked his record – thought maybe he'd done something bad. Was overcome by guilt. But nope. Just the usual speeding tickets, that sort of thing.'

Harry stared at the peeling posters on the brick wall for a minute or so. The pictures kept playing in his mind. *Swipe. Swipe. Swipe.*

'So who was this guy?'

'Zak Godwin. Well-paid executive with the state government. But not so high up the chain you'd consider him into anything serious.' He flicked his eyes from the iPad to Harry. 'You know, corruption. He's sitting on a couple of boards. Wife, daughter. Wife says he's been mostly happy. No massive arguments. No inkling that this was coming.'

Harry went to say, *But there often isn't, with suicides,* but stopped himself. This wasn't your standard suicide. Godwin killed himself by eating shards of mirror.

'Do you want me to write a story on this? This would be right up the *Brisbane Mail*'s alley, you know.'

'God, no. No story. Not yet, anyway.'

'Then why…'

'I'm not finished.'

The waitress returned with their coffees. Phil played around with the iPad until she had returned to the bar, then handed it back to Harry. With dread, Harry took it. He realised he was getting to see the letter after all. But not just one letter – four. *I have sinned. I give my life for the Goddess.* Harry's eyes flicked from one to the next. Cream writing paper. A scrap torn from a cereal box.

A shorthand notebook. A piece of white A4 printer paper, the top half of which featured a printed ticket for the next Brisbane Roar game. The writing on this one was so bad Harry wouldn't have been able to interpret it if not for the other letters.

'Did they all die the same way?'

Phil shook his head. 'One of them threw himself in front of a train. One gassed himself in his garage. The other shot himself with his service pistol.' Phil saw Harry's eyes widen and answered the unspoken question. 'Yeah. A cop. Constable Brad Brooks.'

'So is that why...'

Phil shook his head. 'That's part of it. But not all of it. Swipe to the next one.'

Harry looked back down at the next photo. Again, it was a montage of four photos. Four victims. These photos were well lit though. The photos zoomed in on the victim's backs. Harry could just make out the aluminium surface of the coroner's examination table on either side of the bodies. It was easy to pick out Godwin's body – the back was a mess of black blood and cuts, some still with glass in them. Harry was pretty sure he could make out the train victim's too: the body seemed out of proportion, and was mottled with bruising. But that wasn't what stood out to him. Even though Phil hadn't directed him to it, he noticed the incisions in the men's backs. Five small lines: one on each shoulder blade; one on either side at the bottom of the rib cage; one at the base of the spine. Harry squinted, pulled in for a close look.

'Coroner said they're not new wounds. Says they were made by a scalpel, and scar tissue suggests they were made over the course of a few months.'

Harry nodded and handed the iPad back. 'I'm still not sure what you want from me.'

Phil looked nervous now for the first time. 'Harry, I remember last year you asked me to look into that SAS guy, Rob Johnson.'

'Yeah, so what?'

'I was looking at the photos we had on file of him. The tattoos. You try and hide it with that long hair, and it's faded, but I know you've got the same tattoo on the back of your neck.'

Harry tried to get a hold of his anger. His hand involuntarily went to his neck, where his last tattoo remained, and he forced it back onto the table. 'So?'

'So. What is it, a tribute tattoo?'

Harry looked down and realised he was gripping the table so hard his knuckles were white. He let go and got up to leave.

Phil reached out and grabbed Harry's forearm. Harry could have easily twisted out of the grip. Could have left Phil on the ground, gasping for breath. But something in Phil's eyes stopped him.

'Please, Harry. Sit down.'

Harry sat.

'Your scars are healing well,' Phil said. 'Pretty incredible, what happened last year. You surviving the lightning strike like that.'

Harry nodded. 'I have a lot to be thankful for.'

'It's kind of strange though, the way your scars directly correlate with where Rob was tattooed.'

'Are you going somewhere with this?'

'Harry, this didn't make it into the press, but there's a theory being bandied around HQ that there was an aborted attempt on Andrew Cardinal's life on the day of his campaign launch.'

Harry's blood ran cold. He struggled to keep his face impassive. Phil was gone. All he could see was crosshairs converging on Cardinal's head.

'Someone broke into an office across the river. They'd cut a hole in the window. We've got footage of a man walking down Queen St, holding a case that we believe was used to carry a sniper's rifle. It's not enough to go to court with. Jesus, we haven't even got a suspect.' He stared into Harry's eyes for a few seconds.

'And, you know, Cardinal wasn't exactly the golden child he made himself out to be. Given what you discovered about him, if the guy had pulled the trigger, he would have been doing the world a favour, right?'

Harry sighed. 'That's one way of looking at it.'

'Look, I'm not really a believer in ghosts or UFOs or any of that shit, and my bosses certainly aren't,' Phil said. 'But I can't help think that... something, I dunno, weird happened last year. And that you were at the centre of it.'

He tapped the iPad. 'We need help. Despite the fact the methods of death were different, there's an obvious link here, which leads the detectives to believe there could be more deaths.'

'I'm pretty sure serial killers don't work that way,' Harry said.

'Exactly. It's weird. Whatever happened to you last year was weird. We're desperate, but we can't officially bring in psychics or anything like that. Which is why I'm sitting here, talking to you.'

Harry thought of all the possible responses. Everything

from outright denial to choking the shit out of Phil and going on the run. Phil read the expression.

'Don't shoot the messenger, Harry. My bosses just want your help.'

CHAPTER 4

T he email subject line was intriguing – *Unionist linked to sex workers*.

```
Dear Mr Hendrick,
I'm writing to secure your assistance with a
matter that I feel is of the public interest.
    My husband is Don Clack, the secretary of
Australian United Workers. I have recently
suspected that he has been seeing sex
workers — yes, plural — under the guise of
'working late'.
    Please contact me if you're interested
in knowing more. I'm wary of giving out too
many details via email.

Yours sincerely,
Lee-Anne Stewart
```

Harry welcomed the distraction. He'd spent most of the night tossing and turning, still stewing about his meeting with Phil. Was he being blackmailed? There was definitely an implied threat, but Phil himself had said there was no case yet, not even a suspect. Not officially, anyway. Harry wondered what sort of evidence they'd collected at the architect's office where he'd almost taken the shot that would have ended Andrew Cardinal's life. Did they have DNA maybe, that they hadn't gone to the trouble of testing because they weren't pursuing the case? Was there CCTV footage of Harry walking through the Queen Street Mall, disguised as an air conditioning repairman, that would identify him if they went to the trouble of analysing it properly?

Thing was, he was intrigued. Phil had given him a business card with his contact details on one side and a time and date on the other, like a dental appointment. An arrangement to meet at the most recent crime scene.

When he'd finally drifted off, he'd dreamt of the walking dead. Men with pieces of mirror sticking out of their faces, men cut in half by trains, men blowing their brains out. He fell towards the piece of mirror, saw himself reflected there, shards sticking out of his face, fell towards the piece of mirror, saw himself reflected again. Over and over, a loop of pain and fear. He woke sweaty, despite the chill, as the first rays of dawn pushed through his windows.

Harry returned to the email. There was a contact number under Lee-Anne Stewart's name. He picked up his phone and dialled.

'Hello?' the woman's voice sounded sleepy.

'Hi. Is that Lee-Anne Stewart?'

'Yes, who's this?' More alert now.

'Harry Hendrick. You emailed me?'

'Of course. One moment.'

There was a pause. Some muffled voices. The sound of a door closing.

'He's here… for a change.'

'Ms Stewart…'

'Lee, please.'

'Lee. You said you didn't want to say too much in the email. And you said it's in the public interest.'

'I'm pretty sure he's using union fees to pay for his whores.'

Harry blinked. Opened his mouth. Closed it again.

Lee-Anne laughed at Harry's silence. 'Yeah. That's why I emailed you. I mean, I would love to see him burn, but the thing that really pisses me off is that it's members' money. My dad was a metal worker. The fucking job killed him. It's a disgrace.'

'How do you know he's using union money?'

'We have a shared bank account. Have for years. I mean, he could have set up a separate account somehow, but I do the household accounts and tax returns, so I'm pretty sure I'd know.'

'Have you spoken to him about it?'

Lee-Anne laughed. 'Nope.'

Harry waited for her to elaborate, but when she didn't, he pressed her. 'You want to publicly humiliate him?'

'Sure.'

'You know you'll be in the spotlight too, once other media organisations get their hands on this?'

She hissed in frustration. 'Yeah. I'm not stupid. It's not just about humiliating him. If I confront him about it, he'll shit bricks and then find a way to cover it up. And that's not acceptable to me.'

Harry considered. It could be a great story, but he didn't want to get caught up in this woman's vendetta against her husband. Even if the vendetta was justified.

'I can pay you,' she said.

'I'm not sure that would be ethical.'

'Ha! You sure you're a journalist? Look, it says on your website that you're crowdfunding, right?'

'Well, yeah, but...'

'There's no strings attached to this money, Harry. All I'm saying is, do a little digging. I don't care how you write the story. If you don't end up writing the story, I won't be asking for my money back.'

Harry sighed.

'Harry. It's a piece of piss. I'll text you when he's next "working late". You follow him. See what happens.'

Harry nodded, even though she couldn't see him. 'Okay. I... I'll look into it.'

'Thanks. I've got to go make Lothario here his breakfast. See you, Harry.'

CHAPTER 5

It was a cold morning but Harry sat outside anyway. He pulled his coat up around his chin. From where he sat he could see the set of stairs that led from the bookshop into the cafe. He felt like he needed some strategic advantage. He'd been thinking about the unionist Don Clack all the way over. He didn't know much about him other than what he'd seen in the news. He was a strident unionist, not militant – the days of militant unionism were over. Some touted Clack as fodder for the federal Labor Party at some point down the track, but others said he was too much of a firebrand, even though he'd toned things down significantly since his glory days in the nineties. The most recent blow-up had been when someone had secretly recorded him at an ALP fundraiser, telling the cheering crowd that the captains of industry should be tied to the stake and burnt alive. But that was a couple of years back. He'd been keeping a low profile since then.

Harry had been so caught up thinking about what Lee-Anne had told him that he hadn't really had time to think about Bec. But now he was sitting outside in the cold, playing with his phone and waiting for her to arrive. The sound system went quiet, then fired up with Jonathan

Wilson's 'Ballad of the Pines'. He wanted to see her so badly. He wanted to hold her hand and kiss her. But he also felt angry, even though he accepted their breakup was as much his doing as hers. They had been in a rut. Well, Harry had been in a rut. He had been taking her for granted for months before the break-up. He never would have admitted that at the time, but it was so clear to him now. Bec pulled the trigger, but Harry loaded the gun. And he was scared. He remembered the uncontrollable sobbing as he packed his things from her place. And even though it wasn't fair, he remembered what had happened after they had split. He didn't think he could bear being hurt that badly again.

And there she was. Bec paused for a moment at the bottom of the steps, looking around for Harry. She'd had her hair cut short; it suited her. Her cheeks were rosy from the cold. She wore jeans, a dark jacket and a rainbow scarf. It seemed a bit bohemian for the Bec he knew, but he liked it. Maybe she had changed too? Harry felt his heart stutter in his chest, followed by a rush of borderline panic. What if she didn't feel the same way? What if she just wanted to touch base? Be 'friends'? Then she saw him, through the glass, and her face lit up with a smile. Harry wasn't sure he could stand, but he did anyway, holding onto the table for support. He tried to smile back. It felt as though his face was cracking.

She pushed through the door, came out onto the deck. 'Hey, Harry!'

One of the things Harry had been obsessing about since she called was how they would greet each other. A wave? Kiss on the cheek? Handshake? It seemed ridiculous and yet so much seemed to be riding on it. But in the end Bec crossed the distance and wrapped her arms around him before he could think about it. He hugged her back. Smelt her hair and her perfume. Their coats, and the brevity of the embrace, kept it just shy of intimate. And then Bec backed off, shuffling slightly on her feet, not looking at Harry, as though worried she'd gone too far.

'It's good to see you, Bec,' he said.

'Yeah! You too.' She gestured to the counter. 'Have you ordered?'

'No, I'll…' Harry reached for his wallet.

'I'll get it. You still on the flat whites?' she said.

'No. Just straight bourbon these days.'

She looked at him for a beat then laughed. 'Right. I'll see what I can do.'

She pushed back through the door and Harry watched her go to the counter, then collapsed into his chair. By the time she'd returned he'd calmed himself.

'They said they'd bring it out,' she said. 'I got you a double.'

Harry smiled.

'So, what's happening?' she said.

Harry considered trying to tell Bec about everything that had happened, not just in the past couple of days, but in the previous few months, as he struggled to pull himself back together after the Rob incident. He felt exhausted just thinking about it. He didn't want to go back through all that pain right now. Not when he didn't know what was going on here, and how she felt about him.

'Bec, let's not fuck around,' he said and stopped. He'd surprised himself.

Now she did look at him.

'I can't pretend that everything that happened between us didn't happen. I just can't.'

'Oh. Okay. Shit. I thought we'd at least get to drink our coffee first.' She smiled. It was a genuine smile, but it faded when she saw Harry wasn't yet ready to share the joke.

'I'm sorry…'

'No, that's not…' Harry shook his head. 'I'm not fishing for apologies. Shit. If anyone owes apologies, it's me. I didn't realise what I had with you. But…'

The waitress appeared with their drinks and placed them on the table. Harry raised his glass to his mouth and tasted whisky. Bec grinned.

'Sorry. No bourbon, but I got them to put a shot of whisky in it for you.'

Harry laughed. 'Well played.'

Bec glanced at the table, then back at Harry. Those eyes! She reached out and put her hand on his.

'Harry, the truth is, I don't know. But I know that I missed you. I still miss you. That's why I called you. But I don't know where this is headed. I can't make any promises. I know this sounds corny, but I feel like I've changed. I feel like you've changed. I just want the opportunity to get to know you again.' She sipped her coffee. 'Okay?'

Harry took time to think about it, then nodded. It was worth the risk. 'Okay.'

There was a brief, awkward silence, filled by wind whistling through the eaves, and traffic on Latrobe Terrace. Then, bit by bit, they started talking again. They had a lot to catch up on. Harry gave Bec the short version of all that had gone on last year. He didn't tell her everything. He hoped that some day he would be able to, but that time wasn't now. In return, Bec told him about Paul, the former fiancé. She told him it was a rebound, that it was obviously a rebound, in hindsight, but Harry got the feeling that she wasn't telling him everything, either.

'So, how's the freelancing going?' she said, moving them back into safer territory.

'Yeah, there's a bit on.' He paused as images of the dead bodies rose unbidden to his mind. 'I'm working on something with Queensland Police,' he said. 'I can't really go into too much detail yet. It may be nothing.' He tapped the side of his nose, smiled to hide the feeling that he wasn't being honest with her. 'And I had the strangest conversation this morning.' He recounted the phone call with the unionist's wife, playing it for laughs. He'd forgotten how much he loved to hear her laugh.

'So, I may be visiting a few brothels in the not-too-distant future – just for research.'

'Of course! You can probably claim it on tax.'

They both laughed this time, and Harry realised he hadn't felt so good for a long time.

'How about you? How's your work going?'

'Ah, you know. Same old, same old. Trying to do more with less. My boss wants me to go on one of those leadership camp things.'

'Leadership camp? Isn't that what you do in high school?'

'Basically, except probably about a thousand times more expensive.'

'Are you going to do it?'

Bec sighed. 'I'll probably have to. Try and keep all those fucking Millennials in their place.'

Harry grinned. 'They've got nothing on you.' He drained the last of his coffee, gestured to the counter. 'Going again?'

Bec checked the time on her phone. 'Nah. Better not.

The apartment looks like a bomb has hit it. And I've got to get shopping done.' She stared at her empty cup. There was another awkward silence. 'But it's been fun, Harry. Just...' She stopped, waved it away.

'What?' Harry said, not sure if he actually wanted an answer.

'Nothing. I was going to say, "Just like old times." But I think it's been better than that. Do you know what I mean?'

Harry nodded. He remembered the last couple of months of their relationship. It was like they were both on autopilot.

They stood. There was that awkward moment again, when they weren't quite sure how to say goodbye. In the end, Harry leant forward awkwardly and put an arm around Bec, and gave her a peck on the cheek. Then he followed her back inside, up the stairs, into the bookshop. Out the front of the shop, they paused.

'I'm this way,' she said, pointing away from the city.

'Okay,' Harry said. 'Do you... do you want to catch up again?'

Bec smiled. 'Yeah, sure. I'd like that. See you, Harry.' She gave him a small wave, then walked away.

Harry watched her go for a while, then walked back to where he'd parked his car.

CHAPTER 6

Phil pulled up outside the house. Beige walls, big white garage doors. Police tape still roped around the colonnade holding up the portico above the front door.

'Are you ready to do this?' he said, pulling on the handbrake and turning off the engine.

Harry looked at the house. His stomach was doing slow, queasy rolls. 'Not really. And I don't really see the point.'

'Let's just get it done,' Phil said.

He got out of the car and Harry followed, his feet like lead. He watched them crunch over the dry grass and folded his arms against the cold. Phil unlocked the black gate.

'His wife's taken their daughter out of school. They're spending some time up the coast, at their holiday home.'

Harry grunted. Despite the chill, he could feel sweat beading on his scalp. He ran a hand through his hair, then wiped it on his jeans. At the end of the pathway, Phil snapped the police tape. It drifted to the ground.

'Scenes of Crime have finished with this place. Cleaners are coming tomorrow. So this is the only chance we've got.'

He unlocked the front door and stepped inside. The smell hit Harry first: the coppery tang of blood. He could only imagine how much worse it would have been if Godwin had killed himself in summer. He glanced at the faded welcome mat outside the front door. It looked out of place at the entrance to such a grand house.

In the hallway, Harry noticed the shoes by the front door. The girl's – pink Sketcher sneakers. A set of black pumps for the wife. Shiny brown brogues for Mr Godwin. Harry started slipping his shoes off; Phil rolled his eyes.

'Sorry,' Harry mumbled, leaving his shoes on and taking in the blood-stained carpet.

The house was unusually quiet. It was more than empty. There was something palpable about the atmosphere. It seemed heavy and humid despite the cold. Outside, a crow cawed.

'Is this your first crime scene?' Phil said.

'Yeah. I mean, a couple of years ago when I was with the *Chronicle*, there was a body dumped out at Boondall Wetlands. But I only got within a couple of hundred metres.'

'That was that drug dealer guy – what was his name?'

Harry couldn't remember. 'How about you?'

'I've seen a few. As part of the media unit training they take us out to a few crime scenes to show us how it all works,' Phil said. 'I think the real reason is that they want us to appreciate some of the awful things police have to deal with.'

Harry shoved his hands in his pockets. 'So what exactly do you want me to do?'

'Just have a look around. I'll wait here.'

'Gee, thanks.'

Harry didn't know where to start. His anger at being coerced into this was being replaced by grim humour at the ridiculousness of the situation. Maybe this was the real story – that police were so desperate to solve these crimes, and so clueless (literally) that they hoped Harry could come up with some supernatural solution. The *Brisbane Mail* would be all over it. But then what? End up facing charges of attempted murder? The *Brisbane Mail* would love that too. It could have been paranoia, but he felt as though many in the media industry were just waiting for him to fail.

He walked into the dining room, where the frame of the mirror still hung. It hadn't just been smashed: the glass had been repeatedly hit so that not one scrap of it remained. The frame and the wall around it were smeared with dried blood. Harry got down on his haunches and examined the floor. More blood here – round drops and smeared footprints.

'Would forensics have swept the floor or anything like that?' Harry said.

Phil looked up from his phone. 'No, they may have taken some of the shards away to look at, but that's about it.'

'There's no broken mirror on the floor.'

Phil turned back to his phone.

Harry walked down the hallway, following the bloody footprints. In the bathroom, most of the floor and the marble counter and basin were covered in dry blood. The window was closed and the smell was overpowering. Harry held his shirt over his nose. Again, the mirror had been completely removed from its frame.

He looked over at the bath, got up on his tiptoes so he wouldn't have to actually enter the room. There was more blood in the bathtub, and some broken mirror. Not a lot. Harry didn't even want to think about that. He stepped back from the threshold, and immediately felt a little better. Whatever it was about this house – maybe it was just his imagination – was stronger in that room. The death room. Harry shivered.

He walked further up the hallway. The master bedroom. More blood, but here the stench was masked by the overpowering scent of perfume. The mirror on the dresser had been removed and, once again, there was not a scrap of glass anywhere. Harry entered the room, examined the dresser, pulled out the drawers and rummaged through them, not really sure what he was searching for. On one of the bedside tables there was a wallet and keys. Harry opened the wallet, flicked through the cards. Pulled out a faded picture of Zak Godwin and his wife, cradling their baby girl. Harry was about to put the wallet back when he noticed a slit in the leather, on the inside. He pressed the sides so it opened. A business card. Harry pulled it out. Black and shiny, with pink writing: *Hunted – Gentlemen's Club*. On the other side, someone had scrawled a phone number. He flipped the card over in his hands, drew it to his nose. Perfumed. Different to the perfume that had soaked into the carpet under the dressing table. Harry thought of Mr Godwin, lying in the bath, eating shards of glass until he died. He pocketed the card, and put the wallet back.

Harry continued down the hall and found the girl's room. More blood in here, but not as much as the other rooms. He looked around, wondering why Godwin was in here at all. Then he remembered the photos Phil had shown him. Half under the girl's bed was a small hand mirror. The forensics team must have also found it, as there was more fingerprint dust in here, but they'd left it there, smashed and bent out of shape. Like all the other mirrors in the house, every shard gone. Harry had a vision of Godwin sitting on the edge of the bed, bloody hands full of glass, crying. Tears dropping into his cupped hands to mix with the blood and the glass.

Harry's stomach tightened. His mouth filled with saliva. He backed out of the room, misjudging the doorway. His shoulder clipped it and pins and needles exploded down his arm. He spun in the hall and saw the toilet door open, but the room was coated in fingerprint dust. He gagged.

Harry ran back down the hallway, through the open-plan living area, past Phil, who was still goggling at his phone. He heaved again and tasted acid in his mouth.

The front door was open. He tripped over the doorway, then slipped on the welcome mat. He made it to the garden bed, vomiting at the base of a neat row of rose bushes. Bile rose again, but this time nothing came out. He stared at the mulch through watering eyes.

'You right?'

Harry snorted a thick laugh. 'Does it look like it?'

Phil handed him a handkerchief.

'Thanks.' He wiped his mouth, blew his nose.

'You can keep that, by the way,' Phil said.

Harry looked at him, caught the smirk on his face.

'Don't worry. I was the same, the first time. And it doesn't matter if there's no body here – it's clear that something bad went down. I almost think that sometimes, when something like that happens, it leaves a, I don't know, a kind of residue.'

Harry nodded, remembering the sensation in the

bathroom – the death room. He looked past Phil's legs, to the mat. It was askew. He looked away, then back at the mat. There was something underneath it. A piece of paper, folded into a small rectangle. He hefted himself up. The paper was crinkled and stuck to the concrete. It had been there a while.

'What is it?' Phil said.

'Don't know.'

Harry gently prised it off the ground. There was writing on it. He started unfolding it, carefully freeing the stuck edges.

'We can get forensics to do that, Harry,' Phil said, reaching for the paper.

Harry turned away from him. 'Bullshit. You wanted me here. I found it.'

'Only because you tripped over the mat.'

'Well, maybe your crime scene guys should've tripped over the mat. Or maybe looked under it? Jesus Christ.'

Harry gently unfolded the paper. Symbols. But not like those on his neck. These were more familiar. Well, culturally familiar. A pentagram. And at the corners of the pentagram, sigils, and another in the middle of the design. But it was faded, much of it barely legible in places. He held it to the light.

'Harry, I really think I should get forensics to look at that.'

'Fine.'

Harry pulled out his phone. He laid the paper on the ground and took a series of photos, then handed it to Phil, who pulled a plastic bag out of his back pocket and put the piece of paper inside. Then he looked over Harry's shoulder at the image on his phone's screen.

'Do you think it's important?'

'Could be. Or maybe the victim's kid's just been watching too much *Supernatural*.'

CHAPTER 7

Harry parked his car and peered at the darkening sky. It had been a dry winter but maybe it might finally rain. He grabbed his umbrella and got out of the car, striding along the footpath past a row of run-down houses, some dark, some with the flickering glow of television pulsing through the front windows. He pulled out his phone and checked the time. His best mate Dave would probably be late anyway. He'd never been the most punctual of people – always figuring that everyone else was as laid-back as he was – but things had gotten worse now that he was heading into the final stages of his medical degree.

Thunder rolled ominously through the air. Thick dark splotches landed on the pavement, and Harry opened the umbrella. The week had passed in a blur. After visiting the crime scene on Monday, he'd emailed the psychic, Sandy, a copy of the image. She had so much arcane knowledge in that head of hers, it wouldn't surprise him if she knew what the mysterious symbols meant, but he hadn't heard back from her yet. Harry hadn't had much to do with Sandy since she had been dragged reluctantly into his crisis last year. For a while afterwards they'd kept in touch via email. But then the emails drifted further and further apart, the responses shorter and shorter. She'd told him last that she was thinking about getting into consulting again, that the Rob situation had made her a beacon once more in the spirit world, and that she may as well do something about it, given she was getting hassled anyway.

West End was bustling. A blend of long-time locals tending their stores, suited-and-booted business types winding down after a busy week, and the rough sleepers attracted by the area's more tolerant attitude. A posh Greek restaurant with starched white tablecloths and sparkling wine glasses sat across the road from a dingy pub that hadn't been refurbished since the 1990s.

Harry opened the umbrella as the rain started coming down in earnest. A woman in a bright yellow dress jumped a puddle with more grace than her stilettos should have allowed. He thought of Bec. Their coffee date had been less than a week ago, but it seemed like longer. It seemed like a dream. He'd wanted to call her, but didn't want to come on too strong. Part of him still couldn't believe she wanted to have another go.

Archive Beer Boutique was filling up. Harry pushed through the press of hipsters supping their craft beers and lounging in a mish-mash of chairs that looked as though they'd been salvaged from op shops. Harry wondered that Dave could handle this place, given how lo-fi trendy it was. But then again, Dave did like his beer. Harry searched for his best friend, walking past a wall papered with old comics to the bar. He assessed the beers chalked on the board and chose a chocolate stout.

'Well, well, Mr Harry Hendrick.'

Dave. And for once not in his hospital greens – every

time Harry had seen him in recent months he'd been in his nurse's uniform, stinking of antiseptic, usually hunched over a stack of books.

'Dave!'

Dave had never really been comfortable with the hug, whereas Harry figured after all they'd been through, the pair of them were definitely in hug territory. So they ended up doing an awkward half-hug, half-handshake, before Dave ordered his beer.

They found a couple of bar stools looking out over Hardgrave Road.

'Cheers, big ears,' Dave said.

They clinked glasses and drank, both just enjoying the beer for a few moments.

'Long time, no see,' Harry said. 'How's things?'

'Getting there. Just got the big exam coming up in a couple of months. And then jostling for intern placements.'

'So soon it will be Dr Dave.' Harry grinned. He'd seen his best friend slugging it out for years. It was amazing to think he was almost there.

'Hopefully.' He took a big gulp of beer. 'What about you? How's work?'

'Ah, getting there. A few things going on.' Harry felt exhausted just thinking about it.

'Come on, man, details, details. I've been living like a fucking hermit. Give me something!'

'Okay.' Harry told Dave about Phil and the mystery suicides, careful to play down the fact that he was being coerced into it.

Dave drained half his glass. 'Well, you know, if I was in one of those CSI shows…'

Harry could almost imagine it. *CSI: Dave.*

'... if I was in one of those shows, I'd be looking for connections between the victims.'

'Yeah, I'm on it. The most obvious is the markings. Five lines on the back. Like the points of an inverted star.'

'Satanists?'

Harry nodded. 'But it could also depict a pentagon. Could mean anything. Could mean nothing.'

'But the police think it's something... something weird.'

'Yeah.'

'And they've contacted you because...'

Harry sipped his beer, then looked around the room to give himself a bit of time to answer the question. Dave would do anything to help him. But he'd also nag Harry to death if he thought he was being made to do something he didn't want to.

'To be honest, I think they're just desperate...'

Dave raised his eyebrows. 'They must be. Next thing they'll be calling in a psychic.' Dave laughed, and Harry joined him. It had been too long.

'Thing is,' Harry said, 'There may be nothing... supernatural about it. Could just be someone has fucked with all these people. Tortured them or something. Threatened their families. Who knows?'

'Do you really want this shit right now?'

'It could be a big story. And Jesus, I need another big story.'

'Fame sucks?'

'It's not that. It's just... I dunno. I guess there are people who think I fluked it with Cardinal. And, to be honest, I did have a bit of help there.'

'Bullshit, Harry. Come on. Believe in yourself. If anyone

else'd had that shit happen to them, they'd've ended up in a mental asylum. Seriously.'

'Thanks, man.'

Dave smiled. 'Don't thank me, just buy me another beer. I'm dying of thirst here!'

Harry laughed again, and reached for his wallet.

CHAPTER 8

Harry thought the knocking was in his head, then realised someone was at the front door. He sat up, winced, then slumped back against the bed, head swimming and sweat chilling his body. Maybe it was JWs, or someone who wanted to paint the house. He closed his eyes, willing them away.

'Harry? Harry?'

Ah shit.

Harry couldn't quite place the voice. He should have been able to, but he couldn't. Because the banging was in his head after all, pulsing in sickly synchronicity with the knocking on the door. He pushed himself off the bed. Got his feet on the floor. Tried to ignore the sensation of the world trying to spin out from under his feet.

Harry shuffled through the house, wishing he had his sunglasses but not having the mental capacity to remember where they were. He opened the door, squinting to try to block the sunlight, squinting so much his eyes were basically closed. Through the gap he saw a small shape, a big broad-brimmed hat, the smell of lavender. And then he felt Sandy's warm hands on his skin.

'Have I caught you at a bad time?' Sandy didn't wait

for an answer, she just pushed past him. 'Don't worry. I'll put the kettle on. We'll get you back in the fight, Harry Hendrick.'

Harry pivoted slowly, battling the urge to gag. 'Fight? What fight?'

But Sandy was already in the kitchen, rummaging through his cupboards, making such a racket he wasn't sure the effort was worth it. He slumped down at the dining room table, sipping on the glass of water he didn't remember pouring for himself the night before. Never again. *Never* again.

He couldn't believe he'd drunk that much. Bloody Dave. After what had happened with Rob, Harry'd been extremely careful about drinking. Part of it was that he loathed the feeling of not being in control of himself. And part of it was just that he was more committed to looking after his body.

Sandy hummed to herself. Harry was pretty sure it was a Céline Dion tune.

'Kill me now,' Harry groaned.

'What's that, dear?' Sandy said.

'White. Two sugars, please.'

Sandy returned with two mugs of steaming tea. She set one in front of Harry. He watched the bubbles swirling on the surface, and for a moment thought he was going to be sick. Then he looked at the walls, let out a deep breath, and looked at Sandy.

'Thanks, Sandy. I'm a bit… a bit under the weather,' he said.

'Yes. You look a bit… under the weather. But you're well otherwise.' A statement. Not a question.

'Yeah. Yeah, thanks.' And he immediately thought of Bec.

'She's a good one,' Sandy said, smiling. 'You both lost your way for a little bit. But I think you two are going to be okay.'

Harry felt the floor drop away under his feet, and struggled again to keep his stomach under control. He hadn't told Sandy anything about Bec. He hadn't even told Dave – although, come to think of it, he could have told Dave anything last night. He'd decided he wanted to keep it to himself for now. He was worried about being judged. He supposed Sandy could have asked around. Maybe Bec wasn't playing her cards so close to her chest. But no, he didn't think that was what had happened. Harry struggled to keep a straight face.

'Rob's still watching over you,' Sandy said. 'He keeps me up to date on your comings and goings.'

Harry self-consciously rubbed the back of his neck. 'Oh great. Thanks, Rob. So, what did you manage to dig up about the symbols?'

Sandy's smile faded slightly. She reached for her bag and fumbled around while Harry sipped his tea. It was good. She pulled out a piece of paper, unfolded it and flattened it on the table. It was a printout of the photo Harry had sent her, of the note he'd found under public servant Zak Godwin's front doormat.

'Let me guess,' Harry said. 'It's not some random scribbling.'

'I'm afraid not.'

Harry's hands shook so badly he had to use both of them to pick up the cup. Sandy looked up from the piece of paper, peering over the top of her reading glasses.

'You right?'

Harry nodded.

'There's the pentacle. A pentagram in a circle. That's a given, okay? It's inverted. That's a Satanic thing. Again, not necessarily any biggie.'

Harry raised his eyebrows.

'Well, you know. Kids. Mucking around with the occult. Most of the time they don't know what they're messing around with. Most of the time anything they think they conjure is just a figment of their imagination.'

'Uh huh.' Harry recalled a seance he'd been to as a kid. Someone had brought one of those creepy china dolls and positioned it outside the door, so that the first person who fled the room would find it staring at them.

'But, inverted pentagram is inverted pentagram. Signifying the triumph of matter over spirit. There's a mixture of stuff from different cultures. This one here is from the Romani people...'

'Gypsies?'

Sandy gave him a disapproving look. 'No, Romani. And this one... you might recognise this one.'

Harry peered at the symbol, and reached instinctively for the tattoo on his neck. 'Yep, that's from Afghanistan.'

She spun the piece of paper to face him. 'But then it fades. I can't read the rest of it. If there's anything to read.' She sighed. 'You look at this and you would think it was some crock of shit cooked up by schoolgirls. To scare a mate, or maybe to scare themselves. Or maybe a horny kid hoping to get some randy MILF into bed.'

Harry raised his eyebrows again.

'Don't bother, Harry. Come on, I watch TV. I've got the internet.'

'Okay, so it's bullshit?' Harry said. The pounding was returning to his temples.

'No, of course it's not. That's what scares me, Harry. It's not, because it compelled this poor man to kill himself by eating shards of mirror.'

Harry nodded.

'And the marks on his back,' Sandy said.

The hairs on Harry's arm stood on end. He hadn't told her about the marks on the victims' backs. He'd wanted her to concentrate on the inscription without any distraction.

She stared at the wall, but she wasn't seeing the wall – she was seeing whatever it was that she saw when she went to that place. The place that made her special.

'How many victims are there, Harry?'

'Four. That we know of.'

'There's going to be more. At least six.'

'Why six?'

'One for each point of the star. One for the middle. Also, six is a significant number. In the Bible, six represents human weakness, and the manifestation of sin.'

'I was wondering if it was some sort of blackmail thing,' Harry said. 'And I can almost see that with the guy who threw himself in front of the train, and the cop who blew his head off, and the guy who gassed himself in the car. But eating glass? Eating pieces of mirror until he died? Jesus.

'And then I thought, maybe he was on drugs – ice or something. Maybe he couldn't actually feel the pain.' Harry made a mental note to get Phil to check the toxicology report, even as Sandy shook her head.

'There may have been drugs and there may have been blackmail, but that's not what this is about. There were notes. Something about a goddess?'

'"I have sinned. I give my life for the Goddess."'

'They were all blokes. That's something. You need to go looking at all the badass goddesses out there. Kali. Lilith. Ishtar. Louhi.' She noted Harry's distracted expression. 'Don't worry, don't worry – I'll email you a list.'

'Thanks, Sandy.'

'It could also just be a woman. A woman who has set herself up as a goddess.'

Harry considered this.

'I'll keep my ears open, my eyes open,' Sandy said.

'I'm sorry – I haven't even asked about you. How is all that going?'

Sandy laughed. 'If by "all that" you mean the ghost-whispering – yeah, it's okay. I think I've finally come to accept that I'm always going to be this way. I've started doing a bit of "work" for people. But, you know, I'm not making a big deal of it. Trying to keep it low-key. And, you know, it stops me being lonely, right?'

An awkward pause.

'So, how are things with Bec?' she said.

'I don't know, I mean, we had a really great date. It was just like old times. Better than old times. But… trying to keep my hopes in check.'

'Be careful.' Sandy smiled.

They finished their tea, talking about nothing much. Politics. Whether the Labor Party was going to survive. Harry told Sandy about his karate training. Sandy told Harry about her gardening. By the time they'd finished their tea, Harry was starting to feel almost human again.

Sandy checked her watch. 'Well, I'd better get going.'

'What, you didn't come down here just to see me?'

'I do have a life, Harry. Lunch and a movie with friends.'

'So… the world isn't going to end just yet?'

The smile faded on Sandy's face. 'No, not just yet. Not with you on the case.'

CHAPTER 9

Harry spent the rest of the day cleaning and drinking water and Berocca. His body felt sore, as though he'd run a marathon in between drinking pints of stout. But as far as he could remember, he had only walked from the bar to their seats, and a couple of times to the toilet.

Around lunchtime he got a text from Dave: *How did you pull up this morning?*

Harry grinned and replied: *I've been up for hours you lazy bastard.*

He flipped open his laptop, expecting to just spend a bit of time dicking around on Facebook. But then he checked his email and saw a message from Johnny, the guy who said he'd been raped by staff at St Therese private school.

```
Hello Mr Hendrick
Thanks very much for looking into this for
me.
    I don't know about meeting. I guess I
would have to at some point, but as you can
probably understand, that would be a big
deal for me. I just need to process it, get my
head around it.
```

You should go and talk to the groundsman.
Shane Packard. He wasn't involved. I mean,
I don't know that he was involved. He wasn't
one of the ones who... you know... At the
time I didn't think about it, but I've thought
about it a lot since then. Hard to believe
he didn't know about it. He knew about
everything going on in that place.

I remember the time they took me and a
friend of mine in the changing room by the
footy field. The place was a mess. After.

That prick Glengarry, the headmaster,
told us to clean it up, but we just grabbed
our clothes and ran for it, soon as we could.

He never mentioned it. Someone must've
cleaned that shit up.

Johnny

Harry sat there for a long time, thinking about that email.
Thinking about what Johnny must've gone through. Then
he googled 'Shane Packard' and the school's name. Found
an 'About us' page with a grainy black-and-white picture of
an oldish man with glasses and a head of shaggy dark hair.
Harry made a note to follow it up during the week.

He was preparing for a quiet night in. He'd scanned
through the films on Netflix and decided it might be time
to watch *The Evil Dead* remake. A pizza might be good.
His phone buzzed. Lee-Anne Stewart.

*He's 'working late' tonight. Which is funny, because it's a
Saturday. He's going to leave for his 'union thing' from home.*
And then the address.

'Ah shit,' Harry muttered.

He rubbed his face, thought about what to do. He hadn't accepted any money from her. He could just tell her he'd changed his mind. But he didn't like to let people down, and this could be worth following. He'd kick himself if he saw this story in the *Brisbane Mail* next month. Which it probably would be – Lee-Anne didn't seem like a person to be put off easily.

He texted her back.

Harry changed, grabbed a box of muesli bars, and headed for the car. He drove through the Saturday night streets. Felt a slight pang as he passed the Paddo Tavern. It wasn't his scene and, to be honest, he'd never been that into pubs and clubs. But when he saw those places heaving on a Saturday night, he often felt like he was missing out. The people always seemed to be having such a good time and if anything, it made him feel more removed from his peers, more removed from society.

He snaked around the city, made sure his brain was in gear as he pulled into the winding suburban streets where Lee-Anne and her unionist husband lived. What did he want to get out of this? What would make it worthwhile? An address. From an address he could establish who lived at the house, and whether or not they were a sex worker. Or if the premises was a legal brothel – that would be the most likely outcome. Lee-Anne seemed pretty sure that's what her husband was getting up to.

Harry pulled to a stop a few doors from Lee-Anne and Don Clack's place. He could see the black Mercedes sitting out the front of the house. Life must be looking up for unions, Harry thought. He ripped open a muesli bar and checked the time on his phone. The street was a typical one for this part of the city – tightly packed with refurbished worker's cottages. Often they'd been raised on their stumps and built in underneath. This was one of the areas of the city that hadn't gone under in the most recent floods, so building in underneath was still a popular choice to get a bit of extra living space. The Clack place was the grandest on the street. It looked as though at some point they (or the previous owner) had bought the neighbouring properties. This wasn't a worker's cottage; it was a full-sized Queenslander painted in heritage colours, with verandahs all the way around, a bifurcated staircase down the front, and lit up like a Christmas tree.

Harry was about two-thirds through his makeshift dinner when he saw Clack descend the front steps, wearing a long-sleeved shirt tucked into jeans. He looked much like he did on TV and in the papers. Once a big man, a union enforcer in the truest sense of the term, he'd gone to seed – his big frame supported a sizeable paunch. Meaty jowls added a bulldog-like aspect to his face. Glasses perched on his bulbous nose. He climbed into the car.

Harry expected him to head towards the city, or the southside, where most of the legal brothels were based. Instead, he turned in the opposite direction, away from the city, deeper into the northern suburbs. He drove fast, weaving in and out of traffic, and Harry's Corolla struggled to keep up. Harry floored the accelerator, urging his car on even though he knew that talking to cars was the preserve of the crazy and the desperate. *Maybe I fall into both of those camps right now.*

Eventually Clack pulled off the highway and wound through suburban streets. A poorer area than Harry lived in, but not destitute. The houses were mostly built in the 1980s. Lots of brick. Not much thought put into the architecture. But, much like anywhere in Brisbane, the higher the elevation, the grander the houses. At the top of the hill he pulled up outside a large brick home. It had a portico out the front and a stone driveway. The property was fronted by a fence of brick pillars and wrought-iron spikes. Clack pulled into the driveway. He pressed a button on the intercom system (another nice eighties touch). Moments later, the gate opened and Clack drove in. The gate closed after him and the front door opened. Harry couldn't see who opened the door, because the unionist blocked his view.

Harry pulled over and finished his muesli bar. He noted the address and the time in his notebook. Googled the address just to see if there was anything obvious. It didn't look like a brothel and he hadn't heard of one out this way, but then he wasn't that plugged in to the Brisbane sex work scene. Nothing. Not even an old ad on realestate.com.au. Whoever was living there had been there for a while.

He wondered if Lee-Anne was the jealous type and had got it wrong. Maybe this was a legitimate union function. Or maybe Clack was using union fees to satisfy a lover, rather than to pay a sex worker. That would still be a good story. He sat for a while, staring at the black gates, tapping his foot against the clutch, thinking. The property line continued up the road, where a big mango tree stood, its boughs drooping over the fence. Harry got out of the car, idea not fully formed in his head. Just going with his instinct.

Thick curtains were drawn over the front windows. He walked closer to the house, looked up and down the quiet street. Down the road someone had their stereo cranked up. He scanned the property, looking for signs of security cameras or motion sensors. Cameras could be small enough to be invisible, but most people wanted potential intruders to see them, and then move on to an easier target. Harry couldn't see any. He walked along the street in front of the house, then doubled back in the shadows under the mango tree. He told himself all he wanted to do was watch and wait. If it was a legitimate meeting, there would probably be other people coming too. Harry didn't want to be seen lurking when they arrived. If they arrived.

He found a handhold on the tree trunk, then wedged the toe of his boot into a crevice and pulled himself into a fork between two branches. Then up again. He crouched on the branch. The tattoo on the back of his neck itched. He pulled out his phone and took some photos of the car sitting in the driveway. He waited. He wished he'd thought to bring a warm coat and some gloves. When he'd imagined a stakeout, he thought of himself sitting in his car with the heater running, munching on coffee and doughnuts. His stomach rumbled.

He considered his options. He didn't really want to leave here without some indication of what was going on inside. Call it his curious journalistic nature. His impatience. Before putting his phone away, he checked the time. Don Clack had been in there just over ten minutes. If it was a sex thing, then he probably had another fifty or so. If it was a legitimate meeting, then that wasn't going to be over in less than an hour. Why drive all this way, on a Saturday night, for a meeting that was going to last less than an hour?

Overthinking was something the old Harry used to do. Think and think and think about it, and then do nothing.

Repeat for fifteen years. No. Harry edged along one of the biggest boughs that crossed the fence line. He walked with his hands out, like a trapeze artist, squinting through the gloom to watch where he was putting his foot. Above him, something thrashed in the tree. He ducked. One foot slipped off the bough and his hand shot out, grabbing another branch to steady himself. It creaked, but held, and he regained his balance. He peered into the gloom and saw the outline of bat's wings against the deep green of leaves.

He squatted again, staring at the house, much closer now. There was a gap in the curtain, but not wide enough to really see anything. It looked like there was a lamp on in the front room. Probably a lounge room. The front windows of the house were surrounded by garden beds. He peered back through the foliage, towards the street, to make sure it was still quiet out there, then dropped to the grass below.

He crouched, waiting for a sensor light, waiting for a dog to growl through the darkness. Waiting for a voice. When none of these things happened, he rose on the balls of his feet and crept to the front window. Crouching low, he peered through the gap between the curtains. White carpet. A white leather lounge and glass coffee table (more relics of the eighties?). A stained glass lampshade in the corner casting a warm glow over the expensive-looking modern art on the wall.

No people. But in the middle of the floor, a neatly folded pile of clothes. Jeans. Long-sleeved shirt. Boxers. Next to the pile of clothes, Clack's black leather shoes, socks stuffed inside them.

Harry crept along the front of the house to the door. There was glass on either side and Harry risked a peek through one of the panes, but saw only white tiles leading away into the darkness of the hallway through the middle of the house. He could make out harsh white fluorescents to the right, but again, no sign of movement. He looked at the entry area. A couple of pairs of shoes. High heels. Women's runners. A couple of coats hanging on a rack, both women's. Outside, just a raffia mat. On a whim, Harry picked it up. But no, that trick didn't pay off this time. There was just dirt and a dead cockroach. He set it back, and continued around the side of the house.

He could hear the people next door, cranking the barbecue by the smell of it. His stomach growled again. He heard the familiar sound of someone cracking open a beer as he assessed the head-high gate that blocked his path. It was locked. He could climb it, but there was a high likelihood the people next door would hear or see him, and Harry couldn't risk that. Besides, he was hungry and thirsty and his urge to keep exploring had withered away.

Fuck this for a game of soldiers.

Harry started back for the tree then stopped and looked at Clack's car. He walked over, casting another glance back at the front door, then peered inside. Clack had left his wallet in the centre console. Harry looked again at the glass panels beside the front door, and again out into the street. He cupped his hands against the glass, peered through. It didn't look like the car was locked. And if it wasn't locked, the alarm wouldn't be armed, right? He wasn't sure. He'd never owned a car that was worth enough to bother securing.

He grabbed the car door, said a little prayer, and pulled. The door opened. The interior light went on. No alarm. Harry leant into the car, then saw movement inside the house.

Shit! He jumped into the car, closed the door behind him and clambered over the to the passenger side, arm flailing for the dome light as he did so. He flipped the switch and it turned off. The outside light went on, flooding the car. He slid further down, heart hammering in this chest.

Oh fuck. Oh fuck. Oh fuck.

He was expecting Clack to arrive, looking for his wallet. Of course he'd be looking for his wallet at some point. Stupid. Stupid. Stupid. Harry should have just run for it. He could have easily got to the shade of the mango tree, beyond the reach of the porch light. He waited for the inevitable. Tried to think of some possible legitimate reason for being in Don Clack's car. Tried to think how he was going to explain this to Lee-Anne. How he would explain it to the cops.

Fuck. I'm finished.

But Clack didn't arrive. Harry slid up in the seat slightly, being sure to stay in the shadows. He couldn't see anything through the glare. Then the spotlight turned off. Harry blinked away the after-image, still cursing himself. His legs cramped. Sweat ran down his back despite the chill. *Jesus! What are you waiting for?*

As his eyes readjusted to the darkness, he could make out a woman's form. Tall, shapely. High heels. Stockings and suspenders. A black nightgown that flowed like spider's silk around her breasts and slim waist. She turned, and he saw the lines running up the back of her stockings. Caught a flash of red from her fingernails as she disappeared back inside the house and closed the door.

Harry slumped, panting. For a moment, like the spotlight, an after-image of the woman remained imprinted on his retinas. He couldn't remember why he was in the car. Then it came back to him and he wondered how he could have been so stupid. He grabbed the wallet, opened it. No family photos in this one. Barely any money either. Credit cards – yes. One with Clack's name on it, and one with the union's. Harry pulled out his phone and quickly took photos of them, risking putting the dome light back on. He pulled business cards out of the side pocket. If this woman was an escort, she was top shelf, the sort who might have business cards. He flicked through them. ALP. Brisbane Lions. An accountant – Harry took a quick snap of this one. Then he stopped.

The card was black and shiny, with pink writing: *Hunted – Gentlemen's Club*. A phone number scrawled on the back. It took him a moment to remember where he'd seen a card like this before – in Zak Godwin's wallet. Same handwriting. Most likely the same number. He took a photo and returned the card to the wallet, then placed the wallet back where he'd found it.

Harry got out of the car, gently closed the door, then headed back into the shadows.

CHAPTER 10

Harry sat at the computer, staring at the screen but not seeing it. He was thinking about her. The mystery woman. What connection did she have to Zak Godwin, mirror eater, and what connection does she have with Don Clack, apparent adulterer? With the strip club?

God, she was gorgeous. He kept seeing her slowly reveal herself through the shadows. Was she a stripper who moonlighted as a sex worker? Wouldn't be the first time, but it just didn't feel right. She was too beautiful. If she was a sex worker, like he'd thought the previous evening, she wouldn't need to work extra hours at a strip club. He looked away from the computer, picked up the business card. Closed his eyes and raised it to his nose. He could still smell the perfume. His heart quickened as he pictured her turning away, revealing the stocking seams drawing lines up the back of her long, shapely legs.

He opened his eyes, put down the card, rubbed his temples. There was a low buzzing in his ears, and when he closed his eyes the room spun slightly. It was much worse in the weeks after the lightning strike. The doctor said it would get better, and it had – mostly. He was tired, that was all. After getting back to his car, he'd waited for Clack to come out. It took just over an hour. Harry expected him to have a smile on his face, a skip in his step.

But the man looked worried. No, not worried; kind of dazed. As he walked back to his car he'd stumbled and almost fallen. He'd sworn under his breath. Harry remembered thinking he'd looked stoned, in a paranoid delusions way rather than a happy way.

Don Clack had sat in his car for another fifteen minutes. He hadn't moved, just sat there. Then the car fired up. Harry had followed him home, watched him carry his substantial bulk up the stairs.

Harry thought about having a lie down, then picked up the phone instead. He texted Lee-Anne. She called him a few minutes later.

'Well?' she said.

'Hello to you too.'

'Is he or isn't he?'

'Lee-Anne. I told you when I took this on that I'm not a private detective, I'm a journalist. So if I'm going to get this story, you can't confront him about this...'

'The bastard! I knew it! I bloody well knew it.' Her breathing became heavy down the line. Then she let rip with a hacking cough. 'Hang on a sec, love.'

Harry heard a door slide open and shut. Then the familiar snick of a lighter.

'I mean, I knew. But *knowing*, you know?'

'Hang on. I don't know anything for sure,' Harry said. He recounted his adventures from the previous night. He left out the bit about rifling through Clack's wallet. Even though Lee-Anne was the one who'd sicced him on Clack, he didn't think she'd appreciate this detail, for some reason.

She snorted. 'Beautiful woman, dressed in lingerie. About an hour. Doesn't sound like a union meeting to me.'

'I know but... maybe she's his mistress. As in...'

This time she laughed, so loudly that Harry had to pull the phone away from his ear. 'Ha! Did she have a white cane? A labrador?'

'No but, you know. He's powerful. Maybe that's what she's after. Maybe that's a turn-on for her.'

'I'd rather not sit here discussing that slut's turn-ons, if you don't mind.'

'If you want me to do the job and get the story written, I'll need some help. I'm going to need copies of his credit card statements and, more importantly, the union credit card statements. Can you get hold of them?'

'Yeah. Should be able to. Let me see what I can do. I'll catch you later, Harry.'

Harry thought again of the card, and of Zak Godwin's mirror-filled corpse.

'Hey, Lee-Anne.'

'Yeah?'

'In your email to me, you said this started "recently". How long ago?'

'Well, I don't know exactly. He has been working late a lot. The first time I got suspicious was... hang on...' He heard the door slide again. 'About five weeks ago. Yeah, that'd be it. He told me he was working late. I phoned him but his mobile was off. He *never* turns his mobile off. Tried him at the office and he wasn't there. Didn't think much of it at the time, to be honest. I thought he'd just gone to the pub. But the next time he told me he was "working late" I tried his mobile and it was off again. When he got back I could smell the slut's perfume on him.'

Harry thought of Clack, sitting in his car, staring through the windscreen.

'Have you noticed anything odd about him, since then?'

There was a pause. He heard Lee-Anne exhaling smoke. 'Yeah. He's more secretive. He's less... you know. He doesn't want to get intimate. I mean, he hasn't been that into sex in the past year or so. But it's gotten worse since the slut. I guess he doesn't need me for that anymore. Sorry, oversharing.'

'No, that's okay. I'm sorry.'

'Don't feel sorry for me. Just nail the bastard. Okay?'

'Okay. I'll do my best.'

Harry thought she was going to hang up, but then she spoke again.

'Oh, one other thing. He's become modest all of a sudden.'

'Modest?'

'Yeah. When you've been married as long as we have, you lose your modesty. It doesn't matter if you're on the toilet, in the shower. You've seen it all a million times. But last three weeks or so, Don's been locking the door when he has his shower. Comes out in his PJs, if you can believe it. I don't know what that bitch is doing to him.'

A vision of the four autopsy photos jumped into Harry's mind. He thought of the five incisions in each man's back.

'I'll see if I can find out. See you, Lee.'

CHAPTER 11

Harry tried not to think about what was going to happen. He found it easier that way. There was absolutely no reason to think about the process of asking the hard questions. Just ask them. Instead, he concentrated on his feet, walking up the gravel driveway. One foot in front of the other, shiny black leather. These days, he rarely needed to get dressed up. Many days he barely needed to get dressed at all, given he worked from home. This was not one of those days. He'd dressed that morning, already feeling the butterflies in his stomach. Charcoal trousers. Light pink shirt. Conservative striped tie. And the leather shoes that generally sat at the back of his wardrobe, gathering dust.

The grounds were alive with energy that only comes with the end of the school day. Kids surged around him, a sea of slacks, green shirts, straw hats. Most of them had an iPhone out as they jostled with their friends. Some were heading back to the dormitories. Others were kicking balls around on the Olympic-grade playing fields. And others still were trudging down the driveway towards the road, where an armada of school coaches and a cavalcade of luxury cars waited to ferry them home.

The past couple of days had been largely uneventful.

Bec had phoned, asking him out for after-work drinks on Friday. He was still waiting for Lee-Anne to find him some union credit card information. He noticed that she had dropped some money into his bank account. For expenses, she told him. It quickly went on removing the power and internet bills from his fridge. Both of those were more essential to his future earning capacity than food.

Harry checked his phone, looking for the directions Johnny had sent him. Harry wasn't meant to be on school grounds without permission. And he was pretending he didn't know that, because he knew he wasn't going to get permission. But he'd found in his years as a journalist that if you looked as though you knew where you were going, and you were carrying a clipboard or (in Harry's case, a notebook) you could gain access almost anywhere, if you were willing to shelve any legal or ethical qualms you might have. He didn't think his journalists' union membership would be getting renewed this year.

He passed lovingly restored red-brick buildings, and a few more recent additions. A world-class library and information technology facility, designed by a famed architect. An Olympic-size indoor swimming pool. And of course the shooting range, which came up in the election before last, raised by Labor in a disastrous attempt to take money away from private schools and give it to public schools.

Harry made his way down the side of the stately admin block, stopping outside a door with a neatly painted sign that read: *Facilities Manager*. Harry knocked, then pushed the door open a crack because he wasn't sure his knock would have been heard through the heavy oak.

Shane Packard looked up from his computer, peering

over the tops of his glasses. He was in his late fifties or early sixties, with shaggy brown hair, seeded heavily with silver. From his expression, he was expecting a student, perhaps come to collect a ball that had landed on a roof, or a water pistol that had been confiscated. When he saw a grown man there, Packard blinked a couple of times, as though to make sure he'd seen right.

Harry entered the room, knowing that the threshold was always the worst place to be caught.

'Sorry to bother you. Harry. Harry Hendrick.' He crossed the room and offered his hand. Packard took it. He had a hard handshake, his palm and fingers rough with calluses.

'Shane Packard.' He glanced at his computer. It was open on a news site. 'Did you have an appointment?'

'No, no, I didn't. I'm working on a story about the school.'

'A story?'

Harry took one of the chairs in front of the desk. Packard frowned.

'Yes. An article. I'm a freelance journalist.'

'Your name. Sounds familiar. Have you cleared this through the office?'

There was no easy in for this story. No safe territory to gradually work his way into it, get enough information so that when he dropped the bombshell, he had enough to go on even if the interview was terminated.

'You've been with the school for the past twenty years, right?'

'Does the office know...'

'That's what it says on the school's website, anyway.'

Packard looked slightly bemused. But there were worry

lines creasing his brow. *He's trying to remember who I am.*

'So you would have been working here through the early 2000s, right?'

Packard shrugged. 'Clearly.'

'I've got a source who claims there was a paedophile ring operating here at that time.'

The groundsman froze. He didn't look nervous or scared anymore. He looked angry. 'I know who you are now. Get out.'

'My source says he was raped repeatedly at the school. On one occasion, in the changing rooms…'

Packard reached for the phone. 'Get out. Now. Or I'll call security and have you removed.'

'He says it was a mess when they'd done with him. Any of this ringing any bells for you?'

Packard was bright red, pointedly not looking at Harry. He spoke a few words into the phone. Harry found himself struggling to control his anger. The tattoo burned on the back of his neck. In his mind's eye he was performing a number of martial arts techniques on Shane Packard, all of which ended with the groundsman on the floor, struggling for breath. Harry realised he was standing. He didn't remember getting out of the chair.

Packard hung up the phone. His eyes were watering, but whether that was from remorse or anger, Harry couldn't tell.

'They'll be here soon,' he said.

'So you knew it was happening, and you let it happen, and you didn't help those poor kids?'

Packard looked away, at his computer screen. He put his hand on the mouse. The pointer moving aimlessly on the screen.

'You've got nothing to say to me?'

The door burst open and two big security guards strode into the room. Harry held his hands up in a gesture of compliance. They grabbed him anyway, and dragged him to the door.

'I can walk by myself,' he said.

They ignored him, tried to twist his hands behind his back, but Harry knew those moves too. He let them lead him to the door. At the last moment, he shrugged out of their grip.

'Packard.'

Shane Packard ignored him. He was still staring at his computer screen.

'Shane Packard. You didn't deny it. Not once. I threw every accusation at you and you didn't even deny it.'

Packard looked up, as though to say something, then thought better of it as the security guards dragged Harry out of the room.

CHAPTER 12

Harry and Bec sat in a booth at the back of the bar. The place was just filling up with after-work suits. Outside, people streamed past on their way home or to late-night shopping. Bec looked beautiful in her neat white blouse and black skirt.

'Oh my God, I deserve this,' Harry said, holding aloft the pint of Guinness and tapping glasses with Bec, who had ordered a Manhattan. 'Cheers.'

She laughed. 'Cheers.'

Harry took a deep slug of beer, and it really did feel good.

'Tough week?' Bec said.

'You could say that.' He gave her the shortened version of his adventures following Don Clack, and then getting thrown out of the school. By the end of it, Bec was staring wide-eyed at him.

'I won't bother telling you about my run-in with HR then,' she said.

'No, please do,' Harry said, feigning sleep.

Bec slapped him on the arm, and then told him about her office adventures that week.

'So this Johnny guy,' she said, 'do you think he's on the level?'

'Up until Wednesday, I wasn't certain. His email seemed legit, but you can never be sure. I haven't spoken to him yet. Sometimes people have an axe to grind, and they want to use you as their weapon. But now – I mean, if you were Shane Packard, and the story was totally fabricated, wouldn't you try to defend yourself?'

Bec nodded.

'And then the next day I got a call from the headmaster, which was basically a thinly veiled threat of legal action if I tried to go public with any of Johnny's story.'

'Did they know it came from Johnny?'

'She didn't name him and I didn't name him. She said there were some "troubled" boys who'd come through the school as part of the scholarship program. Tried to make out there were kids with mental health issues.'

'There probably were, if what Johnny said is true.'

'Exactly.'

Harry looked at his beer and was surprised to find it half gone. 'Bec, please don't let me get wasted tonight.'

She raised an eyebrow. 'Worried I'll take advantage?'

Harry opened his mouth, closed it again. Bec winked.

'Dave and I got a little…'

'Wasted?'

'Yeah… wasted… last weekend.'

'I make no promises. You're a big boy. You can look after yourself.'

Over in the corner, the band was setting up. It didn't look like a traditional Irish affair.

Bec frowned. 'This looks ominous.'

'Yeah. That's just what I was thinking.'

'Want to go somewhere else?'

'Yeah. That'd be good.'

They drained the last of their drinks and headed out into the throng, just as the band belted out the opening bars of 'Mr Jones'. Bec and Harry looked at each other and laughed.

They wandered through the city, window shopping, talking about nothing in particular. Bec had changed gyms and had dumped pilates in favour of hot yoga. Harry told her about his karate and how the instructor wanted him to think about competing. Bec wrinkled her nose.

'Not a fan of the old MMA?' he said.

'They fight in a cage, Harry. A cage!'

He laughed. Bec snaked her fingers into his.

They stopped walking outside the old Regent cinema, now the foyer for a new apartment complex. He found himself holding both of Bec's hands, staring into her eyes. From inside the foyer came the smell of coffee.

'Do you want a coffee?'

'Nah. Let's get another drink.'

They strolled to the Victory, and any hope of staying clear of cover bands was obliterated by the sounds of 'Blaze of Glory'. They ordered a jug and stood shoulder to shoulder with the hundreds of people crammed into the beer garden.

'This wasn't quite what I had in mind, either,' Bec said.

They finished the jug quickly. 'I thought you were meant to be keeping me on the straight and narrow,' Harry said.

'Let's go back to my place,' Bec said. 'I've got Berocca. And vodka.'

'Uh oh.' But he let her lead him out into the street again, and swipe them into the foyer of her apartment building.

'Not sick of inner-city life yet?' Harry said.

'Well, the four a.m. bin trucks aren't getting any more appealing,' she said. 'But this is good.'

She pushed the lift button. They stepped in, and she swiped again and thumbed her level.

'Come here, Harry Hendrick.'

She pulled him to her and they kissed as the floor fell away under their feet. Harry held her head in his hands. She snaked her arms around his waist. He felt extremely tired, but extremely content.

Bec's apartment was smaller than Harry remembered, or maybe she'd just bought more stuff. He was apprehensive about coming back. The last time, he'd been in tears, frantically packing boxes because he didn't want to be here when she returned. It felt different. Maybe because she'd made this place her own, as he'd done at Paddington. And they were different people now.

He settled himself on the couch, looking out the windows at the city lights. She returned with a tin of Berocca, a bottle of vodka and two glasses.

'I sense interesting cocktails are on the way,' he said.

She put down the glasses and poured two drinks. Handed one to Harry. 'To new beginnings,' she said.

'New beginnings.'

They chinked glasses and drank. Harry refilled the glasses, slightly drunk now.

'To watchful friends,' he said. He was thinking about Bec's promise to keep him from getting wasted, but when they tapped glasses, he remembered what Sandy had said about Rob keeping watch over him. He shivered.

'You okay?' She shuffled over until their knees touched, laid a hand on his leg.

'I am now,' he said, and kissed her.

She pulled away, grinning. 'Did you rehearse that line, or what?'

'I did now,' Harry said, and leant in for another kiss.

'That makes no sense whatsoever,' she said, but laughed and kissed him anyway. They slid down the lounge together, her skirt riding up. Harry put his hand on her waist. They kissed for a long time before Bec pulled away and topped up her drink.

She got up and walked to the sliding door out onto the balcony. Harry had a serious buzz going. He picked up his drink, sloshing a little over the side, and followed her.

The wind whistled through the city at a fair rate of knots, but the drink kept him warm. Thunder boomed, and Harry shuddered a bit. He folded his arms around Bec, nuzzled into the small of her neck. She pressed her body against his. They looked out at the city, still very much alive beneath them. Between the buildings, they could see lights shining off the river.

'I can't really believe this is happening,' she said. 'Can you?' She pulled away from him slightly and sipped her drink.

'Yes and no.'

She watched him. Her eyes glittered from pools of darkness.

'When I think about last year...' Harry started.

'Don't even talk about last year.'

'When I think about back then it seems impossible. Bec, what happened with Paul?'

She pulled out of his grip entirely, but still held his hand. Fifteen stories below, traffic eased through the city. Someone shouted and someone else laughed. She leant on the railing.

'It seems so obvious now,' she said. 'There was us. Together for years. And then not. It ended so suddenly. And I remember thinking, when it happened, that if it was that easy to break, then it would never have lasted anyway.'

'Bec...'

She held up a hand, quieting him. 'And then... Paul was there, he was sweet. It was something new, exciting. It seemed so easy, after those last few months with you...'

'Gee, thanks.' Harry smiled. Bec returned it.

'And then he proposed and I was literally swept off my feet. He actually swept me off my feet. But then as the big date drew nearer, I started to get this feeling of dread in the pit of my stomach. It wasn't even really about you.'

'Again, thanks.'

'But it wasn't, not then. I couldn't see any way it would ever be right again between us. I just knew that I couldn't be with Paul, either.'

'You didn't leave him at the altar – literally?'

Bec thumped Harry on the arm. 'No, almost. Couple of weeks out.'

'Ouch. I wish I could say I was sorry for the guy, but...' Harry put down his glass and moved in again, pressing himself against Bec, holding her. They kissed.

The skies opened up, and big drops of icy rain splatted against the balcony. But Harry didn't feel the cold anymore.

CHAPTER 13

Harry tried to block out the sound of his phone ringing. Beside him, Bec groaned and rolled over. He opened his eyes, squinting at the bright sunlight streaming through the curtains. He couldn't see his phone.

'Harry!' Bec said, as though the sound was physically hurting her. Harry lurched out of bed, realising he was in his boxers. He didn't remember getting undressed, but saw his clothes strewn across the floor. He picked up his pants and the phone fell out, hit the floor and slid under the bed. It stopped ringing. Started again. Bec pulled her pillow over her head.

Harry got down on his hands and knees, and grabbed the phone.

'Hello?'

'Harry?'

'Phil? It's Saturday.'

'Crime doesn't stop on weekends you know.'

'You're a pen pusher.'

'Can we talk, or what?' He sounded pissed off.

Harry went out into the lounge and closed the bedroom door. The almost-empty vodka bottle sat on the coffee table, mocking him. He slumped on the couch and looked the other way.

'Okay. Hit me. But gently.'

'There was an… accident this morning,' he said.

'An accident? You paused.'

'You need to see this.'

'What? I need to see what?'

'You need to get down here. Roma St.'

Harry rubbed his face. 'I had a bit of a rough night last night.' Unbidden, his mind threw him a vision of he and Bec, entwined on the lounge he was sitting on. One of the shot glasses had rolled under the table.

'I'll send a car.'

'Are you fucking shitting me?'

'Harry, do I sound like I'm shitting you? Just tell me where you are.'

'Don't worry about sending a car. I'll get a cab. I'll see you soon.'

Harry hung up and went into the bathroom. There was only one toothbrush. He checked the cupboard. There was a new one, green, soft. He broke it open and brushed his teeth. When he was done he slotted it in next to the other green one in the holder, and looked at them for a moment. He washed his face.

Harry checked in on Bec. She still had the pillow over her head. He thought about kissing her goodbye but felt suddenly bashful. And he didn't want to wake her.

He found a notebook and pen in the kitchen.

Dear Bec,
Sorry — work calls.

Thanks for last night. I have no idea
what we got up to, but it looks like we had
fun. My place next time, okay?

H xx

Harry eased through the front doors of police HQ, clutching the takeaway coffee he'd picked up down the road. He felt like he needed a breath mint. The desk sergeant looked at him with an expression resting somewhere between boredom and hostility.

'Harry Hendrick. Phil asked me to come.'

The desk sergeant didn't seem to register either name. He tapped away at his computer without acknowledging Harry at all.

'Wait over there,' he said eventually, pointing to a bench that ran along the wall. There was another guy waiting there, head in hands, faded jeans, flannelette shirt. He looked like he'd had a bad night too. Harry sat next to him. Flanno reeked of wine and tobacco. He paid Harry absolutely no mind.

Harry pulled out his phone, surfed blindly through various social networks, something he did when he was bored or anxious. In this case he was a bit of both. He wondered what he did before he had a smartphone. But he knew – he would have been sitting there, one leg jiggling up and down, thinking of worst-case scenarios. He saw a picture of an Instagram friend posing with the DeLorean out of *Back to the Future*. He grinned, in spite of the thumping headache.

'Harry?'

Phil was staring at him. He had his iPad under one arm,

as though he'd been carrying it around for the past couple of weeks. He looked tired. Harry pocketed his phone and shook Phil's hand.

'Follow me.'

He handed Harry a pass with a big red T on it. Under that, his name, scrawled in ballpoint pen. Phil led the way through the front room to a door that looked like it had a bit of heft to it. There was a key-code panel next to it, and a security camera above it. Phil pressed the buttons and the door clicked open, then clunked shut behind them. Phil led him through the bowels of police headquarters.

'Big night?'

'Yeah. I caught up with Bec.'

Phil stopped in his tracks. 'As in?'

'Yeah, that Bec.'

Phil whistled. 'So… back on again?'

Harry nodded, although he couldn't actually remember what happened the night before. 'Looks like it.'

'Good for you.'

Phil opened an unmarked door and gestured for Harry to enter. It was a small office. Computer on a bench desk in front of a large mirror. The mirror looked too big for the room. There were a couple of metallic green filing cabinets. A clock on the wall. Another machine next to the computer, but Harry didn't know what it was. Phil closed the door behind him.

'So what's going on?' Harry said.

Phil pulled out the chairs in front of the bench desk. Harry took one and Phil sat next to him, then laid the iPad between them. Harry's stomach filled with butterflies. He wished he'd had something to eat. He pushed the cup to one side as Phil fired up the device.

'We've had another… situation,' he said.

'Another suicide.'

'No.'

'What then?'

Phil paused, then opened the photo album on the iPad. Harry found himself looking at a cherry picker. The gantry was extended. The hopper at the top was just under a set of powerlines. Harry stared at the picture.

'What? What am I looking at?' He was starting to get pissed off. Phil had dragged him all the way in here to look at a photo of a piece of machinery. He could have emailed it. Then Phil zoomed in.

'Oh shit.'

There was a body in the hopper. It was partially obscured by the railing, but Harry could see that it was crouched, arms curled over its head. And the overalls it had been wearing were burnt and black.

'Happened this morning,' Phil said. 'It should have been routine repair work.'

'So… it's another suicide.' Harry imagined the guy using the controls to push himself into the powerlines. The machine itself was probably insulated. But touching two of the powerlines would cause electricity to arc from one to the other.

'No.'

Phil's phone buzzed. He reached for a switch. The lights dimmed. Harry realised he was staring into an interview room. A man and a woman faced the mirror. Judging by their clothes, Harry assumed they were detectives. There was a guy in a high-vis vest sitting slumped in the chair opposite the cops.

'This guy killed him,' Phil said.

'Oh shit,' Harry said. 'I shouldn't be seeing this. I shouldn't be here for this.' He got up to leave and Phil grabbed his arm a little more forcefully than necessary.

'It's cool,' he said.

No, it's not.

'He started yammering on about a goddess,' Phil said. 'You need to see this.'

Harry let himself be guided back to the seat, partly because he felt this was part of what he signed up for, partly just because he wanted to hear what this guy had to say.

The detective on the left had closely cropped blond hair, streaked with silver, and a broken nose. He reached for a button and the speakers on the desk crackled.

'Recommencing interview at...' he checked the clock on the wall, 'eight fifty-seven a.m. Anthony Gillespie, being interviewed by Tom Dullemond and Sharon Evans.'

Harry got out his phone and opened the notepad.

'Don't worry,' Phil said, 'I'll send you a transcript.'

This is so wrong.

'So, Mr Gillespie, can you just run us through what happened again?' Dullemond said.

'Jesus! I told the cops there and I told you guys twice. You want me to live it over and over again?'

Dullemond and Evans just sat there, waiting.

'The storm knocked out some powerlines. We were sent to repair them. Early this morning. Fuck, I dunno. Just after midnight. It all went well. Just routine stuff. We had the power off, fixed the lines, juice back on. And then...'

He stopped. His shoulders shook. The sound of sobbing came through the speakers. Harry's phone buzzed. He peered at the screen. Sandy. He switched his phone off.

'I'd known him for years. I can't believe he's gone. We used to hang out together.'

'Mr Gillespie. If you could just tell us what happened.'

'I pushed him up into the powerlines. And he fucking burned.'

'Why did you push him into the powerlines?' Evans said. She had old-fashioned glasses and was younger than her colleague.

Gillespie just sat there.

'Mr Gillespie? What happened? Were you tired? Push the wrong button, something like that?'

He shook his head.

'Can you tell us? For the benefit of the recording?' Dullemond said, even though there was at least one camera Harry could see.

'No. It wasn't an accident.'

Harry felt his stomach plummet. His fingertips tingled.

'What then? He pissed you off? He try to fuck your wife? Your daughter?'

Gillespie looked up at this, laughed bitterly. Shook his head, then remembered himself. 'No. Nothing like that.'

'What then? You just got sick of working with him? Just tick you off one too many times?'

'No. He was great. Loved him. Like a brother.'

'You fucking shitting me? You fried him alive, Gillespie. He was screaming and you just pushed him further into the wires, you sick prick. If it wasn't for a passer-by dragging you away from the controls, he'd probably still be there, right?' Dullemond looked as pissed off as everyone else about being woken early on a Saturday morning.

Gillespie's head dropped back to his chest.

'Oi!' Evans said, and Gillespie jerked. 'Talking to you. We just want to understand why you killed him. That's right, isn't it, you're basically saying you deliberately killed him?'

'Yeah,' Gillespie said, then coughed. 'He had to die.'

'Why?'

'He had to die.'

Dullemond slammed the table with his fist. 'But why, you sick piece of shit?'

Gillespie laughed, and for a moment Harry thought Dullemond was going to leap across the table and beat the shit out of him.

'For the Goddess.'

Harry felt the hairs stand up on the back of his neck.

'For the Goddess? What goddess?'

'I knew I was going to kill him. It was so fucking good when it happened. When I pushed him into those powerlines...' He paused and his back quivered again.

Harry turned to Phil. 'Get him to show us his back.'

'What?'

'Ask them to get him to show them his back.'

Phil reached for his phone and thumbed in the message. Moments later, Evans checked her phone. She looked past Gillespie to the two-way mirror. Raised her eyebrows.

'Take your vest off, and your shirt,' she said.

It took Gillespie a few moments to register the order. 'What?'

'You heard. Vest and shirt off. Need to make sure you haven't been injured. Get evidence of any injuries you have, so we don't get blamed for them.'

Gillespie shrugged off his hi-vis vest, unbuttoned his shirt, and slipped it down his shoulders. He stood.

'Holy shit,' Phil said. 'The marks.'

Five incisions, invoking the inverted pentagram. They looked fresh. One of the incisions had split open leaving a trickle of dried blood down his back.

'Except this one's alive.'

Gillespie turned around. Evans made a show of taking photos with her camera.

'They need to ask him about the marks on his back.'

But they didn't need any prompting from Harry on that score. Gillespie barely had his shirt back on before they asked him.

'What marks?'

'You've got five cuts on your back, mate,' Evans said. 'See?' She showed Gillespie the picture.

'I don't know.'

Dullemond snorted. 'Someone's been cutting up your back and you don't remember?'

'I don't know.'

Dullemond and Evans looked at him for a while, neither saying anything.

'Okay, so you said you had to do this for the, what… the Goddess?'

'No. I didn't have to do it. I wanted to do it.'

'Who is this goddess? Your mistress? Bit of action on the side?'

Gillespie laughed again. The sound of it sent shivers down Harry's back.

'I want to know why this goddess wanted your work-mate dead.'

Gillespie sat there, chin on his chest again. His shoulders

shook, and Harry thought he was crying again. But then he lifted his head and it was clear it was laughter. Dullemond's face tightened.

'I fail to see what's funny about this. You killed a man this morning. You've admitted it was premeditated. You say you're acting on behalf of someone called the Goddess. If you fail to cooperate with us, you're looking at thirty years in jail. What, exactly, is funny about any of this?'

Gillespie got himself under control. 'You talk about thirty years as though that means anything.'

Dullemond snorted again. 'It means you'll be just about claiming the pension when you get out. Your daughter, if she's still talking to you, will be forty-five. Yeah, that's right. If you can't be bothered doing it for yourself, do it for your daughter, for your wife.'

Gillespie said nothing.

Harry thought again of the woman standing, partially clothed, backlit. He thought about telling Phil, but held it back. He didn't want cops knocking on her door, giving her the opportunity to slip the net. Harry wanted to catch her himself.

Dullemond and Evans glared at Gillespie. Dullemond's stare looked powerful enough to knock a hole through a brick wall. Harry was glad he wasn't on the receiving end.

'So you've got nothing else you want to add at this point? You did it on purpose, for some goddess, and you're not sorry about it? Don't suppose you want to tell us who this goddess is?'

Gillespie smirked. Dullemond's jaw muscles flexed.

'I'm sorry,' Gillespie said.

Dullemond got stiffly to his feet, looking like he was

using all his energy to resist throttling Gillespie. Evans checked her watch.

'Interview suspended at nine twenty-two a.m.'

She followed Dullemond out of the interview room. The door closed. Gillespie's head slumped. His shoulders shook, and this time Harry was pretty certain he was crying.

Harry expected the two detectives to come into the room and swap notes, but they must have had better things to do.

'What happens now?' Harry said.

'Psych test, most likely,' Phil said. 'Drugs too.'

'Drugs?'

'Oh, yeah. He's most definitely high on something.' Phil picked up his iPad.

'So that's it?'

'Unless you want to hang around for tea and cucumber sandwiches with Mr Gillespie here?'

Harry looked through the two-way mirror. Gillespie was still crying. He had his head on the desk.

'Nah. I think I'll pass. Hey, can you send me everything you have on the victim?'

Phil considered. 'Yeah, I mean, we don't have much at the moment, but when we do, I'll send you what I can.'

'Thanks.'

Harry walked down Roma St towards the city, turning on his phone. He saw the message from Sandy. Traffic was starting to build up, and he didn't want to have to compete with that while he talked to her. He found a cafe and ordered a coffee he didn't really want, then disappeared down the back.

He dialled Sandy straight away, without bothering to listen to her message.

'Sandy, it's Harry.'

'What. Happened.' He could feel the strain in her voice. She was scared. He imagined her sitting at her dining room table, staring over a cup of cold tea at her beautifully maintained garden.

'Are you okay?' Harry asked.

'Harry, don't worry about me. What happened?'

'Someone else died. Someone was killed this morning. I think there's a woman manipulating men somehow, blackmailing them...'

'No. No, Harry. This isn't a woman. Or, if it is a woman, she's meddling in stuff she doesn't understand. Tell me what happened, exactly.'

Harry told Sandy about Gillespie, and how he and his partner were sent out to fix some electricity lines and decided to kill one of his workmates for no apparent reason.

'He had the same marks on his back as the suicide victims,' Harry said. 'How did you know something was going down? You don't get informed of every death on the planet, do you?'

'Harry... I didn't know someone had died, but I suspected it. I was asleep. And then I heard this horrendous wailing, a screeching. I jerked awake. I thought it was a nightmare. Then I heard it again. Fury. A furious screaming. Uncontrollable rage. I thought it was someone hiding in the room at first. Usually, when this sort of thing happens, I can tell that it's from the spirit world. It's like I'm hearing it through, I don't know, a wireless that's not quite on the signal.'

'A wireless?'

Sandy uttered a mirthless laugh. 'Don't toy with me, Harry. Not in the mood right now.'

'Sorry.'

'My heart. I thought it was going to burst. I thought… I thought the world was ending. And then I heard whispering. My spirit guides. They were telling me it was okay. It was okay. Except, it's not.'

The waitress delivered Harry's coffee. He pushed it to the other side of the table. He felt sick again. He stared at the formica table.

'Did they say what it is?'

'No. It's not like that, Harry. They don't often communicate in words. It's more like pictures. And for this they showed me…'

'A door. A door opening on darkness.' The vision jumped into Harry's head before Sandy could speak it.

He could hear Sandy breathing on the other end of the line.

'Harry,' she said eventually, 'you need to be extremely careful around this woman. Whoever it is, this goddess is using her as an envoy.'

'Yeah, I figured. Thanks, Sandy.'

Before Harry put his phone away, he saw that an email had dropped into his inbox. He opened it.

Dear Mr Hendrick

Yeah, I can see that you'll need to meet me before you take this any further. I've just been getting my head straight, you know?

Let's do it next Friday, 11a.m. There's a park just near where you used to work.

It's called Marchant Park. There are some benches near the BBQs, near the car park. I'll see you there.

Johnny

CHAPTER 14

Harry sipped his drink, letting the music pump through him and watching the woman on the small revolving stage do her thing. Having discarded the nurse's outfit, she was down to a red G-string and matching bra that barely covered her breasts. He tried telling himself that there was a lot of artistry to the pole dance he was watching, then gave up and admitted it was turning him on. He checked the time on his phone and looked around the dimly lit gentlemen's club. There was a lot of faux leather and velvet. Dark wood-look tables. A few men sitting around, but it wasn't packed. Every now and then a scantily clad woman would lead one of the men towards the back of the club. Harry guessed that's where the lap dances were done. Still no sign of Clarice.

He'd swapped notes with Bec earlier that week, gently pushing for information until he'd established that they actually hadn't had sex after their vodka binge.

'Harry Hendrick! What do you take me for?' she'd said.

All week he'd been trying to imagine the scenario where he'd apparently undressed her out of the smart, sexy business attire and somehow not made love to her. Another reason to not get drunk. He'd sent her some flowers, and she'd phoned him when they arrived. He could tell by her voice that she was blushing.

The rest of the week had been largely uneventful. Phil came through with his promise of a full transcript of Gillespie's interview, and had added pre-death photos of all of the victims, and of Gillespie.

'Harry Hendrick?'

Harry looked from his phone. The woman was tall, dressed in high heels, stockings and a silk camisole that accentuated her breasts. For this joint, it was a decidedly demure outfit. Around her neck she wore a gold chain with a small key dangling between her breasts. She had a blonde bob, but Harry was pretty sure it was a wig.

'Clarice?'

'That's me.'

She slid beside Harry onto the bench seat. Her leg rubbed against his.

'Sorry,' she said, brushing the hair away from her eyes. She peered at him through her fringe.

'That's okay.'

Her perfume washed over him. Harry felt aroused despite himself, and then embarrassed. He took a sip of his drink, then pulled his phone over to him.

'Did your manager explain what I'm after?'

'I *am* the manager,' she said.

'Sorry,' Harry said. He blushed. 'The man I spoke to…'

'Oh, that's Roger. He's in charge of security.'

'I'm really sorry. You just look… so young.'

Clarice laughed and patted the back of Harry's hand. 'Seriously, forget about it.'

'Okay, let's start again,' he said. 'I'm Harry Hendrick. I'm a freelance journalist…'

'I know who you are. I googled you. You broke that big story last year. Good job.'

'Thanks. Anyway, I'm working on a story. I can't go into too much detail at this stage. But two of the people involved came to your club, and both of them went away with a card from the club, with a phone number written on it. So...'

'You're trying to put two and two together?'

'Basically.'

'Okay – have you got the card?'

Harry pulled the card out of his wallet and handed it to Clarice. She studied it, sniffed it and wrinkled her nose. Frowned.

'Nothing immediately springs to mind. The number isn't familiar. Come with me.'

She stood and wove through the mostly empty tables. Harry followed, trying not to look at her legs. A woman lay spreadeagled on the stage, a couple of strategically placed ostrich feathers all that stood between her and the whooping patrons. At the back of the club was a small lectern, something like a maitre d' would stand behind. This maitre d' wore a suit jacket over a black corset and fishnet stockings. Her bright red hair was pulled up in a bun. Beyond her, a heavy velvet curtain. As Clarice approached, a man emerged from between the curtains, a nubile young woman on each arm. He looked very happy. He tipped Harry a wink and a grin.

'Hey Gem – does this number look familiar to you?'

The redhead looked at the card, then shook her head. Through a gap in the curtains Harry caught a glimpse of a lithe body gyrating in time with the music.

'I'll look it up,' she said. She flipped open an iPad and

swiped, frowning. 'Nope. Not one of ours. Although if she was doing a bit on the side, she might have a separate phone.'

'The girls aren't supposed to give out their numbers,' Clarice said. 'We try and be really strict about it. There's no funny business here. But sometimes the girls want to chase a bit of extra money – you know?'

Harry nodded, although he had no idea beyond what he'd read in news articles. He pulled out his phone and scrolled through the photos to a head shot of Zak Godwin, mirror eater.

'Have you seen this guy around?'

Clarice looked at the photo. 'No, but that doesn't really mean anything. I'm not here twenty-four-seven, and as you can see, we try to at least create the illusion that we're not trying to identify our patrons. If he'd been here, he'd be on our CCTV footage, but we don't really have time to go through thousands of hours of…'

'No, no – that's okay. How about this guy?' He swiped through to a photo of Don Clack he'd saved from the union's website.

Gem frowned. 'Oh shit,' she said, shuddering.

'What?' Harry said.

Clarice grabbed Harry's hand and looked at the photo. 'Ugh. Daddy.'

'*Daddy?*'

'Yeah, he used to come here all the time. Always wanted the youngest girls. He was always pestering them to call him "Daddy".'

'*Used* to come here all the time?'

'Yeah,' Gem said, grinning. 'Tell him the story, Clar.' Her eyes had lit up and were sparkling. Behind her, a woman with dark skin and long blonde hair led another punter through the curtains.

'About a couple of weeks ago he came in,' Clarice said. 'Looking nervous for once, which was weird. He ordered a double Glenfiddich like he was totes cool with it, then sat there sipping it like a nervous schoolboy. Krystal drew the short straw and went over to see if he wanted a dance.

'He started muttering something about his mistress and needing permission. So he phoned up someone, spoke to her for a couple of minutes – all "Yes, mistress, No mistress" – then handed the phone to Krys. She told me later that he was to pay for the longest dance we did, but he probably wouldn't take that long. Then hung up.

'So he comes past, pays his money, looking all hangdog and nervous. He was sweating like a pig. Hands shaking when he handed over his credit card. Said he wanted the works, whatever was the maximum. We were happy to take his money off him.

'So she takes him in, sits him down, gets him comfy with his drink, starts to dance and he tells her, No. He stands up, takes her hand – he was really gentle, she said, and gestured for her to sit. And then...'

'He started dancing,' Gem blurted.

Harry did a double-take. 'He... what?'

'He started dancing,' Gem said. 'You know, like trying to do a strip routine. Started with his shirt, undoing the buttons one by one.'

'And what was Krys doing?'

Gem could barely suppress the laughter. 'She was just sitting there. I think she was shocked more than anything. And she knew that I would've seen it on the CCTV...'

Gem gestured at the small screen set low on the lectern. 'He got his shirt off…'

'And he had cuts on his back?' Harry said.

'Yeah!' Gem said. 'You know this freak?'

'No, not really, but I know of him.'

'Anyway, by the time Roger got in there, this character had taken his pants off. Not his boxers, thank God. Rog just grabbed him and his clothes and wrestled him out the door. Guy didn't put up much of a fight.'

Gem had a hand to her mouth, stifling the giggles. Clarice took over the story again.

'He got dressed out on the pavement. We were going to call the cops but he skedaddled pretty quickly.' She shrugged. 'And that was the last we saw of Daddy.'

Harry made a note of it on his phone, although he couldn't imagine himself ever forgetting this story. Lee-Anne Stewart wanted something that would humiliate her husband. Shit, Harry could dig up the CCTV footage and stop right there. What was Clack thinking?

'Did he seem drunk? On drugs?'

Gem shook her head. 'Not really. He'd had a drink, but he was walking okay. Just nervous, like I said.'

'So what's the deal with this guy? You gonna arrest him?'

'I'm a journalist. He's… he's part of the story I'm working on.' Harry nodded. 'Thanks for your help, Gem.'

'That all you want? Anything else I can help you out with?' she said, arching one eyebrow and tilting her head at the curtain.

Harry laughed. 'Maybe some other time.'

'I'll see you then, then.'

Gem returned to her podium. Clarice led Harry to the entrance.

'I don't understand why this number is on the back of our cards,' Clarice said. 'And then one of them turns out to be this weirdo.'

'Me neither.'

'You showed me two pictures. The other guy – he also had a card?'

'Yeah,' Harry said, thinking of Zak Godwin, who'd eaten every piece of mirror in his home. 'But you won't need to worry about him coming around.'

On the way back to the car, Harry had a thought. He pulled out his phone and dialled Phil.

'Hey, Phil, it's Harry.'

'Hey, Harry. What can I do for you?'

'You know how I found that weird note at Godwin's house?'

'Yeah.'

'Did you find anything similar at the other crime scenes?'

'Hang on.'

Harry waited. At the other end of the line, he could hear Phil tapping away on his computer.

'No. But…'

'Someone could have missed it.'

'Right.'

'Have you got anything back from the lab?'

'Nope. They've got a massive backlog.'

'Figured as much. I was wondering, can I have a look at the cherry picker?'

'Ah… yeah, I guess. Hang on, I'll see where it is.' Another pause. More typing. 'They've towed it out to the police compound. I'll get you the address.'

Harry pulled on his sunglasses while he was waiting. Even though it was winter, it was hot. People on their lunch breaks milled around him. He leant against a planter box and watched a nervous punter hanging around outside the strip club. The man glanced up and down the street once before taking the plunge and disappearing into the club's shadowy depths.

'Here you go,' Phil said, then gave Harry an address. 'When you get there, tell them you've got clearance to inspect the vehicle. I'll put a note on the file for them.'

'Thanks, Phil.'

Harry took a one-hour drive west of the city. The compound was surrounded by rusty old fences, entwined with long dry grass and vines bearing purple flowers. The Police Impound Yard sign was faded. It was even hotter out here, and Harry was dripping with sweat by the time he made it to the office.

It was blessedly cool inside. Enough so that Harry could forgive the budget minimalist furnishings: drab grey carpet and matching cinderblock walls. The desk and the wall clock looked like hand-me-downs from police HQ, circa 1974. A bored constable checked Harry's request on a computer that looked like it was thirty years old, and directed him to the rear of the compound. Of course it would have to be right at the back.

'Watch out for snakes,' the constable said.

'Thanks.'

Harry followed the rutted dirt track between rows and rows of cars. Most of them had the tell-tale marks of fingerprint dust around the door handles and inside. Some had been in accidents. Others sat on flat tyres. The further towards the rear of the compound he went, the older the cars got.

The white cherry picker sat in an old corrugated iron shed. It wasn't hard to tell that this was the right cherry picker – it was the only one in the yard. If it was sentient, it would be thinking, 'What the fuck am I doing here?' The basket was wrapped in police tape. Harry could just make out two blackened hand prints. He told himself the smell of cooked pork was just his imagination.

He walked around to the front of the vehicle and pulled the passenger-side door open, then stepped back as a rush of hot air hit him. A copy of a Queensland Police inspection checklist sat on the bench seat, blue ticks jumping off the page.

Harry pulled the glovebox open and rifled around inside it. Rego papers, a faded safety checklist, a dog-eared skin mag, a shopping list (*milk, Winnie Blues, taco kit*). He closed the glovebox. Too obvious.

He searched under the mat on the passenger side, then on the driver's side. Nothing but dirt and a desiccated gecko. He closed the door, stood back from the vehicle. Just behind the cab was a storage compartment marked with a green cross. The press button release was dusted with fingerprint powder. He tried the button, half expecting it to be locked, but it popped open. He pulled and the door popped up on its hydraulic arm. The first aid kit filled most of the space. Next to it, a defibrillator and a fire blanket in its heavy plastic bag. He pulled the first aid kit out, then the other gear. At first glance it looked like there was nothing else, but then – *there*.

A piece of paper, rolled up and pressed into the corner. Harry gently pulled it out. It was stiff and slightly faded, but it was clear it hadn't been here as long as the porn mag in the glovebox.

Harry gently unfolded it, careful not to rip it, but he knew what it was going to have on it. That's why he'd come all this way. The piece of paper was dominated by an inverted pentagram, with symbols marking each point and the centre of the pentagram. He didn't have to compare it with the picture on his phone. He knew it'd be a match.

CHAPTER 15

Harry zipped his jacket and got out of his car, hunching his shoulders against the wind blowing across Marchant Park. A few straggly pines swayed back and forth in the wind, but the park was mostly sportsfields and grassy hills. He'd been here many times in his *Chermside Chronicle* days, usually to interview Little Athletics stars. Kids ran up and down the hills, with parents or coaches looking on. A dad knelt on a kite, holding it while he tried to tie the string. A toddler with red cheeks and a runny nose watched.

There was a graffiti-scarred sun shelter with seats underneath, electric barbecues, and benches overlooking the strange white building that Harry had once worked in. An artefact of eighties architecture, it looked like an alien spaceship that had crash landed. Harry had considered visiting Miles, his old editor, but dismissed the idea. That part of his life was over, but he was worried he would end up getting sucked back into it.

Harry didn't know what Johnny looked like. He'd said in his email, *I'll see you there*, not, *You'll see me there*, so Harry presumed Johnny knew what he looked like. There were certainly enough photos of Harry online and in the papers after his big story last year.

He strode up the hill, glad of an excuse to get his legs working and warm up. He continued past the benches to the top of the hill, then turned and looked back at the car park. This would be a good place to go for a run, he thought, although probably not that good that it would be worth driving all this way. Jim was still pressuring him to join this martial arts tournament that was coming up, and Harry thought he'd give it a go. With so much else going on, the tournament would provide something different to focus on.

Harry walked back to a bench and sat, huddling against the cold wind. Harry wondered why Johnny hadn't suggested meeting at a cafe or a pub, like most of his contacts. But of course Johnny wasn't here to talk shit – he had finally decided to lift the lid on his traumatic childhood.

Harry looked up from his phone and saw a man walking up the hill. Early twenties. Blond hair whipped about by the wind. Tall but not lanky. Finely chiselled features. He just had jeans and a t-shirt on, but the cold didn't seem to worry him. Muscles rippled under the t-shirt. Shit. He looked like a male model.

'Harry Hendrick?'

Harry stood, and they shook hands. The calluses told Harry the tan was from working outside, and not a salon.

'That's me. Johnny?'

'Yep.' Johnny looked away when he spoke, as though ashamed of his own name. 'Did you go and visit the groundsman?'

'Yeah, I did,' Harry said. 'Hey, shall we get out of the cold?'

Johnny nodded. They walked back to Harry's car. He saw a battered ute in the car park and took it to be Johnny's. The tray was filled with bags of cement and concreter's tools. Harry got into his car. Johnny looked around and followed suit.

Harry pulled out his phone and opened the voice recorder. 'Are you okay if I record this?'

Johnny didn't look so sure, but Harry needed the record. He also found that sometimes getting out the recorder made it real for the interviewee. They knew they wouldn't be able to back down on what they said.

Eventually, Johnny nodded. 'Yeah. Fuck it,' he said, then shook his head and stared into his lap.

Harry set up the phone and put it on the dash. A gust of wind shook the car.

'I think we're gonna get some rain,' Johnny said. He shifted uncomfortably on the seat.

'I went and interviewed the groundsman,' Harry said.

'Yeah? And?'

'Well, you couldn't really call it an interview, since he didn't say anything. But you know what?'

'What?'

'He didn't deny it,' Harry said. 'I gave him every opportunity to tell me I was lying. But he didn't. He just looked shocked. The school contacted me the next day, threatening legal action.'

Johnny nodded. A bitter smile touched his lips, then faded. 'The school – they don't give a shit, they just don't want it to come out.'

Harry watched the kids rolling down the hill. The dad had finally got the kite ready. The toddler was holding onto it, not sure what to do.

'When did it start, Johnny?'

'First year I went there. Just funny remarks, you know. From a couple of the teachers. Inappropriate remarks. I was thirteen.'

'What kind of remarks?'

'Things about my body. Things about their bodies. You know, like "nice arse". Or, "I bet you'd like some of this?" It was always when there weren't any other kids around. They were grooming me. Seeing how I'd react. I was too scared to do anything. I was on a scholarship. I was an outsider. So I just used to grin, try and ignore it.'

Johnny shook his head again.

'Then it moved to the next phase. I found a gay porno mag in my locker. I was called to one of their offices and found a European porn video on the desk. There were kids on the cover – I realise now they were kids. But probably not actually illegal. Like borderline, you know? And when they saw me looking they'd put it away.'

'You didn't report it?'

'When you're a kid, you feel like you're on your own, you know?'

Harry nodded. He could relate.

'I was in the school rugby team. Glengarry was the coach. After training one day, when all the others had gone, he called me aside. Invited me over to his place on the weekend – said he had some training videos he wanted to go through. At the time I thought it was for the whole team. It didn't occur to me how he'd waited until everyone else had gone.

'So, that weekend, the parents were both working, as per usual. I rode my bike over to his place. He made some comment about how sweaty I was, but how that didn't bother him. I think now that I saw the hunger in his eyes but I just ignored it. I didn't listen to the sirens going off in my head.

'He sat me down, got me a drink. I thought it was water until I sipped it. Vodka and lime. He said it would relax me. He put a DVD on then said he was going to get himself a drink. It wasn't a training video. It was porn. Not kiddie stuff. That came later. A man, taking a woman from behind, up the arse.

'He came back and was all, like, whoops, sorry about that. But he didn't turn it off. He was watching my reaction. "Does this bother you?" he said. I was thirteen, at a boys' school. Everyone's paranoid they're gonna be accused of being a homo if they don't like porn. So he sat next to me and... y'know.'

Johnny made a wanking gesture with his hand. He choked back tears, then thumped the dashboard.

'Fucking prick. Afterwards he told me there was nothing to be ashamed of. All this bullshit about the beauty of the human body. He... he touched me. Through my pants. I bolted for the door. And the prick just laughs at me. I was going to tell my parents...' Johnny shook his head. 'But I didn't. I was ashamed, and scared, because I thought there was something wrong with me.' He took a deep breath.

Outside, the rain was easing. The wind whistled over the car. Harry let Johnny's silence play out. He wasn't in a rush.

Gradually, Johnny told the full story. It wasn't just Glengarry: he was part of a paedophile ring. There was another teacher from the school, a science teacher, who had since been convicted of child porn possession charges and was serving time in Arthur Gorrie, west of Brisbane. There were other men he could name, but they'd dropped out of sight in the years since. Johnny was raped on multiple occasions. Sometimes at school. Sometimes at Glengarry's place, which had a soundproof room.

'Sometimes, there was this house, out west. Darra, I think. There were girls there too,' he said.

Johnny had dates for a lot of these assaults. The rapes continued until he left school. Shame prevented him from revealing what was going on, then fear.

'They told me that if I said anything, they'd kill me. One of the guys, he was fucking scary. This old dude. Bushy grey hair. Prison tatts. Said he'd murdered a kid a few years back. Said he'd done time, would be worth doing a few extra years just to nail a snitch. I thought he was bullshitting, until he showed me the photos.'

'Why have you decided to break your silence?' Harry said.

Johnny sighed. 'I... I thought Glengarry was the ringleader. After I left school, I kept my ear to the ground. I told myself that if I heard a squeak that it was still going on, I would go to the cops. Nothing. I thought that maybe that day in the changing rooms, Glengarry realised they'd gone too far, how close he'd come to being caught.'

He stopped, wrapped his hands together in his lap. Looked out the side window.

'A couple of weeks ago, I got an email from an old friend. Hadn't seen her since when I was at school. She was another of their... she was abused. It's still going on. Not at the school. But... do you know the name Marcus Wilson?'

It set off a spark in Harry's head, but it didn't catch.

'He's a cop. You would of heard of him during the...'

'Flood clean-up.' A few years earlier, the city had been hit by a massive flood. Marcus Wilson took charge of the recovery effort.

Johnny nodded. 'That's him. He's one of them. He was there. I didn't know he was a cop at the time. He never made a big deal of it, for obvious reasons. But it explains a lot of things. I think he's more than just a part of it. I think he's in charge.'

Harry stared out the windscreen. *Shit.*

'You think I'm crazy, right?'

Harry shook his head. 'No. I'm just thinking about how we can prove this. This friend of yours, is she willing to talk to me?'

'Maybe. Also, they took photos. I can remember someone with a camera at most of the sessions. They were probably selling them. I don't know if any of those photos still exist. But if they do, there's your proof.'

Harry considered. He reached for his phone and turned it off. 'Johnny, thank you for having the courage to...'

Johnny reached out, put his hand up. He was staring out the window. Lip quivering. 'Just get the pricks, okay?'

Johnny got out of the car, slammed the door, and trudged back to his ute.

CHAPTER 16

'This is nice,' Bec said.

Harry looked around. He hadn't really taken in the restaurant, he was so transfixed by Bec. Had been since he'd met her on George St. She was wearing a deep blue dress, high heels, a delicate silver necklace and matching earrings. The blue in the dress set off her eyes, which could look blue or grey depending on the day – and sometimes, Harry thought, her mood.

'Yeah, it is,' he said. He looked around. Crisp white tablecloths. Muted lighting. A candle on each table, creating a sense of intimacy. All the men were in suits. All the women in close-fitting dresses.

The staff hovered, anticipating the diners' needs. After seating Harry and Bec, they'd made themselves scarce before returning with the wine list. Harry let Bec do the ordering – she had always been better than him at that sort of thing – and he was very satisfied with the full-bodied red the waiter returned with.

He took a sip. 'Do you remember that time in France?' he said.

Her eyes lit up and he saw she knew what he was talking about. They'd hired a car and gone on an ill-fated camping trip, where the rain seemed to follow them wherever they went. Just outside of Marseilles they'd pulled into a little town and were coaxed into a small winery to sample some wines. Bec looked at the price tag and saw the bottles were a hundred euros each – about their weekly budget at the time. The guy working there was unperturbed, offering them credit, offering to ship the bottles back home for them. In the end, they'd waited until he went into the back room to get some brochures for them, then bolted.

'I thought he was going to follow us,' she said. '"Your bro-*sewers*. Your bro-*sewers*."'

Harry laughed. 'Just letting you know, that is the worst French accent I've heard.'

She slapped him playfully on the arm.

'I've never told you this,' Harry said, leaning in. 'But I'm pretty sure I saw him at Gare du Nord when we left, running alongside the train.'

Bec laughed. Harry sipped his wine. He'd spotted the restaurant a couple of weeks earlier, filed it away in his mind, hoping he and Bec would get to this point.

'So you pulled up okay after last weekend?'

'Yeah. I'm going easy on it tonight though,' she said. She played with her glass, then glanced at Harry. 'Don't want to get too drunk.'

He felt her foot, under the table, brushing his calf. He wanted to grab it. He wanted to leave the restaurant right now, take her to her place, tear her clothes off.

'I wish you could have stayed longer, last weekend.'

'Me too,' he said. He stared into her eyes. Thought again about just blowing the joint. But she would be furious. He was capable of being a grown-up, was capable of delaying the gratification, just a bit.

'How's work?' he asked.

'Ah, you know, same old same old. You?'

He nodded, guarded. He thought about the week he'd had. Interviewing Johnny the day before. The visit to the strip club. The horrific reason why he'd been dragged away from Bec's place the previous Saturday. He searched for something he could share, something that wouldn't drag the evening down. Couldn't think of anything.

They ordered dinner, then filled the silence with small talk. Around them were the sounds of muted conversation, and the clink of cutlery and crockery. They talked about music, about movies that were out, brushed upon the news of the week.

Harry had the steak. It went perfectly with the wine, and pretty much melted in his mouth. Bec had the lamb, and from the look on her face at the first mouthful, it was just as good.

'Are you okay?' Bec said, out of nowhere.

'How do you mean?'

'You seem a little quiet. Like there's something on your mind.'

Harry watched her for a moment. 'It's just work, just turning the pieces over, trying to make them fit.'

'Anything I can help with?' She took another mouthful of dinner.

'No, but thanks for offering.'

Bec laid her knife and fork on the edge of the plate. 'Harry, this isn't going to work if you can't open up to me.'

Harry dabbed his mouth with his napkin. Nodded. 'Yeah, I know. It's just been a heavy week, I don't want to bring you down.'

She took his hand, interlaced her fingers with his.

'I promise, I'll tell you everything... over breakfast,' Harry said.

Bec smiled. 'A bit presumptuous. But, okay.'

Harry's phone buzzed. He pulled it out and looked at the screen. He recognised the number immediately. It was the same one written on the back of the business cards.

I understand you're looking for me?

He slid the phone back in his pocket. She could wait.

'Is that your other girlfriend?' Bec said.

'Yeah,' Harry deadpanned. 'Which is really annoying, because I specifically told her I'd be with you all night.'

Bec mock-laughed.

They finished dinner and ordered dessert.

'So, are you going to take me to the Ekka?' Bec said. 'Win me a stuffed toy?'

Harry was taken aback by the request. Like pretty much every kid in Brisbane, he'd been to the Royal Queensland Show. The rides, junk food and ridiculously priced showbags were a Brisbane institution. But the only time he'd been as an adult was when he was doing stories for the *Chronicle*. He and Bec had never been, and he'd just assumed she thought it was tacky.

'Do you want to go?'

She nodded.

'Is this some kind of mid-life crisis?' he said.

Her face darkened.

'I mean, early, still totally hot, mid-life crisis?'

'No... just... I dunno. I think we got into a rut. I don't want that to happen again. I want us to do new stuff. Nice save, by the way.'

Harry nodded. 'I'd love to take you.'

Harry's phone buzzed again.

'She's insistent,' Bec said. 'I'll go powder my nose so you can sort it out.'

She rose from the table. Harry watched her head towards the bathroom, then picked up the phone.

I think you need to hear my side of the story. Now.

He thumbed the keyboard: *I'm busy.*

Less than a minute later the reply came: *I'm sure your lady friend won't mind. This is a one-time-only offer.*

Harry felt the hairs on the back of his neck stand up. His 'lady friend'. What, she was spying on him? He looked nervously around the room. The same bunch of people as before. He thought about the walk here. He'd met Bec outside the restaurant. Had anyone been watching? He didn't think so, but he'd been preoccupied. Anger flared.

He dialled the number.

'I knew you couldn't resist,' she purred. Her voice was deep, slightly raspy. Harry's mind flashed to the night he saw her standing in the doorway dressed in lingerie. His body betrayed him.

'What the hell are you playing at?' he said.

The waiter who had been so attentive now swooped, as people looked over from neighbouring tables.

'Sir, if you could please...' He gestured to the front door.

At the back of the restaurant, Bec returned. As Harry rose from his seat, he saw her smile fade.

'I'm not playing, Mr Hendrick. But you seem to be playing detective.'

'I'm not a detective, I'm a journalist...'

'Then you will know the one about hearing both sides of the story.'

'Of course, but I'm busy.' He stood in the doorway,

looking back into the restaurant where Bec was pointedly not looking at him.

The woman sighed. Harry's face burned. 'You want to solve the mystery. I think by the time you get to my place, you'll be most of the way there.'

He knew she was smiling. He imagined red lips. He imagined her in the outfit he'd last seen her in.

'I won't bother giving you the address,' she said. 'I know you've already visited me... you naughty man.'

She hung up.

Harry stared at the phone, then pocketed it. He could feel the tension, not just from Bec but from himself. When he got back to the table, the desserts were there. He didn't sit.

'I'm sorry, but I'm going to have to go,' he said. He could tell she was pissed off, that she knew this was coming.

'What?'

'I'm sorry – it's a work thing.'

Bec looked at her dessert, then around the room. Then she grabbed his hand. 'No.'

'No?'

'You are going to tell me why this is so important, or I am not going to let you go.'

'What?'

'Sit.'

Harry sat. The tattoo on the back of his neck was growing warm. He sighed. 'The texts are from a woman. Maybe a sex worker,' he said. He was trying to keep his voice low, but even so the volume of conversation in the room seemed to drop a few decibels, and a couple of heads turned his way.

Bec's eyebrows lifted.

'I think she's involved with the deaths of five men in the past few weeks,' Harry said. 'And this woman has just offered to tell me her side of the story.'

Bec looked at her dessert again.

'I'm sorry,' Harry said, getting up.

Bec pulled his dessert over. 'On the bright side, two desserts.' She forced a smile. 'Is it safe? To go and talk to her?'

Harry felt a wave of excitement wash over him. *No*. The tattoo on the back of his neck burned.

'I'll be okay.'

'Go on, then. Go and meet your maybe sex worker.'

'Thank you.' He kissed the top of her head and was gone.

CHAPTER 17

Harry stopped outside her house, getting out of his car and heading straight for the intercom. He thumbed the button.

'Hello? It's Harry Hendrick.'

There was no reply, but the electronic gate buzzed, and the lock released. As he walked up the path he heard her heels clicking on the tiles, saw her silhouette briefly as she walked down the hallway. She opened the door as he stepped onto the porch. She had on a pair of tight jeans, a red t-shirt and green hoodie. Her long black hair hung over her shoulders. She was still beautiful, but looked like she was heading out to the movies, not about to wallop some (lucky) guy into submission.

Lucky? Harry caught the thought, surprised at it. He was here to do a job. He tried to remember the anger he'd felt at being interrupted during dinner.

'Mr Hendrick.' She held out her hand. Her grip was firm, her skin warm. 'Lily Sweeney. Sometimes known as Mistress Hel. With one L.' She stood to one side.

He walked into the small hallway, and she directed him through to a lounge room at the front of the house. Harry recognised the décor from his first visit, although the white leather lounge and the glass coffee table didn't look as tacky from up close.

'Drink?' she said.

No, Harry thought. 'Yeah. Whisky.'

'Ice?'

He shook his head.

'A man after my own heart. Take a seat.'

He sat on the couch. He could smell her perfume, and found himself watching her make the drinks. She was still sexy, even dressed like this. She returned to the couch, with the drinks, and sat next to him.

'Bottoms up,' she said.

Harry picked up his drink and she clinked glasses with him. He took a sip. It was good. Malt whisky. At least fifteen years old. Its warmth spread through him; he felt as though he was sinking into the couch.

'I hope your girlfriend wasn't too upset,' she said.

The comment raised a spark of anger. 'I'm not here to socialise, Ms Sweeney.'

She smiled at him. 'I like it when you call me Miz.'

She sipped her drink. Also a whisky, although she'd added some shards of ice. Harry flashed back to Zak Godwin and the shards of mirror they found in his stomach.

'Okay then, let's get down to business. Thanks to you, Mr Hendrick, I've been banned from that lovely gentlemen's club. They seem to think that I'm implicated in some wrongdoing. I have done nothing wrong.'

'Why troll a strip club then?'

'Have you ever been to those places? Exploiting women, treating them as pieces of meat to touch and ogle. It's revolting...'

'Then why…'

'Because I find that sometimes men can be made better, they can be made to respect women… with a little training.'

Harry felt his body respond to the comment, even though he didn't want it to. He wanted to ask what kind of training, but he bit down on it. Covered his reaction by taking another sip of whisky. Interesting. Something… something slightly bitter at the finish.

'They said that Don Clack thought he needed to be the one doing the lap dance,' Harry said.

'Like I said – training. See how they like it.'

'You know he's using union money for this "training"?'

She rolled her eyes. 'How he pays is none of my business.'

'You expect me to believe that he started stripping off because you told him to?'

Lily Sweeney crossed her legs. For a moment Harry remembered how they looked in stockings. He turned away, embarrassed. She leant in closer. The smell of her perfume was intoxicating. He was sweating. The drink was going straight to his head.

'Men are so easy to control, Mr Hendrick. I got you here, away from your lady friend, just by asking.'

'What about Zak Godwin, what did you get him to do? What about Anthony Gillespie, what did you get him to do?'

The smile faded.

'I read about it online. Very sad. But nothing to do with me.'

'And the marks, on their backs?'

'Again, nothing to do with me.'

Harry felt the bulge of his phone in his pocket. He hadn't thought to record any of this.

'I don't believe it,' he said.

'Ask them then. Well, the ones who are still alive. Harry, there are some men who like to be cut – it turns them on. But I don't do that. That's one of my limits. No golden showers, no brown showers, no kids, no blood.'

Harry stared at her.

'If you don't believe me, I can show you the playroom,' she said, eyes twinkling.

For a moment Harry saw himself naked, arms tied above his head. He couldn't see Mistress Hel but he could hear her heels clacking against a burnished concrete floor. And he wasn't scared, just excited.

He put his glass down, surprised to find it empty.

'Another?' she said.

'No, I... I've got to drive.'

Lily Sweeney smiled. 'You could stay here the night. I'm sure I could find somewhere safe to keep you.'

Harry struggled to focus. He was looking at her on the lounge, but seeing her standing in the doorway in her lingerie as he hid in Don Clack's car. He pulled his phone out of his pocket. Opened the images. Swiped through to the one of the piece of paper he'd found in the cherry picker truck.

'What's this?' He handed her the phone.

She raised her eyebrows. 'Looks like some kid's drawing. Doodles.'

She started swiping through the photos. Harry reached for the phone but she blocked him.

'Interesting collection you've got here. Are you really meant to have these on your phone?'

He knew she was looking at the crime scene photos from the cherry picker. He reached again for his phone. She pushed out her arm and held him back. He was surprised at how strong she was.

'You don't really play by the rules, do you, Harry?' she said.

'Can I have my phone back?'

'That's okay. Neither do I.'

Lily Sweeney kept swiping through the photos. 'She's nice, Harry. You've done well.'

He batted her hand away and snatched his phone back, glimpsing the photo of him and Bec drunk. The one that had ended up on Facebook. He shoved the phone back in his pocket, suddenly full of remorse. *I'm such an idiot.*

'Are you actually going to tell me anything useful?'

She pouted. 'I already have, Harry.'

'And what about Don Clack?'

'I'm not going to talk about business arrangements with clients. There's that whole confidentiality thing. You might be familiar with it – or maybe not.'

Harry got to his feet, a little unsteadily.

'You sure you're okay to drive?'

'Yeah. I'm sure.'

She stood, put her hands behind her back. A smile played at the corners of her lips. 'Sure you don't want to come and inspect the playroom?'

Harry didn't answer; didn't trust himself to answer.

'Oh, well. Maybe next time.'

Harry headed for the door. He didn't bother looking to see if Lily Sweeney followed. He tried the handle – locked.

He waited. Turned.

Her grin broadened. 'Women like me have to be careful.'

She took her time unlocking the door, then stepped in front of Harry as he tried to make his exit.

'Oh, just one more thing, Mr Hendrick,' she said.

'What's that?'

'I have cameras all around my house. Like I said, girls like me need to have some... protection.'

Harry felt the hairs on the back of his neck stand on end. Lily Sweeney smiled. She took a couple of steps up to him, so they were almost touching.

'Don't fuck with me. Or I can promise you, I will fuck with you. Good night, Mr Hendrick.'

He backed out of the doorway, almost tripping over the doorsill.

'You can get out the same way you did last time,' she said, and closed the door in his face.

Harry stood on the front doorstep, cursing, until he remembered what she'd said about the cameras. The front gate was locked. He climbed over it and jumped down the other side, looking up and down the street to make sure he hadn't been observed. Well, observed by anyone other than her.

He sat in his car, fuming, looking at the front door. Why had he rushed out here? What had he expected her to do? Own up to it all? Give him an exclusive? He stared into the darkness. A possum walked along the powerline, stopped and sniffed the air.

'Shit. Shit, shit, shit.'

He'd wanted to see her, that was the bottom line. No matter how much he tried to rationalise it, that was why he'd come out here. He felt as though Lily Sweeney had sucked all the emotion out of him, and how he was filling up with guilt.

Harry pulled out his phone and dialled Bec. He wasn't surprised when it went to messagebank.

'Hey, it's me. I'm so, so sorry. I'm... I'm finished here. Call me when you get this.'

He drove. He didn't want to go home. He drove into the city. Revellers roamed the streets: guys with their shirts out, women in tiny dresses, despite the winter wind rushing down Elizabeth St. He drove past the restaurant. It was closed. He hadn't really expected it to still be open and, even if it was, he certainly hadn't expected Bec to be there waiting for him. His mood darkened as he left the city.

He ended up on a lonely road on the edge of the Brisbane State Forest. He pulled into the car park. In a few hours this place would be packed with cars – mountain bikers, bushwalkers, families. But now it was deserted. The wind in the trees sounded like static pulsing from a radio. The stars shone like pinpricks of light.

You could stay here the night. I'm sure I could find somewhere safe to keep you.

Harry found himself considering the offer. He thought again of her long legs, clad in fishnet stockings. Suspender belt cutting a black line across her milky thighs. The riding crop. His head buzzed. He was hard.

He looked up and down the road but there was no-one about. In a daze, he unzipped his fly. Harry started rubbing himself, eyes closed, imagining Mistress Hel working him over. He felt her gloved hand against his bare chest, her breath in his ear. Intoxicating perfume. He gasped for breath, imagining himself in her playroom, strung up like a piece of meat, completely at her mercy.

I know you've already visited me... you naughty man.

The sting of the crop against his chest, his arse, his legs.

You fuck with me, and I promise you, I'll fuck with you.

Harry came. As soon as he did, he woke from his stupor, looking down with a mixture of bewilderment and disgust.

'Shit.'

He searched in the centre console, found a wad of old McDonald's napkins, cleaned himself up. He felt cold, empty, but intensely relieved. He felt calm for the first time that week. But also ashamed.

He zipped himself and drove home.

CHAPTER 18

Harry bowed, jumped into the ready stance. His heart rate quickened as he saw Jim getting ready to hand him his arse on a plate. The referee, a fourth dan black belt Harry had only met tonight, stood between them, hand held out, eyeing Harry and then Jim.

'Fight!'

Jim leapt at Harry. For a small man he had a long reach, his legs launching him over Harry's head. Harry blocked the kick but this wasn't like fighting a red belt: Jim was stronger, faster.

Harry staggered backwards, the padding soft under his feet. Jim followed up with a series of punches and strikes, Harry only just getting his arms between them and his body and head.

But he couldn't maintain any control over the situation. Jim was smothering him. Toying with him. *If I could only get some space*. Harry made his move, leaping backwards with the intent of launching a spinning kick as Jim moved in to finish him off.

But no sooner had Harry pivoted slightly than Jim was on him, launching into the air and bringing down a scissor kick. Harry stumbled off the mat as the referee came between them again. Jim pulled the kick at the last minute.

'Break!'

They returned to the centre of the mat. Harry was only vaguely aware of the other students – all black belts – sitting in rows. On the other side of the mats, the club's Australian founder stood, arms folded. He probably wasn't seeing the potential in Harry that Jim had.

'You've got to focus, Harry,' Jim said.

Harry nodded. But he hadn't been able to focus since Saturday, the night of his disastrous date with Bec and encounter with Lily Sweeney. He'd spoken to Bec on the phone and she'd seemed distant, possibly still pissed off at him. He considered visiting her, but worried it might come across as desperate, as though he was still hiding something from her. When he wasn't thinking about Bec, it was Lily Sweeney. Mistress Hel. He kept wondering about what she'd said, about showing him the playroom. He kept wondering what might have happened if he'd stayed the night.

'Fight!'

Jim leapt in again, this time with a roundhouse kick. Harry pivoted, just avoiding the blow. Regardless of the pads they wore, if that kick had connected he would have been on the floor waiting for an ambulance.

But then a rare opportunity. Putting all his effort into the kick, Jim had let his arms drift open a bit, revealing the red circle in the middle of his chest padding. Harry pummelled him with three quick punches – *bambambam!* – and despite Jim's fitness and the padding, he heard the instructor grunt under the force of the barrage.

Jim darted back and Harry was on him, trying to sweep his legs, then driving his heel through Jim's hasty block, delivering another solid blow. Jim ducked to the side and stepped in with a front kick. Harry parried, turning his instructor, and drove his fist into Jim's kidney. Jim wheezed and spun, but Harry went the other way, wrong-footing him.

Harry saw it in his eye, his moment to finish this. Jim had been forced off-balance; all his weight was on his front foot, away from Harry. He was totally exposed. Harry saw himself drop, spin and sweep Jim's legs out from under him. In the moment before he struck, everything was perfect. All he had to do was...

I know you've already visited me... you naughty man.

Long legs. Stockings. Black, black hair cascading over bare shoulders. Sparkling eyes.

Harry saw the kick just before it connected. A fiendish step side kick, delivered from a position of weakness but at perfect range. The side of Jim's foot slammed into Harry's stomach, knocking the air out of his lungs. Harry hit the deck and slid all the way off the mat, onto the hardwood floor.

'Break!' the referee yelled. Quite unnecessarily.

At first Harry didn't think he'd be able to breathe again, then managed to heave in a breath that made his chest feel like it was going to explode.

Jim waited for him in the 'rest' position, fists in front of his belt. Harry struggled to his feet, then hobbled to the centre of the mat. Jim wore a barely suppressed grin.

'Bow,' the referee said. They bowed. Jim gestured to the side of the mat. On the way off, he slapped Harry on the shoulder.

* * *

Harry and Jim walked back to their cars. The wind howled around them, but Harry didn't feel cold.

'What happened in there?' Jim said. 'I saw your eyes go. One minute you were there, the next...'

Harry looked away.

'Weren't feeling sorry for your old instructor, were you?'

'Ha! No, I've just got a lot on my mind.'

Jim paused, waiting for Harry to fill the silence. But Harry couldn't talk about this with Jim.

'Okay. You did well.'

'Thanks.'

'But at the bout you're going to need to keep your wits about you. We go easy on each other here...'

'That was going easy on me?'

'You know what I mean. At the tournament, you lapse like that, you'll probably end up in emergency.'

Harry rubbed his ribs. Nodded. 'It's okay, boss. This... this thing. It will be sorted out by then.'

CHAPTER 19

Harry pushed through the front door, still panting from his run. He was planning to get straight in the shower but on the way to the bathroom decided to check his email. When he saw one from Phil, he sat. The shower could wait. He opened the email and downloaded the attachment. Harry's heart thumped in his chest.

The case files. Fuck. This was so wrong. Harry had told Lily Sweeney he was a journalist, not an investigator, but he could feel himself drifting further and further from one to the other. He flicked through the file.

Zak Godwin. Public servant turned mirror eater.

Constable Brad Brooks. Blew his brains out with his service pistol.

Christopher Lawrence. Jumped in front of a train.

John Moncrieff. Gassed himself in his garage.

Phil had also included Anthony Gillespie, and the guy he'd fried, Jeffrey Stafford.

As Phil had said, Godwin had seemed like a regular guy. Police hadn't been able to dig up anything weird about him. His wife said she didn't know anyone who would want to harm him. Like Phil, he was a civil servant for the Police Department, but much higher up the food chain.

He'd been working on a project to support the families of police officers killed in the line of duty. Very noble. As Phil mentioned, he was on a couple of boards: Queensland Writers Centre and the RNA, home of the Ekka.

Brad Brooks had been a young, promising constable. Then, shortly before he suicided, he began acting strangely. Harry didn't know what exactly he'd been doing – large sections of the report Phil had sent him had been redacted – but it was enough to get him suspended. Two days later, he was dead.

Harry made a mental note to ask Phil about it. They may not want to give it to him in an official document, but maybe Harry could weasel it out of Phil over the phone or in person.

For some reason, when Phil had told him about the guy who jumped in front of the train, Harry had imagined it happening in Central Station. Maybe it was him harking back to his time in London, when it wasn't unusual for trains to be delayed due to 'body on tracks'. But it wasn't like that at all. It happened out at Ipswich, west of Brisbane. Chris Lawrence had been on his way home from Walloon Quarry, where he worked as a blasting technician, AKA a powder monkey. Witnesses say his ute pulled up at a railway crossing as the boom gates came down. He put the ute in park, switched on his hazard lights and got out. He stood on the road as the crossing lights flashed and the bells rang. Just before the coal train reached the crossing, he sprinted around the boom gates and threw himself in front of the train. The driver didn't even have time to sound the horn, let alone hit the brakes. Wouldn't have mattered anyway; at that speed, the train needed three-quarters of a kilometre to stop. Police found his note on the passenger seat: *I give my life for the Goddess.* Same as the others.

Harry looked up from his computer, thinking about Chris and his sprint in front of the train. Clear blue sky, yellowing grass on the sides of the road, someone cursing as he made his dash. He thought about what Lily Sweeney had said to him about men being so easy to control.

John Moncrieff had also lived out west. Actually not too far from Chris, although according to the police reports, they'd never met. John had been a cattle farmer, but his sons didn't want anything to do with diesel and dust. They'd moved away to Sydney and Melbourne. John's wife had died three months previously. He had no close friends, and lived on the edge of a small town. The neighbours – if you could call people living a kilometre away neighbours – said the Moncrieffs were friendly enough but kept to themselves. One of the them had seen John in town a few months prior to his wife dying. Said they were looking at selling up. The local cops said he'd been saying that for years and had never done anything about it, hadn't even got a valuation done on the property.

The sons returned for the funeral but didn't stay long, and didn't seem fussed on selling the old farm house. Neither of them could explain the note he'd left, about giving his life for the Goddess. The best they could guess was that he'd gone a bit loopy over losing their mum.

Harry squinted at the police notebook. The page had been scanned in but no-one had transcribed it. The notes said the sons didn't seem that upset, but when asked what their dad had been like, were non-committal.

'Just the usual,' one of them said. 'Bit strict.'

Harry rose from the desk and stretched his legs. Had Lily Sweeney found all these men at the gentlemen's club?

Zak, definitely. The cop, yeah maybe. And while Chris had been out west, Ipswich was only a forty-minute drive away. Harry could see a young guy like Chris wanting to let loose in the big smoke every now and then. But John Moncrieff? Didn't seem to fit. Older guy. Wife dead. Maybe that pushed him over the edge.

He returned to the desk and scrolled back through the reports, looking for dates. Six weeks. It had all happened over the course of six weeks. Harry thought again about Lily Sweeney. Was she really responsible for this? Or was it just a coincidence that they'd all visited her? He didn't have any proof she had cut them. There could be another connecting factor he couldn't see.

Harry went to the bathroom and turned on the shower. He undressed, his body stiff. Goose bumps rose on his flesh. He stepped into the shower and let the hot water pound him.

Jeffrey Stafford was the odd one out. The only one who'd been harmed, rather than taking his own life. Harry needed to talk to his wife, if he could. Anthony Gillespie was another odd one out. He was still alive, although locked up tight. And of course, Don Clack, alive and on the loose. Harry should probably tell Phil about him, or tell Lee-Anne. Warn her. But he wanted a bit more time to try to figure out what was going on. Stafford needed to be his first priority.

Harry sat in the car, took a deep breath, and looked up at the house. It was a high set, looked like something that had been thrown up in the eighties. Double garage underneath, both doors down. The lawn, framed by garden beds full of wilting roses, was dry and unkempt. He wondered if looking after the garden was one of Jeff's jobs. He wondered if his wife – he checked his notes – Kala, used to nag him about it.

You're stalling. Get on with it.

He hadn't had to do many death knocks in his time. While he was at the *Chermside Chronicle*, most of the deaths had been expected, such was the demographic. He got out of the car, prepared what he had to say. The mission brown stairs creaked as he climbed them. At the top was a rusty screen door. On the left of the landing was a window, with Thomas the Tank Engine curtains. Harry tapped on the door, and peered into the dim interior. A woman emerged from the gloom, walking on the balls of her feet. She had a finger to her lips.

'Hello?' she whispered. 'I've just put the little one down.' Her eyes were red, dirty blonde hair hanging down the sides of her face. She held one hand protectively on the door handle, as though Harry might try to barge in at any moment.

'Hi,' he said. 'Kala Stafford?'

'Yes?' She peered past Harry, down to the street.

'My name is Harry Hendrick, I'm a reporter…'

'No. No, not interested.' She started to close the door, then paused. 'Did you say Harry Hendrick?'

'Yes.'

'You're the one who…'

'Yep.' Harry smiled. It could go either way. Since the election, he'd found the split about fifty-fifty. Half the people who recognised him still thought he'd made it all up; the other half wanted to buy him a beer.

Kala stared at him and blinked a couple of times. 'What do you want?'

'I'm sorry for your loss,' Harry said. And he meant it. 'I

wanted to talk to you about Jeff.'

'Are you doing a story on him?'

Harry pointedly stared at the window with the Thomas curtains. 'Might be better if I came in,' he said.

A fragile smile formed on Kala's lips. She opened the screen door and invited Harry into a lounge room dominated by a large TV and a tattered red sofa.

'Can I offer you a drink?' Kala said. She rubbed her eyes.

Harry waved it away. 'No, but thank you.'

She gestured to the sofa. Harry took a seat. He felt something hard. He reached around and pulled out a *Thomas the Tank Engine* DVD and handed it to Kala.

'He can't get enough of the damn things,' she said, and put it on a coffee table crammed with old magazines, kids' books, and a half-eaten mandarin. There were pieces of dried-out peel on the stained brown carpet.

'I've already spoken to the police,' Harry said. 'They said they couldn't see any reason why Anthony would've wanted to hurt your husband. Is that true?'

'Yeah, I mean they worked together. Jeff would come home bitching about him from time to time, but you know how it is. Just sounds like a… like a…' She held the tissue to her mouth, as though trying to hold the grief in, but it bubbled out anyway. A tear ran down her cheek. 'I don't know what happened. From what the cops told me, sounds like Ant had a brain snap.' She shook her head, willing it away.

'How was Jeff in the days leading up to… his death?'

'Ah, y'know, he was fine. Cops wanted to know the same thing. I had trouble remembering anything specific about him. The days just blend into one another. That's how normal it's been.'

Harry thought about Don Clack, union official, trying to give the stripper a lap dance. And about what Lee-Anne had told him, about his behaviour in the bedroom, wanting to cover his marks.

'Any unusual behaviour?' Harry said.

Kala sighed. 'I just told you. No. Well, not lately.'

'Not lately?'

'Are you going to print this?'

Harry considered. 'I don't know. How about this? I don't think I'll need to. But if I do, I'll come back to you and get your permission. You'll have final say.'

Kala stared at the blank TV screen. 'I don't see what this has to do with what happened anyway.'

Harry waited. She wanted to talk to someone about it, otherwise she wouldn't have raised it.

'He had some issues earlier this year. He got all weird.'

'In what way?'

Kala sighed. 'I thought he was having an affair. He went on a boys' night out. He was all quiet the next day, like distant. I let it go. Told myself I was being stupid. Then a couple of weeks later, he was fixing the car, leaning over the bonnet. And I saw blood on the back of his shirt. Spots of blood.'

She closed her eyes and put one hand to the side of her face. 'He didn't want to talk about it. He got really defensive. So when he had his shower that night I used a five-cent piece to get into the bathroom. He had cuts all over his back.'

'All over?'

'Like, lines. About an inch long. Four, maybe five of them. Sort of in a circular pattern.' She stared at Harry.

He looked at his notebook and waited.

Kala took a deep, shuddering breath. 'I... that's about it.'

'What happened?' Harry said. 'When you saw the cuts.'

She pushed her hair back on her forehead. She was sweating. 'I'm sorry... I don't really want to... I shouldn't have...'

Harry shuffled closer to her. 'Kala. This is important. I think your husband may have been murdered...'

'By Anthony? Bullshit!'

'No. Well, not exactly.' Harry closed his eyes for a moment, thinking about the best way of putting it. 'I think Anthony may have been coerced. And I think the person responsible is also responsible for those cuts on your husband's back. If you decide that you've had enough, that's fine. And I'm really sorry to have to ask you. But if there is anything else you can tell me...'

Kala cried silently, staring into her lap. She grabbed a tissue and blew her nose. 'Jeff broke down. Collapsed in the shower. Bawling his eyes out. I got in there with him, I was so worried. When he'd calmed down enough to talk to me, he said he'd been stressed out. More than stressed out. Depressed. He'd been having this treatment where they cut his back. Some new-age bullshit. But he was over it, he said, it was over. It wasn't working. Said he just had to visit his therapist one more time to let her know...'

She shook her head again. 'And I thought, he's not telling me the truth. This sounds like an affair. But the cuts? What sort of weird shit was that? Anyway, he goes to meet her. Comes home. Seems rattled but okay. Next day, he tells me we're going on a second honeymoon.'

She noticed Harry's expression. 'Yep. A week at Noosa. Some fancy resort. He's organised to send the little tyke to his parents. Don't worry about the money, he says, he's been putting a little aside for it.'

'Was it your anniversary?'

'Not even close. I decided to just go with it. I figured he might open up to me, and tell me the full story. But no.'

'So what happened?'

'We went away for a week. We spent the week either getting smashed out of our skulls or...' she looked down, 'you know. It was like when we first met. It was exciting... a bit scary.'

'What happened when you got home?'

'He wasn't back to his old self, but he was close. In some ways better. I think... no one likes to think they've been cheated on... but I think that's what it was all about. That still doesn't explain the cuts though.'

When Harry returned home he checked his email. There was one from Lee-Anne Stewart. He opened it and saw a WinZip folder attached. She'd come through for him.

There was another email from Johnny. The news there wasn't so good. He'd spoken to his friend, and his friend was too scared to go public.

Harry's phone rang. He looked at the screen but it wasn't a number he recognised.

'Hello?'

'Is this Harry Hendrick?' A woman's voice.

'Yes.'

'This is Agnes Rowe, Principal of St Therese. I was wondering if you'd like to come to the school for a chat?'

'A chat? Or an interview?' Harry said.

'I'm happy with either, if you're happy to make an appointment.'

'Sure.' Harry checked his calendar. 'How about Thursday?'

They agreed on a time that suited both of them. 'I look forward to seeing you then.'

On a whim, Harry looked up the charity that Marcus Wilson, the alleged paedophile cop, was involved with. He wasn't expecting to find much about Wilson. But when he navigated to the 'About Us' page he found a short bio, including an email contact. He cut and pasted the address into an email, and thought about what he wanted to ask. Clearly 'Are you a paedophile and rapist?' wasn't the right approach.

```
Dear Mr Wilson,
I'm working on an article about the floods
and the recovery effort, and wanted to see if
I could interview you about some of the work
you did during that period.

Yours sincerely,
Harry Hendrick
```

Given Harry's reputation, it was likely Wilson would drop him a line, even if just to shut him down. It didn't matter. At some point Harry was going to have to get his response to the allegations being made against him, so Harry may as well set the wheels in motion.

CHAPTER 20

Harry sat at the dining room table, headphones on, typing out Johnny's interview. Like every other time he'd done this, the words never had the same impact they did on the first occasion. He'd distanced himself, now they were just words, looking for a narrative. As he typed, he made note of possible quotes. It was deplorable that such human suffering would fit into a mould, but there it was. There were only so many stories out there, repeated over and over again. This particular one had been told so many times, with so many victims and perpetrators. That was the only sad thing.

The small heater under the table was whirring away, only just keeping Harry's toes warm. He could see golden sunlight shining through the front windows, and had promised himself a coffee on the front steps once he'd finished this task.

Harry typed away, thinking not of the words themselves anymore, but of other things. Mostly Bec. She still hadn't called him. Hadn't returned any of his messages or texts over the weekend. He was torn. Part of him was angry. This was one dinner, one time. In their previous life, she'd accused him of being unambitious. And here he was, chasing a story, and she wasn't talking to him. The news, unfortunately, rarely followed a nine-to-five pattern. The other half of him wanted to do whatever was necessary to make things work with her.

A notification popped up. An email from Marcus Wilson.

```
Hi Harry,
Yeah, shouldn't be a problem. My schedule
is pretty jam-packed but we should be able
to work something out. Do you want to do it
over the phone or in person?


Marcus
```

Harry replied that in person was preferable.

Something caught Harry's attention from the corner of his eye. Something small and black, sitting on the floorboards. He looked over – there was nothing there. The tattoo on the back of his neck stung. He needed a break. Johnny kept speaking in his ears. He rewound the file, hit play, and kept typing.

The black spot loomed again. This time, when he looked over, he saw a pair of women's shoes sitting outside the door to his room. Black patent leather. High heels. Pointed toes. Harry blinked, rubbed his eyes. Sweat beaded on his forehead.

'Hello?'

His voice echoed, but there was no response. It was possible someone was in his room. Someone had climbed in through the window, and snuck the shoes out into the hallway when he wasn't looking. It was possible he was going crazy. He rubbed his arms, but the goosebumps were nothing to do with the chill. The previous year, he'd been convinced for a good while that he was going insane. He wanted to put that behind him.

He got up quietly from his chair, crept across the floor. He half expected the shoes to disappear. But they refused to budge.

'Hello?'

No response. As he neared his room, he saw that it wasn't just shoes. They sat outside his room. Just inside were two black stockings lying on the floor like snake skins. Seams up their backs, toes pointing to the bed. He could smell her perfume – and another musky, altogether older and more organic, smell. He felt a stirring in his pants.

In his mind's eye he saw her, stretched out on the bed, pale skin, dark hair. She stretched like a cat, let one hand trail over a breast. Her eyes closed in ecstasy as she pleasured herself.

Saw himself, tied up with the stockings, kissing the shoes. Crawling towards her. Crawling...

Harry blinked. He was on the floor in his bedroom. On his knees, pants around his ankles. Cock bobbing up and down. He turned, as though waking from a dream. No shoes. No black stockings. No naked dominatrix on his bed. It was only then that he noticed his phone ringing, on the dining table.

Harry stood, pulled up his pants and answered the phone.

'Harry?'

He'd been expecting Bec. But no, it was Sandy.

'Sandy. How... how's things?' Harry zipped up. He still felt dazed, as though he had just woken.

'Me? I'm fine. It's you I'm worried about.'

Harry sat down at the table, then remembered how cold it was. He took the phone out to the sunroom, opened the front door and sat in the sunlight.

'Why?'

'I don't know. I'm getting bad vibes about you, Harry.'

'You really know how to make a guy feel good about himself, Sandy.'

She grunted. He had no idea what she was doing, but he imagined her in her garden, weeding, clutching the phone to her shoulder with the side of her head, Mt Tibrogargan in the background. It was a comforting image.

'Did you meet that woman?'

Harry flashed on Mistress Hel lying naked on his bed.

'Yeah. Well, no. I don't know. I met a woman.'

'Harry, you're the award-winning journalist, right?'

'Apparently.'

'Well...'

'Her name is Lily Sweeney. Also known as Mistress Hel. She says she has nothing to do with the deaths. That men are basically led by their dicks and she can't take responsibility for that.'

'Hmm. She has a point there. Do you believe her?'

'About the dicks, possibly. But the other stuff. I know it's cliched, but I don't believe in coincidences.'

'Me neither.'

'She, ah, she also caught me breaking into one of her client's cars.'

'What!'

Harry gave her the short version of the Don Clack stakeout.

'Harry!'

'Yeah, I know. So, she's warned me to keep out of her way.'

'That's probably good advice. You stay away from her.'

'Yes, Mum.'

'Don't!'

Harry laughed for the first time in a couple of days. It felt almost as good as the sunlight on his face.

'What else is going on?' she said.

'Why does something have to be going on, Sandy?'

She didn't reply. She knew when to wait.

'Bec and I had a fight. Well, it's more of a cold war. I got called out on a job on Saturday night, halfway through our dinner…'

'Let me guess, to visit this Mistress Hel character?'

'Yep.'

'Harry…'

'I know, but I had to go. I've texted her, called her. She's not replying. She doesn't want to see me.'

'Again, this is the award-winning journalist? Apply as much effort to her as to your work, and you'll sort it out.'

'What's that supposed to mean?'

Sandy sighed. 'You've broken into some guy's car, you've hidden outside some woman's house. Maybe try that with Bec. Wait for her outside work, with the biggest bunch of flowers you can carry.'

'I dunno…'

'Harry. I don't know if this is exactly what the spirits are telling me, but I feel like you're at risk of losing her.'

Harry shook his head. 'Is that the spirits, or you?'

'Sometimes it's hard to tell the difference.'

Harry sighed. 'Well, I'd hate to ignore the spirits.'

'They've saved your life on more than one occasion, if I remember correctly.'

'Yeah. Fair call. Okay, okay… just stop nagging me about it.'

'Sure. But I'm going to be asking you how it went next time we speak. Take care, Harry.'

Harry ended the call and returned to the table, which now felt colder, after being out in the sun. He picked up the laptop and moved to the front steps, balancing it on his knees.

He looked back over his shoulder to the hallway. No shoes. There were never any shoes.

'She's just got into my head, that's all,' he muttered, and returned to work.

Time dragged. His mind kept lapsing, and he'd have to rewind the audio and listen again. But it wasn't Bec he kept returning to, it was Lily 'I love it when you call me Mizz' Sweeney. Her shoes outside his bedroom. No, not her shoes. There were no shoes. He wondered if she dated. Despite the cold, Harry found himself sweating. He forced himself to think of Bec. He would go out and get her some flowers. He'd suck it up. He imagined himself buying the flowers, taking them to her work, just as Sandy had suggested. But when he arrived at her work, somehow he was outside Mistress Hel's place.

He moved the computer off his lap and returned inside. Had a shower to clear his head, but instead of clearing it he found himself thinking of what Mistress Hel would look like in the shower, water flowing down her perfect body.

He stared at himself in the mirror. 'Stop it!'

Harry felt his tattoo burning again. He needed to sort this out. It was bullshit. Just some stupid crush.

That's all it was. It was this fascination with the unknown.

Harry paused, razor halfway to his face. He had a moment of clarity. The unknown. The best way of dealing with this was to make it known.

Harry finished shaving quickly. He didn't want to lose this thread. It was the only thing that had seemed to make sense in his head all day.

Towel wrapped around him, he went to his room and found his wallet. Rifled through it looking for the card with the number scratched on the back. Reached for his phone. His heart pounded in his chest.

It rang ten times. Harry felt this absurd feeling of sorrow and panic that she wouldn't answer.

'Hello?' She seemed to be talking through a smile. Deep, soft, yet with a firm edge. Harry had this weird feeling that she knew it was him, even though he blocked his number.

'Lily?'

'No...'

Harry felt another blast of panic.

'This is Mistress Hel. Who am I speaking to?'

'This is Harry. Harry Hendrick.'

Pause. 'Harry Hendrick?'

He knew she was toying with him, yet he couldn't control himself. 'I... we... I saw you the other night... I'm the journalist...' He felt like he was in primary school, asking a girl out on a date.

'Oh, yes. Mr Hendrick. What can I do for you?'

'What happened with Jeff Stafford?'

A pause. When she spoke again, there was an edge to her voice. 'Sorry, who?'

'You know who. He... he crossed you, or something. Wouldn't do as you wanted, so you had him killed.'

'Oh, Mr Hendrick. You really should move into fiction writing.' Another pause. 'Do you want to come see me again, is that what all this is about?'

Harry blinked. He saw her lying on his bed, naked. He saw her in her stockings, walking away from him.

'Have you been thinking about me?'

'Yes,' he said.

'Well, I'm a busy lady, Mr Hendrick. You'll need to make an appointment. It's five hundred for half an hour.'

'What!'

He felt as though she was smiling. 'You heard me.'

Harry hissed in frustration. He was hard, in spite of himself. 'Fine.'

Mistress Hel chuckled down the line. Harry felt sick. Sweat dripped off him.

'You need to beg me.'

'What?'

'Beg. Me.'

Harry saw himself hanging up the phone. At the same time he said, 'Please, Mistress, please will you see me again?' He rubbed the back of his neck, where the tattoo now ached.

She sighed. 'There, that wasn't so hard, was it?'

'I'll be over in about half an hour.'

Mistress Hel laughed, so loudly Harry had to pull the phone away from his ear. 'My! You are the eager one. I'm busy, Harry. A little tied up, if you get my meaning.'

He pictured her in her playroom. Somehow, he doubted she was the one who was tied up.

'I'll check my calendar, and I'll text you when I know when I can fit you in, okay?'

'Sure.'

The line went dead. Harry swooned against the bed, pummelled by a mixture of relief and dread. His towel slipped off his body.

He pulled his clothes on quickly, ignoring the desire burning in him. For the first time that day he could think clearly. He thought of Bec and experienced an overwhelming ache of warmth for her. He smiled, thinking of her response when he turned up at her work with the flowers.

By the time he headed out the door, the phone call with Mistress Hel seemed like nothing more than a bad dream.

CHAPTER 21

Harry waited outside Bec's work, big bouquet of roses and cornflowers gripped in one hand. He'd changed into his charcoal suit and white shirt, because he knew Bec liked it. He wished he'd thought to wear his coat, as he turned his back to the wind.

On the drive into the city he'd thought about Mistress Hel but there was none of the compulsion he'd felt before. The events of that morning seemed like a fever dream. Harry started to think about the prospective appointment with Mistress Hel, and his heart skipped, but then he pushed it away. It was just a follow-up interview.

Harry checked his watch. Men and women in smart business clothes streamed out of the building, checking their phones and reaching for cigarettes. Harry watched as Bec descended the escalator from the mezzanine level. She removed her glasses and put them in her smart leather attaché. Harry tried to gauge her mood but her face was impassive. As she reached the ground floor and headed for the doors, one of her colleagues called out to her. Bec turned and smiled, her face lighting up. Harry felt like he was on his first date. Not his first date with Bec – his first date ever. He took a deep breath to calm himself.

'Showtime.'

He walked to meet her, holding the flowers out in front of him. 'I'm sorry,' he said.

She took the flowers and smiled. Harry touched her arm, and she pulled him to her. They kissed, squashing the flowers between them.

'I really am sorry,' he said.

She kissed him again. 'Oh, Harry.'

They parted. Harry felt warm, filled up. Bec admired the flowers.

'They're beautiful,' she said.

'Here,' Harry said, carrying her attaché so they could hold hands. The day didn't seem so cold anymore and, even though it was a Tuesday, the city seemed alive with possibilities.

'Do you want to get something to eat?' he said.

Bec pulled him to her again, her mouth brushing his ear. 'How about we just go home and fuck?'

After clumsily kissing and staggering through her front door, Bec unbuttoned Harry's shirt. He slipped his jacket off, letting it fall to the floor, and Bec yanked his shirt over his shoulders. Harry kicked the door shut and Bec pushed him against it. She kissed him hard on the lips, holding his arms. She smelt of perfume, sweat and excitement. Their mouths still joined, he grabbed her arms and they shuffled into the dining area, until she bumped up against the table.

Bec ripped the chair out of the way so hard it toppled and clattered on the floor. She spread her knees apart, her skirt riding up her legs, and pulled Harry to her. He could feel her heat, rubbing against him. She undid his pants. The soft material dropped around his ankles and he stepped out of them. He pulled down his boxers.

Harry felt the absurd need to apologise again.

'Bec, I just wanted to…'

She silenced him with her mouth, then reached down, pulling her undies to one side and guiding him into her.

'Jesus, you're so wet!' he said.

He slid into her as she leant back on the table, sighing. Harry drove his cock into her, again and again. He expected to finish quickly. But every time he felt he was close, he saw Mistress Hel in his mind. Guilt washed over him.

Bec came, grinding against him. 'Come, Harry. I want your come inside me.'

Harry thrust hard into her, got to the edge, couldn't finish. He pulled her up off the table.

'Get to the bedroom,' he said.

She walked to the bedroom, removing her blouse and skirt on the way, and lay on her belly. He followed her, slipping his shoes and socks off. He yanked her undies off and spread her legs. Harry was sweating, skin tingling, delirious with lust as he slid into her again. Bec writhed against him. Time and again, Harry hit the edge, but there was no release. Finally, exhausted, he pulled out, throbbing and hard.

'I can't,' he said, sliding onto the covers. 'Sorry.'

She faced him, still panting and gently slapped his cheek. 'Don't… ever… apologise… for that.' She pulled him close and they kissed again.

They pulled off their remaining scraps of clothing and glided under the covers. Bec dozed a little, but Harry lay staring at the ceiling, his whole body vibrating. He rolled his shoulders to try to relieve the headache he could feel building in his temples. He lifted his head and looked down. Still hard. Jesus, it was like he was eighteen again. There was a dull ache in his stomach. Harry wasn't touching Bec and yet he could feel her firm breasts, soft skin, her wet pussy. It was as if he was touching her all over, with every part of his body. He tried to think of something else.

He thought of Johnny, and everything he must've been through at the hands of Marcus Wilson and the other predators. He thought of Zak Godwin, eating pieces of mirror until it tore his insides apart. He thought of Anthony Gillespie, the hapless contractor who'd fried a friend because... because...

You need to beg me.

Oh shit.

But as soon as he thought it, the memory popped out of his mind, pushed away by thoughts of his beautiful girlfriend. He imagined her tying him down, riding him until he begged for mercy. Maybe that's what he needed. Maybe that's what all this was about.

After a while, Bec reached out for him.

'Oh! What's going on?'

'I want you to ride me. Hold my hands and ride me.'

'Oh. Okay. I'll get some lube.'

She climbed on top of him, smiling. The light was fading out of the sky now. Shadows claimed the room. Bec slid over him, and he groaned in pleasure and pain. She leant her body close to his and pressed her breasts against his chest. He felt her heartbeat. She reached behind her and guided him into her.

In that first moment, the sensation was so pleasurable he thought he might come. His whole body tensed... then nothing. Bec reached down and held his wrists, then bucked her hips, slowly at first, then faster and faster. She closed her eyes, bit her lip as she focused on the sensation.

'Is this what you want, huh?' she whispered, then bit Harry's earlobe.

'Yeah, uh, yes!'

Bec rolled her hips back and forth, rubbing the head of his cock. Her nails dug into the soft flesh of his wrists. Time and time again he felt the muscles in his cock contract, but there was no release, only the increasing ache in his abdomen. Eventually, it was pure pain, and still he was hard.

Finally, Bec slumped against him, then slid off him, panting and sweaty.

'You've worn me out!' She trailed a finger across his chest. 'It's okay, you know. That you didn't come.'

Harry couldn't think of what to say. 'I'm just stressed, with work.'

His phone buzzed. It was like a bolt of electricity passing through him. He jumped out from under Bec's grasp and almost fell off the bed, reaching for his phone in his pocket. Bec laughed a little uneasily.

He looked at the phone.

I can squeeze you in next Tuesday.

Harry felt an insanely disproportionate feeling of release. Not coming. Something that transcended any physical feeling. He let out a shuddering breath. Felt on the verge of crying.

'Harry? What is it?'

He shoved the phone back in his pocket.

'Nothing,' he said, realising too late that this was the worst possible thing he could say.

He reached for Bec, but she pulled away. She was backlit

by the evening sky, a silhouette, yet he knew the expression on her face.

'Nothing?'

'It's just something to do with work.'

She shifted away from him on the bed. He realised that he was no longer hard, but there was no relief there. It felt as though all the tension had been transferred to his abdomen. His head felt like it was being gripped by a vice.

'The prostitute?'

'She's a dominatrix.'

'Oh, sorry,' Bec said, not sounding at all sorry. 'I didn't realise there was a difference.'

'I'm trying to tee up another interview with her.'

Bec rolled onto her side and looked at him, frowning. 'Did you not get what you need from her?'

Harry blinked. Remembered his disappointment when Lily Sweeney had opened the door dressed in casual clothes.

'Something like that.'

His head pounded. Bec looked as though she was going to make something of it, then rolled onto her back and stared at the ceiling.

'Sorry,' she said. 'Just being stupid. Jealous.'

Harry felt guilt wash over him. He touched her face. 'You have nothing to be jealous about. This woman is…' *Beautiful? Dangerous? Sensual?* '… nuts.'

Bec rolled towards him, laying an arm over his shoulder. Her bare leg brushed his cock, which was hard again. She smiled.

'Are you taking Viagra or something?'

Harry forced a smile. 'No, it's all you, babe.'

Bec closed her eyes. 'Sorry, but this babe needs to sleep.'

She pulled him close. Harry closed his eyes, hoping for some relief from the pounding in his head and his gut. None came. Eventually, exhausted, he drifted off to sleep.

CHAPTER 22

Harry took a deep breath, trying to quell the sick feeling in the pit of his stomach as he waited outside the headmistress's office. The state school he'd been to had been all fibro and cinderblock. This place was sandstone and rosewood. The walls were lined with trophy cabinets, honour boards, thankyou certificates and oil paintings of past principals.

He yawned. The previous night had been one long fever dream. Bec riding him with his hands held over his head. Bec morphing into Mistress Hel. The handcuffs digging into his wrists until his skin was chafed and bloody. He'd woken up sweaty and hard. He'd tried to give himself some relief, but just ended up even more frustrated and sore.

'Mr Hendrick?' the secretary said, looking up from her computer. 'Dr Rowe will see you now.'

Harry got to his feet, using his notebook to hide the fact that he was still hard. He opened the door and found Dr Agnes Rowe waiting for him. She was in her late fifties with silver hair pulled back from her face. She wore a smart pantsuit that was probably worth more than Harry had earned in the past six months. He thought of the bills still piling up on his fridge. Make that a year.

Like the antechamber, the office was all rosewood and lush carpet. There was the desk, a large picture window that looked out on the grounds, and a leather lounge. Outside, kids were playing football.

'Mr Hendrick.'

'Dr Rowe.'

They shook hands. She gestured to the lounge. Harry took a seat and crossed his legs. Dr Rowe sat opposite him.

'Thank you for coming to see me, Mr Hendrick.'

'Harry – please. I was surprised to receive your call. The last time I visited, I was thrown off the grounds.'

Dr Rowe smiled. 'To be fair, you had not been invited. And Mr Packard – well, he's very loyal to the school.'

'Yes, that's what I've heard too. Loyalty isn't always a good thing.'

Dr Rowe cleared her throat. 'Mr Hendrick…'

'Harry.'

'Harry. We take any accusations of inappropriate behaviour…'

Inappropriate behaviour? Harry thought of what Johnny had been through.

'… very seriously. But in order to act on them, we need information.'

'Dr Rowe. Is this on the record? Because if it is, I'd like to record it, if you don't mind.'

'Of course. We have nothing to hide here.'

Harry set up his phone. 'Dr Rowe, if I could just start by asking, how long have you been here at this school?'

'This isn't an interview, Mr Hendrick, but I can tell you that. I've been here for eight years.'

'Right. So you weren't actually here when the alleged incident took place.'

'No, but this is the thing, Mr Hendrick. I have gone through the school records. I have spoken to the former deputy...'

'What about the former principal?'

'He's no longer with us, unfortunately. But he was a great man. He did a lot for the community.'

'How did he die?' Harry said, trying to quell the anger.

'He... he died suddenly.'

'Committed suicide, you mean?'

'I didn't say that.'

Harry grunted. He stared out the window. The kids formed a scrum and packed down against the scrum machine, on which the coach stood, bellowing.

'Dr Rowe, my source tells me that he went to the school chaplain, and nothing was done.'

'Who is your source?'

'I can't tell you that.'

Dr Rowe raised her hands, wrinkled her brow. 'And this is the problem. I have no record of any inappropriate behaviour taking place at this school – ever. If you give me the information, I can follow it up and take action on it.'

'Did you ask Mr Packard about it?'

Dr Rowe looked out the window. 'Mr Packard and I had a long conversation about it, yes.'

'And?'

'I've told you. He's very loyal to the school.'

'Are you saying he's covering something up, out of loyalty to the school?'

'Of course not, Mr Hendrick! I'm saying to you that I want to work with you. It will do you no good, publishing information that is wrong. In fact, part of the reason I invited you here today was to make sure you're aware that

I will do everything within my power to defend the honour of this school.'

Harry shook his head. 'Is that a threat?'

'You have someone, one person, a former student of this school, who is telling you that he was abused here. By several people. And that other boys were abused. Don't you think, if this were the case, that something would have come to light by now?'

'Dr Rowe. It takes someone with real courage to open up about something like that. If I thought this person were lying, I wouldn't be chasing the story.'

'You're going on your instincts. That's admirable. But don't you think that's a huge risk to take?' She smiled again. Harry thought she was going for the 'caring' look, but it didn't touch her eyes.

'Dr Rowe. You've got your lawyers. Bring it on.'

On the way back to his car, Harry's phone buzzed in his pocket. He pulled it out and saw Sandy's name on the screen. He answered.

'Elizabeth Tawny,' she said. She sounded slightly out of breath.

'In my country we usually start conversations with "Hello", or sometimes the informal "Hi".'

Sandy hissed in frustration. 'Harry! This is important.'

Harry stopped and looked back at the school. Rugby training was over. The grounds really were quite beautiful. If it wasn't for the pain in his gut and the crazy woman breathing down the phone, it would be almost pleasant.

'Okay, so tell me why,' Harry said.

'I... I don't know,' she said.

Harry rolled his eyes. 'Of course you don't.'

'Harry, how many times have I told you…'

'I know, I know, there's no email in the afterlife.'

Silence.

'Sorry, Sandy,' he said. 'I appreciate it. Elizabeth Tawny. Tawny as in the port?'

'As in the owl.'

'I'll look into it. Did you see what I did there? Look. Owl.'

'Harry… are you okay?'

'No, not feeling great.'

'Hmm. Just…'

'Yeah, I know. Be careful.'

Sandy chuckled. 'Maybe it's you who has the clairvoyance.'

CHAPTER 23

Harry stared at the screen, not really seeing anything. He was having trouble concentrating. He was having trouble thinking of anything except Mistress Hel. The relief he had felt after booking the session had been brief, and now he was back to thinking about her, wondering what it would be like. Fantasising about what she would do to him. He was sweating, despite the cold.

'Come on, come on!' He took a slug of coffee and forced himself to focus on the words. After his interview with the school headmistress he'd returned home and typed out the conversation, but he wasn't helped by the fact that she kept morphing into Mistress Hel, telling him that he'd been a naughty boy, reaching for the cane. He knew there was nothing sexy about being sued, or being threatened with legal action. And yet his whole body craved discipline. He was hard. Had been all morning. His lower abdomen was aching so badly it felt like gastro. But without the shitting.

The back of his neck burnt. What Would Rob Do? It was a question he asked himself often, when he was trying to draw on the knowledge the former SAS soldier had. There were no answers there this time, so he fell back on the basic breathing techniques he'd been perfecting in tandem with his karate training, focusing on the sensation of the breath coming in through his nose, out through his mouth. Concentrating on the everyday sounds he could hear through the front windows. Just trying to let it all go.

Harry opened his eyes. In the moment of clarity he remembered the name Sandy had given him. Elizabeth Tawny. Like the owl. He plugged it into Google. It spat out just under six hundred results. Harry considered. Tried combining it with 'Lily Sweeney'. Nothing. Already, the clarity was fading. Harry rubbed his face. 'Come on!'

He typed 'Elizabeth Tawny' and 'Brisbane'. He got one hit. A news story from a few years before: SUSPENDED SENTENCE FOR 'SUICIDE PACT' TEEN, read the headline.

A Brisbane teenager who survived a suicide pact with a friend has been spared jail time...

Harry scanned the article. Elizabeth Tawny, sixteen, had died after swallowing a cocktail of alcohol and prescription medicine. A friend, who also went to Darra High and wasn't named for legal reasons, had been given a two-year suspended sentence. The article said the magistrate had taken into consideration the defendant's grief at her friend's death, and a statement from a psychologist saying that she believed the teenager was suffering psychosis at the time of the incident, with a recommendation for ongoing treatment.

Harry's phone rang three times before he realised it was his. He turned, disorientated. Where had he left it? He got out of his seat, went into his room and found his phone. He was half expecting whoever it was to hang up.

'Hello?'

'Harry? It's Phil.'

Harry felt a stab of annoyance. He'd told Phil that if

there were any developments he'd let him know. Part of the annoyance was guilt that he hadn't really been thinking about the case, hadn't really been thinking of much of anything lately, except her.

'Nothing new, Phil, I told you…'

'No, it's not about that.' Phil's voice quivered slightly.

'Oh?' Harry walked through his sunroom.

'I hear that you're chasing a story about paedophiles, at that posh school?'

Harry opened the door and walked out onto his front steps. He stared up at the stark white water tower and the pure blue sky behind it. Telephone wires leading up the road. An old black cat, sunning itself.

'Yeah?'

'Just wondering if there's anything I can help you with?' Now Phil sounded distinctly uncomfortable.

'If there was, I would have told you. Who told you about the story, Phil?'

Phil cleared his throat. Said nothing. Harry's impulse was to ask him about Marcus Wilson, put it all on the line and see what he said. Wilson wasn't a cop anymore, but he was part of the brotherhood. Once a part of it, always a part of it.

But Phil was fishing.

'Is someone recording this, Phil?'

Silence.

'Is someone recording this? Because if I find out I'm being recorded, without a warrant…'

'No, Harry. No-one's recording it!'

'Good.'

'Harry, listen very closely.'

Harry tilted his head to one side. This was something

new. Anger. He'd never heard Phil angry in his life. Why had his fear transformed into anger? What had Harry done to deserve this?

'I'm listening.'

'You need to be very careful about what you choose to do from this point forward, okay?'

Harry paused. Closed his eyes. Laughed. 'This is incredible. I've had this same speech twice in two days. I must be on the story of the fucking century here!'

'Look… most of the cops here, they hate paedophiles. Have devoted their lives to bringing those fuckers to justice…'

'That's comforting…'

'But there are others, others who believe that protecting other cops – regardless of what they've done – is more important than anything else.'

Harry blinked. He'd suspected as much, but having someone connected to Queensland Police actually lay it out for him was still shocking.

'You just need to be careful.'

'Phil…'

'I gotta go.'

The phone line clicked off.

Harry paced up and down in the sunroom. Emotions fought for dominance. Excitement. He must really be onto something if the cops were trying to shut him down. Fear. Could he really trust Johnny? Could he get enough corroborating information to make the story stand up? Would these bad apples come after him? Why hadn't Wilson cancelled the interview he'd scheduled with him? Relief. To be finally thinking about something else. He felt free, for the moment. Free from… from her.

At the mere thought of Mistress Hel, he felt himself drifting back under. He thought of her legs, her waist, her breasts. He thought of sweat dripping off her body. He thought of the taste of it on his lips. The sting of the crop against his back. The taste of his own blood…

'No!'

He ran. Left the front door open and ran, out of his garden, up the road. Sprinting up the steep hill, focusing on his body, on his breathing, on the gentle burn at the back of his neck. Arms pumping. Sweat beading on his forehead, in spite of the chill air. He ran to the top of the hill, pushing all thoughts from his mind as he did so.

He ran, taking random streets, trying to get lost, trying to exhaust himself by running further and further from home, knowing that eventually he would have to find his way back again. And when he did, she would be waiting for him.

CHAPTER 24

Harry put the buds into his ears and clicked through his music collection to the *HEAVY \m/* playlist. He'd put it together partly as a joke a year or so before, and partly because he was going through a phase where he was nostalgic about his angry youth. Rage Against The Machine, Rollins Band, Metallica, some early AC/DC. He cranked the volume. He'd lost the best part of a week thinking about Mistress Hel. It wasn't even thinking, it was just like white noise, some sort of porn supercut that looped over and over again. By the end of the day he'd feel disgusting, worn out, but not satisfied. Never satisfied. Pain pulsing up into his stomach. He couldn't get relief.

The adrenaline rush when Phil called him was the only thing that spiked through the haze, but it was enough to show him that something could get through it. The only thing that came close was listening to heavy music too loud, and so that's what he did.

And it was weird. At first, it was worse than thinking about her. But after he got used to the music, he found that he could ignore it, and yet it still blocked her. And with her blocked out, he could keep fighting. But it was so exhausting.

He cranked the volume up another couple of notches as the opening riffs of 'Bombtrack' blasted through his brain. If this carried on beyond his 'session' with her, he was going to kill his hearing. But he could worry about that later.

He scanned through the documents Lee-Anne Stewart had sent him. Photocopies of union credit card statements. She'd helpfully highlighted all the ones that marked payments to Mistress Hel, or the Lilith Foundation, as it appeared on the statement. Harry didn't know how Clack was explaining it away, but he could see the payments: $500 every time. He rifled through the pages and checked the calendar on the computer. Every fortnight, regular as clockwork. It was almost unbelievable. Every fortnight. None were on Clack's own credit card – every one was being paid for by the union. Shit. Clack just didn't care anymore. Harry went back through the pages. Six months this had been going on. Six months. Despite the thrashing guitars and howling vocals, he felt his cock twitch in his pants, wondered what it was that she could offer that would make this man so blind to the danger he was facing. He was going to lose his wife, his job. He was going to go to jail too.

Harry stopped, gazed over the keyboard to the aqua tongue-and-groove wall. For the briefest of moments he had it in his mind to cancel his appointment with her. Fuck her, he just wouldn't keep the appointment. Then the track ended. Silence. Like a gate opening, his body filled with lust, the sensation so strong he actually grabbed the table, trying to stop himself from being swept away. Then the next track started and when the drums were beating so hard he felt like his brain was going to start leaking out of his ears, the feelings receded like a tide. This was fucked.

He googled 'Lilith'. *A female demon from Jewish*

mythology. He tried 'Lilith Foundation'. There was a company in Texas, but no information about what they did, and one in Brisbane. Harry clicked. A basic brochure-ware website. *Lilith Foundation – Making a Difference.* Vague text about Outward Bound-style camps for abused kids. A bunch of obviously stock photos of smiling children in outdoor gear. No address. No phone number. An *info@* email address.

He picked up the phone and dialled Lee-Anne, then stood and stretched his back as much as he could with the earphones tethering him to his laptop. The phone rang and rang, went to messagebank.

'Hey, Lee-Anne. It's Harry. Call me back when you get a chance?'

His phone bleeped, drowning out the music for a couple of seconds. He checked it. *Coffee with Dave.* Shit. He'd forgotten all about it. That's why he'd started putting every little appointment into his calendar – he was forgetting a lot these days. He pulled the headphones out of his ears and almost immediately felt a veil of fuzziness descend. Desire, lust, frustration. He rubbed his face. Saw Mistress Hel smiling at him.

He packed up the documents and put them in his room. Caught the photo pinned over his bed. Him and Bec before the break-up. He'd put it away then but it was back out now, because he liked it so much. He and Bec, sitting on a low rock wall, with the Irish Sea in the background. He liked it because they both looked a bit rough around the edges – they'd been backpacking for a while by this point – but they both looked happy and satisfied. For a long while, he didn't recognise either of them.

Harry grabbed his keys and headed out the door.

Harry met Dave at one of their usual haunts in the West End. Harry chose a booth at the back but, even so, being out was almost too much. He was edgy and disorientated. He tried to remember the last time he'd left the house. With a bit of effort he recalled meeting the headmistress, but he couldn't remember much of their conversation, nor how long ago it was.

Dave was big, loud, impossible not to love, even when he was offering advice that Harry didn't want to hear. Same as usual, in other words. Harry looked at the coffee he'd ordered, realising he didn't want it.

'Look, all I'm saying is, you've been through so much,' Dave said. A smile touched the corners of his mouth, as though this were some sort of soap opera. From Dave's point of view, it sort of was. Harry should have been angry at that expression. It wasn't impossible to get angry at Dave, but it was extremely difficult.

'Yeah.'

'Yeah? Are you okay? Expecting someone?'

Harry forced himself to focus on Dave's face. Managed it for a couple of seconds before his eyes darted outside again.

'No. I… I've just got a lot on.'

'So tell me about it. Set Bec to one side for a moment, if you like…'

Harry found the idea comforting: setting Bec aside for a few weeks, so he could pull her back when he had his shit together. But would he ever have his shit together? After what had happened the previous year, Harry should have been dead, or in jail, or in psychiatric care. He thought that was enough excitement for one lifetime, and yet here he was again, neck deep. He rubbed his tattoo.

'Harry?'

'Sorry, Dave. Okay, where do I start?'

'Well, you know what Dame Julie says.'

So Harry started at the very beginning, unpacking it. He had no idea if it meant anything to Dave. Had no idea if the words he was stringing together would mean anything to anyone who hadn't lived through it. But it helped to talk. And Dave was listening. Really listening: brow furrowed, smile gone. He could see why Ellie loved him so much. Harry realised this was the reason he found it so hard to get angry at Dave – when Harry needed him, Dave was there.

Harry laid it all out. The police invitation to the mystery case. The alluring Lily Sweeney, aka Mistress Hel. Don Clack – the scumbag using union dues to pay a dominatrix. The paedophilia investigation, and Phil's warning. Everything that had happened between Bec and him. Well, not everything. He left out the sex part – he was a bloke; there were some things blokes just didn't talk about. And he left out his looming appointment with Mistress Hel. Even though that was the one thing that had been dominating all his thoughts for the past week.

Dave nodded. 'Yeah, you've got a lot on,' he said. 'But at least it's not up there with all the shit you went through last year, right?'

Harry nodded, slowly.

'And you got through that all right, yeah?'

Harry nodded again. 'With a little help.'

Dave smiled, held his big hands up, palm out. 'And I'm here now, to help you, if I can.'

Harry shook his head. 'I think I've got it. I mean, thanks.'

'But you don't want your work destroying what you've just got going with Bec, right?'

Harry sipped his coffee, even though stimulants were the last thing he really needed. 'Of course not.'

'So you have to talk to her, man.'

'She thinks I'm hiding something from her.'

'And are you?'

Harry stared at his hands. Clenched them into fists. 'It's not like that. I'm... I'm trying to protect her.'

'And are you trying to protect me?'

Harry groaned in frustration. He didn't want to talk about Lily Sweeney any more than necessary. It was as though the mere mention of her name made that deep, hot pit of longing even deeper, even hotter.

'Okay. Look. I thought... I thought I could draw the mistress out by making out that I wanted to...'

'Wanted to what?'

'You know. Wanted to see her.'

'*See* her?' Dave's face lit up, his mouth opened and he bellowed laughter. He slapped the table so hard Harry's mostly full cup slopped over the edge.

'Yeah, laugh it up. Anyway, so she texted me to confirm my, ah, my appointment. And that's what Bec wanted to see – that's what she wanted to know.'

Dave was still laughing. His laughter was so infectious that it melted Harry's anger away. For a moment it even melted the befuddlement away, and things didn't look so bad.

'Shit, Harry. You're fucked.'

'Thanks a lot.'

'You're seriously fucked.'

Harry nodded, sipped his coffee.

'Why didn't you tell her it was an interview or something? Tell her you were confirming an interview time?'

'I dunno. Just got caught flatfooted.'

Dave nodded, getting that thoughtful expression again. Harry looked over Dave's shoulder. He didn't want his friend digging down that hole anymore. He'd lied. And Dave's bullshit detector was only slightly less effective than Bec's. Which, of course, was the real reason he hadn't lied to her.

Walking through West End, Harry found it increasingly difficult to concentrate on what Dave was saying. Instead, he saw Mistress Hel everywhere, taunting him. He adjusted his pants to try to disguise the bulge there. Harry wished he could put his headphones in and crank the volume, but even if he hadn't been with Dave, his head ached and his ears were red raw from having buds in so much. Then his eyes focused on the front of West End Tattoo. Other than the name, it looked like an accountant's office: sky blue blinds, black door.

'Hey, Dave,' he said.

'Yeah?'

'Does that mate of yours still work at West End Tattoo?'

'Sian? Yeah. Why?'

'Can you see if she can do a favour for me?'

Sian looked from Dave to Harry and back to Dave. 'We don't usually do walk-ins,' she said.

'Yeah, I know...'

'And as you can see, it's not actually quiet today,' she said, flicking through the dog-eared diary on the counter. The bench-seating around three sides of the reception area was crammed with people: a middle-aged man in a business suit, checking his iPhone; a young woman in a TISM t-shirt, her knee bobbing up and down to whatever was pumping through her headphones; another woman nervously flicking through an art portfolio. Tattoo machines buzzed away behind the Japanese screen at Sian's back, and also from the room up the stairs to Harry's right.

Sian slid her finger down the day's appointments, and tapped on an entry scrawled in pencil. 'Hang on.' She picked up the phone. 'Hey Jaya, did your eleven thirty show? Uh huh. Can you do a walk-in? Cool, thanks.' Sian put down the phone. 'You're in luck. Go on up.'

Dave grinning. 'Thanks, Sian. I owe you one!'

'No probs.'

'Thank you,' Harry said. 'Seriously.'

Sian smiled. Then the phone rang. 'West End Tattoo. Sian speaking.'

'Thanks, Dave.'

'Want me to come up and hold your hand?'

'Ha ha,' Harry deadpanned. 'I'll catch you later.'

Up the top of the stairs was another reception area with a black leather sofa and low coffee table covered with tattoo magazines and art books. From behind more Japanese screens came the sounds of tattooists at work. Jaya emerged from one of these workspaces, dressed in a purple t-shirt and old jeans. She smiled and offered her hand.

'Jaya.'

'Harry.'

She gestured to the lounge. 'Take a seat.'

Harry sat, and Jaya perched on the armrest.

'So, what can I do for you?'

Harry bunched his hands into fists, curling his fingers so hard his nails dug into his palms.

'I... uh... got a tattoo last year, on the back of my neck,' Harry said.

'Oh yeah? Let's take a look,' she said.

Harry leant forwards so Jaya could see the strange tattoo.

'Interesting,' she said. 'Was that done by hand?'

'Yeah, it was.'

'Those symbols, what do they mean?'

'It's Afghan in origin. It's a protective design. Kinda to ward off bad luck.'

'Cool,' Jaya said, but she didn't sound so sure.

'So I wanted to get some companion tattoos,' Harry said. He focused hard and managed to picture Bec. 'I was thinking swallows.'

'Uh huh. Well, if you wanted something to go with the Afghan theme, there's the wire-tailed swallow.' Jaya pulled her phone out of her back pocket and did a quick search, then showed Harry a picture of two birds in a nest: black wings, white chests, and a flash of red on their heads. She swiped to another picture, this one of one of the birds in flight, the bifurcated tail trailing to a fine filament on each side.

'Wire-tailed swallows?' Harry said.

Jaya shrugged. 'I do lots of birds.'

'Sounds good.'

'Where were you thinking?'

Harry considered. Should he get them over one of the burn scars from the lightning strike? No. It felt wrong. The burns had removed almost every one of Rob's tattoos. This was about him, not Rob. A vision of Mistress Hel came unbidden to his mind, and he flexed his hands into fists again. He stared at his hands.

'My hands. One on the back of each hand.' So the swallows were apart, but could be together.

Jaya frowned. 'Have you had any other tattoos, other than the one on the back of your neck?'

'No,' Harry said. He didn't want to get into all that.

'Because some people find the hands quite painful,' she said. 'There's not much fatty tissue or muscle in your hands.'

'Perfect.' Harry noticed the look Jaya was giving him. 'I mean, I want to feel this. This is for someone who means a lot to me, so I want to feel it.'

'It's your funeral. Let's rock 'n' roll.'

Harry thought he was ready for the pain but it still caught him by surprise. He sucked air through his teeth, then laughed when Jaya stopped the machine and raised her eyebrows at him.

'Told you,' she said.

Harry took a deep breath. 'Okay, good to go.'

The first five minutes were the worst. The sensation of the needle piercing his skin sixty times a second felt like an intense scratching, and then when Jaya went over the bones in his hand the vibrations coursed up his arm like an electric current. Harry closed his eyes and leant back in the chair, focusing on his breathing. He visualised the picture of the swallow Jaya had shown him in her book of tattoo designs. He visualised a wire-tailed swallow, soaring through the clear blue Afghan sky, darting down through the poppy field below, twisting and turning and taking in the vistas of the vibrant greens and browns of the land below, and the blue-greys and whites of the mountains in the distance. For a few hours he forgot all about Mistress Hel, and paedophiles, and corrupt cops.

'Hey,' a voice said. 'Hey! Harry!'

Harry opened his eyes. He was covered in sweat. The tattoo on the back of his neck was on fire, as was his hand. Jaya was staring at him.

'You okay?'

Harry blinked a couple of times. His head felt woolly but it was a good feeling, like waking after a good night's sleep. He nodded.

'Here,' Jaya said, passing him a can of Coke. He took a swig, enjoying the sensation of the fizzy bubbles in his mouth, then set the can on the side table next to his chair.

Jaya wiped the blood off his tattoo. 'Just about done,' she said. 'What do you think?'

The swallow was beautifully shaded and even though his flesh was red and swollen, it was a great piece of art. He turned his hand this way and that. 'Looks fantastic,' he said.

'You sure you want to get both done today?'

Not really, Harry thought. But he could feel Mistress Hel back there, hidden momentarily by the pain, or maybe by the chemicals his brain was producing in response to the pain. He had two tattoos now, but there was power in the number three. When he closed his eyes he visualised an equilateral triangle, glowing in the darkness.

'I can book you in for a couple of weeks,' Jaya said.

'No, today,' Harry said. 'If you have the time, I'd love for you to finish today.'

Jaya smiled. 'No probs.'

CHAPTER 25

Harry sat awkwardly in the doctor's surgery, while Dr Boyd went through his file on the computer. His hands throbbed. Harry bunched them into fists and smiled at the pain. He looked down and couldn't quite believe he'd gone through with it. Two swallows, one for each hand. Both shaded beautifully. Harry glanced from his hands to the doctor's boots. Cowboy boots. Tooled leather, deep brown. Harry remembered that last time he'd been here, Dr Boyd had told him about his Johnny Cash tattoo.

'So, how are things?' Dr Boyd said. 'It's been a while. New tattoos, I see?'

'Yep. Just got them done.'

'Nice birds.'

'Swallows. The old mariners used to believe they were a good luck charm, to get them home safe. And a sign of fidelity.'

'Make sure you keep them clean, okay? Other than that, you're well?'

'Yeah, good.'

'Headaches?'

'A couple but nothing too bad.'

'Ringing in the ears? Dizziness?'

'Nope. That's totally cleared up.' *Other than that caused by the loud music.*

'Good.'

He grabbed the ophthalmoscope and checked Harry's eyes, then swapped it for the otoscope and had a look in both his ears.

'Any problems with your vision?'

'No. Right as rain.'

He got Harry to roll up his sleeve, then wrapped the black cuff around Harry's upper arm and checked his blood pressure. When he was done he returned to his computer and typed some notes.

'Do you mind if I check how the scars are healing?'

'No, that's fine.'

Harry pulled his shirt off. Dr Boyd put on his magnifying glasses and peered at a couple of areas on Harry's back.

'Remarkable. The human body's ability to heal itself.'

He looked at Harry's arm, where there used to be a tattoo of a drowning man. Now there was just some mostly healed scar tissue, a little pinker than the rest of the skin around it.

'Amazing. It's just amazing how it lifted the tattoo off your arm.'

Harry blushed. He thought of Phil's vague threat against him, telling him of all the footage they had of Harry carrying a sniper rifle through the mall on that fateful day the previous year. There was this, too. Medical records. The only reason no-one had really picked up on the issue with the tattoos and the scar tissue was that they couldn't conceive of what had happened to Harry. And even if they could, they wouldn't believe it. What else was out there?

Would he ever be free of this? Ever be truly normal?

Harry slipped his shirt back on.

'Well, that's it then. You're cured,' Dr Boyd said. 'Anything else I can help you with?'

'Yeah, actually. It's, ah… it's a bit personal.'

Dr Boyd looked straight at Harry. He didn't even blink. 'That's okay. I'm your doctor. You can tell me anything.'

'I can't come. I mean, I can't ejaculate.' Harry looked at the carpet.

'Oh. Okay. Since when?'

'I'm not sure. A couple of weeks?'

'And can you still get an erection?'

At the mere mention of the word, Harry started growing stiff in his pants. He crossed his legs, praying Dr Boyd wasn't about to have a look.

'Yeah.'

'You're still able to have intercourse – maintain the erection throughout intercourse?'

Harry thought of Bec, sweaty, telling him that she'd had enough. 'Yeah.'

'Are you in a sexual relationship at the moment?'

'Yeah… no… it's complicated.'

Dr Boyd returned to the computer. 'Okay, that's good. It's probably not much comfort to you, but I can tell you that there are most likely a lot of guys who envy you. I bet your girlfriend is impressed.'

'Yeah, well… no. You know, she wants to know what's going on.'

'Uh huh. Well, let's take a look. Do you want to undo your pants and hop onto the examination table?'

Harry nodded, glad that the erection had gone back down. He undid his pants, climbed on the table and lay down. He was glad, too, that he didn't have to look at the doctor.

'If you could just slide your pants down for me, Harry.'

Harry did as he was asked.

'And pull your foreskin back.'

Harry complied.

'Have you had any itchiness?'

Harry shook his head.

'Any pain?'

For a moment Harry's mind flashed with Mistress Hel, lashing him with a whip. Then it passed.

'It feels heavy down there. I'm getting some pain, a pulsing sort of pain, up through my abdomen.'

'Uh huh. Okay, you can pull up your pants now.'

Harry buttoned up while Dr Boyd washed his hands at the sink next to the door.

'Well, I can't see anything physically wrong with it. Your testicles are a bit swollen. That would explain the discomfort you're experiencing. Take a seat.'

Harry got off the table and sat at the doctor's desk again.

'There are two possible causes. It could be something physical. We can send you for a scan to rule that out. It could also be psychological. Sometimes, the brain can get some aversion to ejaculation. So everything else feels fine, the brain just associates some negative connotations to ejaculating. And then, if it happens once, your mind fixates on it, so that when you're in a position where you feel you should be able to come, the brain steps in, getting anxious about it, and that detracts from the pleasure you're experiencing, and then you can't. So it feeds on itself.'

'Right.'

'Generally, if it's a psychological problem, you can work through it with a bit of cognitive behavioural therapy. I can give you some fact sheets on that. If it's physical, the blockage can clear itself. Otherwise, we can give you some treatment to clear it. Most of the time though, that's not necessary.' Dr Boyd paused. 'Can I ask – you said that your relationship status is complicated – do you feel comfortable talking about that?'

'It's nothing that interesting. Just... on-again, off-again,' he said. He gave Dr Boyd a brief history.

'That could be it. I'm no psychologist, but it could be that you've built it up so much that now you're worried that it won't live up to your expectations. You can't let go.'

Harry nodded. He hadn't mentioned anything about Mistress Hel, but he had a feeling she had at least something to do with it. It was as if he was saving himself for her.

Dr Boyd turned to his computer, brought up some information, printed it out and handed it to Harry.

'Check these out,' he said. 'The good news is that, although it's good for your prostate to give the old tubes a flush out regularly, it's not essential. The seminal fluid will get reabsorbed into your testes. Obviously, it's not something you want to live with but my advice would be to take a look at the handouts and see how you go.'

'Okay. Thanks.'

Harry sat in the park, flicking through the handouts. The key, if it was psychological, was to gradually break down the association between coming and sexual fulfilment. To focus on the smaller things. Kissing, touching. Taking a more mindful, holistic approach to sex.

Harry looked into the cold, blue sky. Everyone seemed to be suggesting he needed to make up with Bec. But as he read through the pamphlet, all he could think about was Mistress Hel. Kissing her. Her touching him, gently. That half-smile of hers. That husky voice.

The desire filled him. He closed his eyes. No matter what the doctor said, it felt like nothing was being reabsorbed. It was all collecting inside him, these feelings, growing to a point that he couldn't bear. He flexed his hands, the burst of pain giving him a moment of relief.

Without thinking about it, he pulled out his phone and dialled her number. The phone rang and rang until he was sure it was going to go to messagebank. Then she answered.

'Hello?' Soft, silky voice.

'Hello, Mistress. It's me. It's Harry.'

'I know who it is.' She was smiling. He could hear it in her voice.

'I was wondering... is there any chance you can see me any earlier?'

She laughed. 'I'm busy.'

'Please!'

'Beg me.'

'Please, Mistress. I'll do whatever you say. I'll do anything!'

'Get on your knees.'

'What?' Harry looked around the park. Cars passed by on the road, a personal trainer put some people through their paces.

'You heard me. Get on your knees.'

Harry slid off the seat onto his knees. 'Okay. Please, Mistress. I'm on my knees.'

She laughed again. 'No, Harry. You can wait, like all

the rest. But it's good to know you're so compliant. We're going to have fun!'

The line went dead.

CHAPTER 26

Harry's phone buzzed as he walked back to the car, pulling his coat tight against his sweaty karate uniform. The wind rustled through the trees. Harry retrieved the phone with one hand, absently rubbing his right thigh with his other. A narrow miss. A kick that had almost got through, because he wasn't paying attention. He'd been thinking about Mistress Hel again.

He checked the screen. *Hey.* From Lee-Anne Stewart. *Don't call. He's here. You wanted to talk to me?*

Harry unlocked the car and got in, slamming the door behind him.

Hey. Have you heard Don talking about a Lilith Foundation?

Harry stared through the windscreen, watching the dark leaves rustle against each other. He flexed his free hand. The tattoo was healing quickly but looking at it and feeling the burning sensation blocked her out. That and the loud music were getting him through somehow. He plugged his earphones in and slotted the buds into his ears, then chose something loud to listen to.

Yeah. I don't know who this Lilith mob are, but I know Don was talking about this big payment coming to the union.

Rubbing his hands together. He said he was working on something with...

Harry sighed. Tapped his fingers against the steering wheel. Behind the car, silhouettes formed and then disappeared into shadow. His phone buzzed.

Sorry. Almost got busted. He was working on something with some cop. Dunno what. Some function or event or something. Dunno if the fact he was a cop meant anything. Don't know what the connection was. Just know that the cop had something to do with the Lilith mob.

Harry tapped out a reply. *Do you know this cop's name?*
Yeah. Sorry. Constable Brooks. Dunno his first name.

Harry's brain was so fried it took him a couple of seconds to place the name. Constable Brad Brooks. *I have sinned. I give my life for the Goddess.* Service pistol. Blood and brains all over his bedroom wall. Note on the bedside table. Marks cut into his back. Some cryptic note probably hidden in his house somewhere. Harry stared into the darkness. Goosebumps rose on his flesh. His breath plumed in front of his mouth. The music – he hadn't been aware of it until that moment – 'Revolution 9', by The Beatles.

Harry's phone buzzed in his hand.

Maybe you could try and get in contact with this Brooks character?

Harry laughed. Just a small exhalation of air. Dry. Lifeless. He stared at his phone until the screen faded.

Harry?

Yeah. Got it. Thanks for the info.

He switched off the music, and was almost instantly deluged with sights, sounds, smells. His cock throbbed. His breath came in short, sharp gasps. He groaned in frustration. Bit his lip until he could taste his own blood.

The pain cleared his mind enough for him to dial Phil's number.

'Hello?' Harry could hear the TV on the background. Some kid's show.

'Phil? It's Harry.'

'Hey, Harry,' Phil said. He sounded cautious. Guarded. 'You okay?'

No. 'Kinda.'

'Hang on.'

The background noise died out. Harry pictured Phil going into a bedroom, pulling out a notebook and pen. 'Go on.'

'Constable Brooks. Did you ever hear him mention anything about the Lilith Foundation?'

'Lilith?'

Harry spelled it for him. 'Yeah. As in the Jewish demon.'

'Well, I didn't work with him, but I can ask around if you like?'

Harry considered. There was a risk that whatever this was to do with was also the reason Brooks was dead, but Harry didn't see that he had any option at this point.

'Yeah, if you could. But be discreet, okay?'

'Sure thing, Harry. And, Harry?'

'Yeah?'

'Thanks.'

Harry smiled. 'Phil, I'm still chasing that other story. If I can nail that bastard for what he's done, I'll do it.'

Phil lowered his voice, as though that would save him if his phone was tapped. 'I know, Harry. Thanks for that, too.'

Harry switched the music back on, letting it blast through his brain, cleansing him. All this would be over soon. He started the car. He didn't really understand why this had transfixed him so strongly, why he hadn't been able to think of anything else. Or maybe he did, but... when he started to think that way everything began to go fuzzy. But he felt confident, deep within him, that seeing Mistress Hel would make it all much better. Everything would be clearer.

He put the car into gear and drove out of the school grounds. The Lilith Foundation. Brad Brooks. Don Clack. What did they have in common? What was pulling together this young cop and this grizzled old union official?

CHAPTER 27

Harry pulled up outside Mistress Hel's place, heart thudding sluggishly in his chest. For the first time in what felt like weeks, he had clarity, but it was a kind of tunnel vision. He looked at the swallows on the backs of his hands. He bunched his hands into fists. He would make it through this. He and Bec would make it through this.

And yet, although he told himself he could totally fire up the car and drive away, he pulled the keys out of the ignition, climbed out of the car, locked it and walked to Mistress Hel's front gate.

He pressed the buzzer. 'Hello?'

He waited. *What the hell am I doing?*

Press the buzzer; wait for her; it will all be okay.

The speaker buzzed and the gate opened a crack. Harry pushed through, heard it clang shut behind him. He walked up the front path thinking no further than the next step ahead.

She was waiting at the door when he arrived. He smelt her first. Perfume and a deeper, musky scent. She pulled the door open wide and smiled. 'Mr Hendrick, how lovely to see you.'

Harry thought he would cry. She was so beautiful. She

had a silk gown wrapped around her, but he could see her perfect body underneath. Fishnet stockings led to high heels.

Harry's legs gave way and he staggered over the threshold. Mistress Hel grabbed his forearm with surprising strength and kept him on his feet.

'Not out here,' she said. 'There will be plenty of time for that later.'

Harry grinned. He felt like an idiot. A moron. He felt wonderful.

'I... I don't...'

She paused, looking at the tattoo on the back of his hand. 'Hmm. Didn't take you for someone who'd get their hands tattooed. Still waters run deep, huh?'

'Yeah... I...'

'Shh,' she said. 'Follow me.'

She led him through the house, heels click-clacking against the white tiles. Past the lounge room, kitchen, bedrooms. She opened a door, switched on a light. Stairs descended to a basement. Even through the fog, Harry's face registered his surprise.

'The house was made to order, with my special playroom. After you.'

Harry walked past her, feeling so grateful to be here. The doorway led to a set of stairs, going down.

Get out! Now!

Mistress Hel closed the door behind her.

Down the stairs there was another door, standing ajar. Harry pushed it open. The room was as big as Mistress Hel's lounge room. Black and red were the dominant colours. There was a cross-shaped rack against one wall. A table off to one side, like a doctor's examination table, but with wrist and ankle restraints. Ropes hung from a pulley system in the ceiling. Sex toys and whips and paddles were lined up on one wall. On the far side of the room was a doorway through which Harry could see white tiles. In the centre of the room stood a throne.

Lily removed her gown and hung it on a peg by the door. She was dressed in a leather corset, like a fantasy warrior princess. She smiled again, revealing bright white teeth between blood red lips.

'There's a bathroom through there,' she said. 'Go and wash yourself. Leave your clothes folded on the bench. I'll wait for you here.'

She sat in the throne and crossed her legs.

Harry stripped, trying to get out of his clothes so quickly that he almost fell over. He dashed under the shower. The room filled with perfumed steam. Harry felt dazed. His heart slammed in his chest, sending blood pulsing through his excited body. He washed quickly then dried himself, then folded his clothes and hung up the towel.

'My, my!' Mistress Hel said. 'You are eager!' She laughed. 'You know what to do.'

Harry dropped to his knees and crawled across the floor. He felt exposed. He felt ashamed. He felt alive. He looked at the swallows on his hands, but couldn't quite remember what they meant. He felt nothing except the gloriously warm air on his skin.

'Jesus,' Mistress Hel said, 'what happened to you?'

At first Harry didn't know what she was talking about. He was so used to seeing the burn scars on his body he didn't notice them anymore.

'I... I was struck by lightning,' he said.

'And you survived,' Mistress Hel said. 'Wow. There's

more to you than meets the eye, Harry Hendrick. Over here, quickly.'

Harry crawled to her feet.

'Now, before we get to the fun part, Harry, I have some rules,' Mistress Hel said.

Harry looked up at her. She launched herself forwards. He saw the hand coming but did nothing to stop it. The slap rocked his head, sending stars across his vision.

'The first is that you never look me in the eye. You can look at my pretty shoes. Do you understand?'

'Yeah.'

She grabbed his hair with one hand, pulling it so hard that he cried out. She slapped him on the other cheek then tilted his head towards hers. He frantically looked away.

'Another rule. You address me as "Mistress" or "Mistress Hel" at all times. Do you understand?'

'Yes, Mistress.'

'That's better.'

She let go of his hair and he slumped. He watched her shiny black shoe bob up and down in front of his face. He could see his reflection. Shame bloomed, and then wilted, drowned out by desire.

'Kiss my shoe, slave,' she said.

'Yes, Mistress.' Harry leant forwards. The shoe was still bobbing up and down. She moved it from side to side, making it hard for him. She laughed. Eventually, he managed to plant a kiss on the tip of her shoe.

'You asked me how it was that I could make men do what I want. Do you understand now?'

'Yes, Mistress.'

'No. No, you don't. But you will. Follow me.' She

got up and brushed past him. He crawled along the floor behind her. 'Stand.'

Harry stood. She went to the wall and grabbed a pair of handcuffs. They looked like the real deal, not the sort of thing a sex shop would sell. Harry's mind flashed to Constable Brad Brooks' brain splattered across his bedroom wall. And then the image was gone.

'Hands out.'

Cold steel dug into his wrists. Mistress Hel yanked down a rope and tied it to the cuffs, then disappeared behind him. He heard the pulley wheels over his head, then raised his arms to make it easier for her. She pulled the rope until his arms were stretched over his head and he was standing on the balls of his feet.

She returned to his field of vision.

'Ta da!' she said, grinning. She sauntered to the far wall, running her fingers over the wide range of whips, crops and paddles.

'Men are so easy to control. It's so easy to get into their heads. I've been in your head this week, haven't I?'

Harry looked down. 'Yes, Mistress.'

'Of course I have. And I'm going to stay there.'

She returned with a riding crop. *Smack, smack, smack!* Harry cried out. Mistress Hel cooed in his ear, her body pressing against his. Then more of the crop. *Smack, smack, smack!* Harry dropped into a trance, his mind engulfed by the pain coming from his wrists, from his calf muscles, from his back and arse and legs where the crop kissed his skin. And yet the pain became pleasure. Every smack was followed by the warm glow of relief. The physical relief matched the mental relief. He was no longer in control.

'Slave, what's this?'

Harry came to. Mistress Hel was still behind him, gloved hand entwined in the hair at the back of his head.

'My hair, Mistress Hel?' he said. He couldn't concentrate.

'No, idiot! This!' She slapped the back of his neck.

'A tattoo.'

She hissed. 'I can see that. What is it?'

Harry opened his mouth and was about to tell her all about the tattoos and everything else that had happened the previous year. And then he stopped. He tilted his head back and looked at his hands, strung above him. He couldn't see the birds but he could feel them.

NO!

He closed his eyes and envisaged an equilateral triangle, burning bright in the darkness. His neck tattoo burned hotter than he'd ever felt it burn before. He gritted his teeth.

'I don't know. I was drunk.'

She held his head. For a moment he thought she was going to snap his neck, but then she let him go. His hands were numb. His calf muscles screamed.

Mistress Hel returned to him with a piece of chalk. She drew a circle around him, muttering under her breath. As she completed the circle, Harry felt the atmosphere in the room thicken. She walked around him a second time, drawing symbols outside the circle. Harry's ears hummed.

She stood, looked at Harry. Grabbed him. 'Are you ready?'

'Yes, Mistress.'

She smiled. 'I can feel that you are.' She threw the chalk into the corner of the room and disappeared behind him. The rope slackened a bit, so he could stand normally.

He curled his hands into fists to get the circulation

moving again. He felt so grateful he thought he would cry.

'Thank you, Mistress.'

As soon as the pain in his wrists and calf muscles was gone, Harry could fully appreciate the waves of pleasure washing over him. It felt as though his whole body was being covered in soft kisses. He gasped, panted.

'It's good, isn't it?' she whispered in his ear. 'But it gets better.'

Mistress Hel sauntered over to the end of the bench where she kept her toys. She pulled out a small wooden bowl and a bunch of bottles and brown paper bags. Harry found it hard to focus, as though he was watching her through waves of heat coming off a furnace. She hummed under her breath as she worked, the sound both distant and intimate.

She returned with the bowl, and something in her other hand. She held it in front of his eyes, let the light glint off the small blade.

On some level Harry recognised the scalpel, understood what she was going to do with it.

'You... you said no blood, Mistress.'

She assessed him. He looked at her shiny shoes. She twisted the scalpel in front of his eyes and let the light reflect across his face.

'Yes... maybe you're right,' she said. She clamped the scalpel handle between her teeth, grabbed the base of his cock and slowly pulled. Harry felt the lip of the bowl press against his glans. He let out a shuddering breath.

'No, please!'

She let him go and took a step back. She took the scalpel from her mouth and gently stirred the liquid in the bowl. 'No, I really think I'd better not.'

Harry started crying. 'Please... please, Mistress.'

'Oh. Okay, then. If you insist.'

She disappeared behind him again. He felt her hand against his back. She muttered under her breath. He waited for the sting of the scalpel, but none came. Instead, he felt an intense burst of heat and vibration, starting at his upper back and quickly moving through his body. When it hit his groin, he tensed.

'Easy,' she whispered in his ear.

She cut him again and this time, although Harry wouldn't have thought it possible, the pleasure doubled. He thrashed against the cuffs holding him in place. His knees buckled. He didn't realise it was possible to experience such pleasure without orgasm.

Mistress Hel cut again, and again, each time sending a wave of intense pleasure through Harry. All the while, she muttered. Harry understood that she was using words, but couldn't recognise them. Not English; not any language he was familiar with. The atmosphere in the room thickened more still. It reminded Harry of the tropics, thick balmy air washing against his sweaty skin. He opened his eyes, blinking away the tears of joy, and the room seemed hazy, smoky.

'Are you ready, Harry?'

Harry's skin was so alive he could feel the tip of the scalpel against the middle of his back.

'Yes, Mistress.'

She cut. An explosion of pleasure tore through Harry, ripping him to pieces through the abdomen to his cock. Despite being held by the wrists, Harry fell into a warm, dark cave. He could hear Mistress Hel laughing at him as he fell away from her into the intense darkness.

Harry woke up on the floor, still naked. His whole body hummed. He was sleepy, but his mind was clear. For the first time in a week, his mind was actually clear. He felt no guilt. No fear. Just relief.

He sat up, looked around. Mistress Hel was back in her throne, smiling slyly at him.

'Well, hello there.'

'Hi… Mistress.'

As his eyes focused he noticed the mess he'd made. His semen and blood on the floor.

'Don't worry about that. I've got a slave who'll clean it up.'

He rubbed his face. He could see it all now. How it all fit together. It was as though he was looking at a map. It was so simple.

'That… was… incredible.'

'You understand now. Good. Go take a shower.'

Harry picked himself up on shaky legs. He felt like he'd just done an intense workout after taking a few weeks off. He gently walked to the shower and put the water on full, as hot as he could take it, cleansing his face and chest. He turned, wincing as the jets burrowed into the fresh cuts on his back. His mind flashed to the photos he'd seen, the other victims, with the cuts on their backs. But still, he felt no fear.

He got out of the shower, dried himself off and saw his clothes still sitting there. It felt like a thousand years since he'd taken them off. He pulled his shirt over his head, then yanked his pants on. When he walked back out to the playroom, Mistress Hel was waiting with a handheld EFTPOS machine.

'Cash or credit?' she said.

For a moment Harry was rocked by the juxtaposition. He'd just had the most incredible, the most spiritual, experience of his life... and now she wanted money? She seemed to know what he was thinking, but just sat there smiling at him. He fumbled in his pocket for his wallet, handed over his card.

'Credit.'

She put through a transaction for $500. Harry punched in his PIN.

'Pleasure doing business with you, Mr Hendrick.'

She put the machine down on a bench, placed a hand at the small of his back and aimed him towards the door. Her hand felt warm. She guided him through and up the stairs.

'I'll see you again next week. Same day, same time,' she said.

'Okay,' Harry said. His mind still had that calm feeling. He told himself that there was no way he'd be back here in a week. He was 'cured' now. But another part of him wanted to experience that massive relief once more. He had never felt so good.

CHAPTER 28

Harry woke before sunrise, feeling refreshed, and decided to take a run. He got out of bed, not noticing the small bloodstains on his sheets. He scrounged around in the semi-dark, looking for his running gear and threw on a singlet, shorts and pulled on his shoes.

As he started running, he assessed his condition. He felt great, except for his calf muscles. It took him a moment to recall why they hurt so much, and when he did, it seemed like something out of a dream. He pushed it away. The morning was too glorious to bother with any of that. His breath plumed out of his mouth. The air felt so fresh. Had it ever felt this great? So crisp and sweet?

He passed a guy delivering newspapers, cut towards the water tower, legs pumping up the steep incline. At the top of the hill he paused, staring out at the city lights, standing underneath the big old fig tree. He vaguely remembered feeling as though he could pull all the pieces of the puzzle together. That wasn't quite true but he felt like it was at least possible. He was on the cusp of something. He kicked off, through the winding streets at the top of the hill, until he stood under the water tower. There was a security fence and cameras. They only let people in during the day.

There was also a plaque to Rob Johnson and his girlfriend. Rob's dossier, revealing the despicable acts of Andrew Cardinal and his minions, had been hidden in the water tower for years, until Harry found it. He stared at the tower, remembering the night when he thought his life was over. Everything was clear in that moment after Cardinal fell to his death: a sudden death putting everything in perspective, clearing all the crap away and letting Harry see what was truly important.

'Bec.'

He wasn't aware he was even thinking of her until the name passed his lips. He knew what he had to do.

'Jesus, Harry!'

Bec pulled her apartment door closed behind her. Red skirt, matching shoes and jacket. White blouse. Harry knew when she usually left for work, and knew that her first stop was always the coffee place downstairs.

He offered her the cup. 'By way of apology,' he said.

She frowned, but took the coffee. 'Thanks. But...'

'I'm sorry I didn't just tell you. Her name is Lily. Lily Sweeney. She was texting me to confirm an appointment I'd made with her... for an interview.' His mind flashed to that feeling of release, as Mistress Hel made that final cut.

Bec stared at him so intently that he feared she'd somehow seen what was going on in his head.

'Harry...'

In that moment, Harry couldn't tell which way it was going to go. Harry's phone buzzed in his pocket. He ignored it. It kept buzzing. Bec's eyes darted down.

'Are you going to get that?'

Harry grinned, pulled the phone out of his pocket.

Inwardly, he breathed a sigh of relief when he saw Sandy's name pop up.

'It's Sandy. Sandy Flores.'

'The psychic?'

'Yeah… you'd have thought she'd know I was busy.'

Bec laughed. 'So, are you going to answer it?'

The phone stopped ringing, and this time they both laughed.

'Can I walk you to work?'

She nodded.

'I'm sorry,' Harry said. 'I just – I've been neck deep in this stuff. I haven't felt I could talk to anyone about it. And I just didn't want to get into it. Especially not after I bailed at dinner because of her.'

'Harry, you can tell me anything.' She took his hand and squeezed it.

'Ow!' Harry said, as a bolt of pain shot up his arm.

Bec looked at his hand, then gently lifted it. She blinked. Harry showed her the other one to save prolonging the conversation.

'Um…'

'Yeah, got them done the other day.'

'They're… they're pretty,' she said. She stood on tiptoes and pecked him on the lips.

They walked out into the street together. Harry's back thumped in time with his heartbeat. When he blinked, he could see Mistress Hel, looking down and laughing at him.

'So,' Bec said. 'Do you want to try me out?' She offered him a wry smile.

'Huh?'

'The telling-me-anything thing.'

'Oh. Right,' Harry said, looking at the stained pavement. 'Do you mean the tattoos?'

'If you like, but I'm more interested in this dominatrix.'

'Okay. Lily Sweeney. AKA Mistress Hel, with one L.'

'Jesus, what is she? A hipster or something?'

Harry laughed. 'Anyway, it seems like she's implicated in some murders, or suicides.'

'Which are they? Murder or suicide?'

'It's as if she has somehow compelled four men to take their own lives. And one man to kill a workmate.'

'Blackmail?'

Harry thought of Godwin, choking down pieces of mirror. 'Maybe. Anyway, the police wanted me to look into it. They thought, given what happened last year with Cardinal, that I might be able to come at it from... I don't know, a different angle.'

'Uh huh.'

'One of her clients is a high-ranking union official, and he's using union money to pay her.'

'Shit.'

They stopped to cross the road. Around them, people huddled in big coats and scarves, eyes on their phones. Ahead, sun was streaming down Elizabeth St, turning the buildings gold. He hated this city sometimes, but at moments like this it was hard not to love it.

'Yeah, and that's not even going into the paedophile ring,' he said.

Bec gave him a sideways glance. 'Now you're just showing off.' She squeezed his hand. He squeezed back.

His phone buzzed in his pocket. Harry took it out, looked at the screen. It was Sandy again.

'It's okay. It's just Sandy.'

The lights changed. They walked across the road.

'Harry, I don't mind if you take it.'

'Nah, it's cool. I'll phone her back. I'm enjoying this walk with you. So anyway, enough about me. What's going on with you?'

'Ah, you know. Work is work. My boss wants me to apply for this management leadership thing, but I dunno…'

'You should.'

'Yeah, he says it will be really good for my career.'

'I think you'd be awesome at it.'

'Harry. Do you even know what I do?'

'Something to do with money?'

She gave him a playful punch in the arm. 'I'm a risk assessor.'

'Yeah. I totally knew that.'

'You live on your own planet a lot of the time, don't you?'

Harry thought of his battle with the tattoos. He thought of himself strung up in Mistress Hel's playroom.

'Yeah, I guess. I'm sorry.'

'Anyway, this thing – it's overseas… It's a twelve-month placement in London.'

'Uh huh.'

'Still want me to apply for it?'

Harry stopped and looked at Bec. 'Only if you take me with you.'

Bec grinned at him, then wrapped her arms around him. It was almost comical, their bodies bulky with winter clothes. And Harry found himself crying. The tears erupted out of him, down his cheeks, cooling his face as the wind blew on them. She squeezed him harder.

Harry wrapped his arms around Bec and lifted her off

the ground. The cuts in his back flared. The pain seemed worse than it should have. Harry lowered her to the pavement.

'I'm serious,' Harry said.

Bec placed her hands on the side of his head. 'Let's... let's just see how it goes. I haven't even applied for it yet.'

'Okay.'

They walked the rest of the way to work together, not talking, just holding hands. Harry felt torn. Full of love but also full of guilt for the secret he was carrying.

'Well, this is me, Harry Hendrick.'

She put her cool fingers on his face again, stood on tiptoe so she could kiss him on the lips. He held her head between his hands, ran his fingers through her long hair. In that moment he had clarity. He would phone Mistress Hel as soon as Bec was in the building. Cancel the appointment. The story wasn't worth it. He'd give up journalism, if that's what it took. He fantasised about working in London. They'd be away from it (*her*) all. They'd be safe.

The kiss ended. Bec put her arms around his waist.

'Do you want to come over for dinner tonight?'

'I'd love to.'

'Six-thirty?'

'Perfect. Love you.'

'Love you too.'

Bec walked towards the revolving door. She turned and waved. Harry waved back, then pulled out his phone.

Harry dialled Mistress Hel's number, worried that if he didn't do it straight away he'd forget about it or change his mind. He felt a heavy ball of lead in his gut. Tingling in his fingers.

'I'm all tied up at the moment. Leave a message.'

At the sound of her voice, it all came flooding back. His knees buckled, and he staggered to a nearby bus stop.

'Ah... it's Harry... call me back, please.'

Harry hung up and stared at the phone, shakes rolling through his body. Did he need to cancel? Maybe he was being a bit hasty. He put the phone away, stared at his feet. Why did he make the first appointment? *Because I needed to see what it was like.* Why did he need to make a second appointment? *Because I need her to trust me. I need her in order to get the story.*

Harry shut his eyes, rubbed his temples. Was that even true? He wasn't sure. She was the story, right? Without her there was nothing.

'Without her there's nothing,' Harry muttered, not sure if he was talking about Mistress Hel or Bec.

The day seemed colder now. He pulled his coat tighter about himself and headed for his car.

CHAPTER 29

Back at home, he put the heater on and walked around the house, restless. He thought of Bec. He thought of them living together in London. Away from all this. But it didn't seem real. It felt like remembering a movie he'd seen a long time ago. His mind kept returning to Mistress Hel. Red lips. High heels. The sting of the crop against his back.

His back.

He reached under his shirt and gingerly fingered the wound on his right shoulder blade. It stung at the touch. He pulled his finger away and looked at it. The tip was stained with blood. But there was something else. Something black.

'Shit.'

He pulled his shirt off and walked to the bathroom. He felt like he was experiencing deja vu. He looked over his shoulder, into the mirror. Blinked. Wiped his eyes. Looked again.

'No.'

His phone rang. He immediately thought of Mistress Hel, but he wasn't sure what he would say to her now. It had seemed so obvious mere hours before. He strode to the table and looked at his phone: Sandy.

'Hello?' he said, irritated.

'Harry! Oh, I was so worried. Are you okay?'

'Yeah.'

A pause. 'Are you sure?'

Harry clamped down on the anger. Bit his tongue until the taste of blood filled his mouth. Clenched his fist.

'Of course I'm sure. Why wouldn't everything be okay?'

'Oh. I… well…'

'Sandy, I'm really quite busy so…'

'The spirits. I'm hearing that you're in trouble.'

'You've been wrong before, Sandy. Remember?'

It was an awful thing to say. Years before, Sandy had believed she had located the body of a missing boy. She did find a body, but not the one the authorities were looking for. Anger swamped his guilt.

'Sandy. I know that you were a big help to me last year, with the whole… you know…' Harry's back pulsed. He could feel five points of fire, burning. When he closed his eyes, he could see them in the darkness: tiny slits, gateways. He heard Mistress Hel muttering in his ear. Smelt her perfume. 'But it doesn't mean that I'm always in crisis. I had my crisis, remember? I'm leading a normal life now.'

'But Harry, what about the symbols under the doormat?'

Harry suppressed the anger again. Why had he ever even told her about that? She was a crazy old woman. A lonely, crazy old woman.

There was a pause on the other end of the line, and for a moment Harry thought he'd spoken those words aloud.

'Okay, Harry. Sorry I bothered you.' The line went dead.

Harry felt a momentary stab of belated guilt, but then

the lines on his back flared, so hot and bright that he cried out. He returned to the bathroom and checked out his back again in the mirror.

He was marked. Five cuts, swollen and red. Infected?

'No,' Harry whimpered. 'No, no, no.'

He reached over and pressed the one on his right shoulder, gasping at the pain. A few drops of blood trickled down his back, and then the black stuff, like hot tar.

'What the…'

He wiped his hand across the cut then pulled it back so he could look at it. The black stuff was sticky. He lifted his fingers to his nose, and immediately wished he hadn't. He heaved. The smell was like rotting meat crossed with burning metal.

He took a deep breath and centred himself. He put his shirt back on, walked out into the sunroom at the front of the house and stared at the water tower.

Could it be to do with the tattoo at the back of his neck, a tattoo with the sole purpose of protecting its wearer from harm? All the others had disappeared in the lightning strike. Why not that one?

'I lied to her,' he said quietly, remembering when Mistress Hel had asked about his tattoo.

His phone rang. Harry pulled it out of his pocket and saw Mistress Hel's name on the screen. He considered ignoring her, letting it go to messagebank. Make *her* wait, for a change. But even as he thought it, he was answering.

'Hello, Harry,' she said.

Harry dropped to his knees, not even aware he was doing it.

'We had a rule, do you remember?'

Harry opened his mouth, closed it again.

'You are to address me as Mistress. Even on phone messages. Is that understood?'

'Yes, Mistress.'

'I'll forgive you this time, Harry.'

'Yes, Mistress.'

'Okay then. What did you want anyway?'

Harry swallowed. He couldn't remember. 'Just to hear your voice, Mistress.'

'Liar,' she said. He could tell she was smiling. 'What have you been doing this morning?'

'I made up with my girlfriend, Mistress.'

'Aw, cute. Now, just to be clear. Who is the number one priority in your life?'

Harry tried to remember Bec's kiss. He tried to remember the feeling of her arms around him. It was hazy. Unreal.

'You are, Mistress.'

'That's right. Don't forget it. I'll see you next Tuesday night. And Harry?'

'Yes, Mistress?'

'Don't waste my time again.'

The line went dead. Harry gasped for breath.

Harry paced in the lounge room, nervous energy coursing through him. His neck felt like it was on fire, and his back pounded in sickening bursts that sent black spots blooming across his vision.

He was drawn to the memories of his session with Mistress Hel, to that moment of release. It was comforting. It made him feel like he was safe and that everything would be okay. Harry slapped himself, grabbed his phone and dialled Phil.

'Queensland Police Media Unit. Phil speaking.' Phil sounded bored.

'Phil, it's Harry.'

'Hey, mate, how's things?'

Harry felt himself slipping again and bit his knuckle. 'The suicides. I know who's responsible. You need to get someone to bring her in.'

'Okay, I'm listening.'

'She goes by the name of Mistress Hel.'

'Okay.'

Harry felt sick. Sweaty and nauseous.

'So... what's the story?' Phil said.

The world spun around him. Harry crouched, worried he was going to fall over. He sucked in a breath to steady himself.

'Harry, you okay?'

'Yeah... just not feeling too great. The cuts. I'm pretty sure she's doing the cuts...'

'Oh yeah, why's that?'

Because she did them to me. 'There's another guy... seeing her... a union official...'

'You sure you're okay, Harry?'

'No, not really. But this... this is important...'

Shut the fuck up. Her voice was in his head. Not just him imagining her – actually in his head. *Shut the fuck up or I'll flay you.* And then he saw it: her playroom floor covered in blood and him hanging there like a piece of meat.

'Harry, are you in danger? Has this woman threatened you?'

YES! 'N-no... nothing like that.'

A pause at the other end of the line. 'Do you have any evidence?'

Shut the fuck up, Harry.

Harry tried to blink the vision away, but it wouldn't go. Eyes open, eyes closed, it made no difference. Mistress Hel dropped the scalpel to the base of Harry's cock. *And now I end you...*

Harry cried out.

'Harry?'

'Yeah, I'm here,' he said. He knew what he had to do. And it wasn't blab to Phil. He lay on the floor, taking deep breaths.

Mistress Hel stared into his eyes. She smiled and took a step back. Harry opened his eyes and he was back in his lounge room, staring at the ceiling.

'Do you have any evidence?' Phil said. 'Anything at all? If the boys have reasonable suspicion a crime has been committed, they can get a search warrant.'

Harry took another deep breath. A crime? He recalled questioning Mistress Hel about the scalpel, while he was strung up, and then giving her permission to use it on him. Shit, he begged her to use it on him. If there was any evidence of someone else being at the crime scenes, other than the cryptic scrawls he'd found outside Zak Godwin's place, Phil hadn't mentioned it.

'No... I... sorry...' Harry said.

'That's okay, mate. Why don't you call me back when you're feeling a bit better?'

'Yeah, yeah, maybe that's for the best.'

Harry hung up and then crawled into his bedroom and into bed. He fell asleep almost straight away, the stench of blood in his nostrils.

* * *

Harry waited for Bec outside her office building. There was no trace of the optimism he'd felt that morning. In fact, it was the opposite. Any attempt to try to remember what had actually happened was like trying to look through a thick layer of fog. He knew in his head it was something significant, he could replay the moment in his mind, but he was divorced from any feeling associated with it, as though he was watching a TV show but he'd come in halfway through.

His hand probed his shoulder. The cuts weren't bleeding anymore, but he could feel them through his shirt, rough under the fabric.

He had a few moments to watch Bec before she saw him. Then their eyes locked and she smiled, and all he could think of was how he'd told Mistress Hel she was his top priority.

Don't ever waste my time again, Harry.

He forced a smile as Bec walked towards the revolving door. She came out and, if possible, her smile grew even wider. She wrapped her arms around him, squeezed him. It was like a jolt of electricity.

Bec let go of him slightly. 'You okay?'

Harry smiled. 'Yeah.'

'No, you're not.'

Harry felt tears welling inside him. 'No. No, I'm not. But can we talk about this at your place?'

'Of course.'

They walked back through the city together, holding hands. Skin on skin. He felt a thread of hope among all the confusion. He could do this. As long as she never let him go, he could get through this. He couldn't speak. It was hard enough just putting one foot in front of the other.

His fingers tingled. He felt disconnected from himself. In his peripheral vision, he could see Bec glancing at him from time to time, worry lining her face.

She guided him into her building, into the lift, through the door to her apartment, then to the couch, where he could watch dusk settling over the city.

'You stay there. I think we need tea for this,' she said.

'Whisky,' Harry mumbled, through numb lips.

'Tea first. Then whisky.'

The sounds of her rummaging around in the kitchen, those lovely, everyday sounds, kept him calm. He zoned out, and came back to himself when Bec handed him the tea.

'I put sugar in it. I don't know if you still take sugar, but you look like you could use some,' she said.

'Thanks.'

She sat next to him, set her cup on the table. 'Look, if this is about the London thing, I don't even know if I'll go and even if...'

'It's not about London.'

'Okay. Then spill it. The words, not the tea.'

Harry concentrated on the warmth going into his hands, and on the surface of the tea. 'I didn't tell you everything about what happened last year,' he said.

Bec nodded.

'Because it sounds crazy,' Harry said. 'But after last year, I get the feeling that crazy is going to be a part of my life. And if you're going to be a part of my life, then...'

She put a hand on his leg.

'I had a bit of help getting that big story last year,' he said. 'In fact, without the help, I wouldn't have got the story at all. No one would have.'

He laid it all out for her. The tattoos, the nightmares, how they connected. Rob and his girlfriend. Andrew Cardinal and his sick little hobby.

When he'd finished the story, his tea was gone. Bec hadn't touched hers. For a long time, she said nothing. There was just silence, punctuated by the wind whistling around the building.

'Harry, that sounds...'

'Crazy. I know. Look.'

He showed her the tattoo on the back of his neck. She must have seen it before. She must have assumed it was something he'd done post break-up. A drunken mistake.

'This is still with me. And sometimes I think Rob is still with me. Did you know I'm going to compete in a martial arts tournament next week?'

'You mentioned something about it.'

'I've been doing karate for nine months. I'll be competing against people who've been doing it for years. That's Rob. I still have some of Rob's abilities.'

'Harry...'

He stared at her. In the semi-darkness it was hard to read her expression, but she still looked worried. Harry sighed. He unbuttoned his shirt. Turned his back to her to show her the cuts. She gasped.

'Harry! Harry, who did this to you?' She sounded scared.

He put his head in his hands and cried. He didn't want to tell her. But now he had no choice. He'd gone too far.

'Mistress Hel.'

Silence. Somewhere in the city a siren went off.

'The dominatrix?'

Harry nodded. Bec took her hand off his leg.

'Harry, what the hell is going on?'

Harry tried to get it straight in his own head. Why had he booked the session with Mistress Hel? He saw the photos of the marked backs. All dead. He closed his eyes, saw strange symbols floating through the darkness. Made fists with his hands and saw the triangle, burning through the darkness.

'I'm caught in a trap,' he whispered.

'You're not making any sense.'

He sat up, rubbed his face. 'I'm caught in a trap. Like a spider's web.'

'Harry… sit down.'

Harry didn't realise he was standing. He didn't sit. Instead he walked to the window and stared out at the city. Bec didn't follow him.

'We can figure this out, Harry. I can help you. Just sit.'

He shook his head.

'Tell me what happened.'

Harry sighed. 'I didn't just interview Lily Sweeney. I went there for a… a session with Mistress Hel. I don't know why. I couldn't get her out of my head. I mean… I couldn't stop thinking about her. I needed to know why those men had…' He walked behind the lounge. Couldn't bear the feeling of her eyes on him.

She didn't get up. She didn't face him.

'So I went to see her. She tied me up. Cut me. It was… it was… amazing. Terrible. Horrific. It was pure ecstasy.'

'Harry…'

He waved her away. 'And now I'm trapped.'

'Harry, I think you should leave,' Bec sobbed.

'I'm sorry,' he said, and walked out the door.

CHAPTER 30

The ashen six-storey block looked as though it had been airlifted from Soviet Russia. UNION HOUSE was stamped on the side in faded red letters. The portico out the front bore the names of six different unions, the letters time-worn and almost illegible.

Harry pushed through the front door, glad to be out of the chill. His pulse rate lifted, but he was glad. Despite pumping loud music into his brain, despite the tattoos on the backs of his hands, his head was a maelstrom, filled mostly by Mistress Hel and the massive orgasm he'd had at her hands. Then the break-up with Bec. He was assuming it was a break-up. He found he cared less than he should, which worried him. But when he worried about it, his brain fogged up. But this, what he was about to do, this was real. Real and highly unethical, not to mention illegal.

The receptionist was on the phone. Harry surveyed the foyer. Grey walls with tacky red tiles and union posters. VALUE ME, one of them screamed. It seemed a bit needy. Harry walked to the counter. The man behind the desk was in his late fifties. His work area was covered in slips of paper and Post-It notes, stacks of printed reports, and overflowing in/out trays. Several lights on his phone were flashing.

The receptionist hung up from a call and peered at Harry.

'Chad Brunswick,' Harry said. 'Here to fix Don Clack's computer?' He lifted the briefcase, which was mostly empty. The receptionist looked none the wiser. 'He's the Australian United Workers secretary.'

'Hang on a sec.' He dialled a number, listened for a while, then cut off the call. 'Sorry, he's not in, is he expecting you?'

'Yeah, it's okay...'

'I can call up and get someone to let you in?' His tone suggested he'd rather he didn't have to.

'Nah. That's okay. I'll just pop up.'

'Thanks. Have a nice day.'

'You too,' Harry said, and headed for the lift.

It was a small workspace, four desks and a tiny office at the back, sectioned off with glass partitions and blinds. Two people were at their desks. The man closest to the door was in his forties, with a paunch and sweat stains under his arms. When he glanced up, Harry smiled.

'G'day,' Harry said. He didn't stop, didn't ask for directions, just kept walking.

The next occupied desk was closer to Clack's office. The woman with frizzy brown hair and a matching cardigan didn't even look up. He pulled out his set of lock picks, slid them into the lock and eased them back and forth. He'd bought the picks on Amazon late one night a few months before, an impulse buy that he didn't remember until they arrived in the post. He'd decided he might as well try them out and discovered, as with karate, he'd picked up another obscure skill from Rob. That afternoon he'd managed to pick every lock in the house.

'You okay there?' the woman in the brown jumper said.

'Yeah,' Harry said. 'The lock's just a bit stuck.'

And then it popped. He left the door open, put the picks into his pocket, went to the computer and switched it on. He peered through the blinds. The guy was staring at his computer. The woman watched Harry, but then returned to her work when he met her gaze and smiled. He let the computer boot up.

He turned to the battered green filing cabinet behind Clack's desk. This lock was even easier to pick. He pulled out the drawers and rifled through the files.

There was a tap at the door. Harry looked up, smiled at the woman standing there. She'd put glasses on.

'Can I help you with anything?' she said.

'Nah, I'm okay,' Harry said. 'I'm trying to find the registration code for Clack's antivirus software, which is horrendously out of date, by the way.' He returned to the screen and made a show of tapping some keys. 'This old thing is riddled with viruses. Wonder what he's been looking at.' Harry tipped her a wink and she smiled back at him, then retreated to her desk.

He returned to the files, slid the drawer closed and moved to the next one down. There it was: EKKA FUNDRAISER, in bright red letters. Harry lifted the file out and opened it. He flicked through the mass of documents. A quote from a catering company: red and white wine, beer, canapés; staff to serve. Another quote from a hire company for tables, chairs, linen and potted plants. Harry noted the date – just over two weeks away. He took photos of the two documents. He shuffled through the rest of the documents, looking for anything mentioning this mysterious Lilith Foundation. Harry froze when he saw the Queensland Police letterhead.

```
Dear Mr Clack,
I hope this finds you well. Apologies for the
formal nature of this letter but I wanted to
reach out to you in a more traditional way
before moving to email.

    As you know, the Queensland Police Union
and Australian United Workers have a long
history of solidarity. I'm contacting you for
help setting up a charity fundraiser.

    Forgive me for being candid, but I know
you've had some issues with the press in
recent years. I think this could be a good
opportunity to show you're a good bloke, as
well as raise some money for the kids and
get the boys together for a few beers.

    If you're interested, please give me a call
on the number below and I can organise a
meeting to take things further.

Best Wishes,
Constable Brad Brooks
Queensland Police
```

'Holy shit,' Harry whispered.

'Everything okay?'

Harry closed the folder and looked up, forcing a smile. The woman was back, this time holding a cup of tea.

'Yeah, just, y'know – I didn't realise they actually had

antivirus software this long ago,' Harry said, gesturing at the computer.

'I thought you might like a cup of tea,' she said. She set it on the desk for him.

'Thanks,' Harry said.

'No worries,' she said, and backed out of the room.

Harry sipped his tea. Checked the time. He reached for the back of his neck, where the tattoo burned on his skin. His back throbbed. He opened the folder again. There were a lot of printouts of emails. Didn't Don Clack know one of the advantages of email was that it saved on paper? To-ing and fro-ing between various public servants in the Department of Police and union representatives. Marketing and social media strategies. Documents from Brisbane City Council regarding use of public facilities and public liability insurance. Jesus, the bureaucracy. It would have been cheaper and raised more money if everyone involved had just chipped in five bucks each.

Harry was about to close the folder when another name caught his eye: Zak Godwin. An involuntary shudder passed through Harry as he recalled the bathtub black with blood. It was a passing reference to use of facilities at the RNA Showgrounds, stating that Zak Godwin, who sat on the RNA board, was supportive of the project and would smooth out any problems with access and insurance. Harry took a photo of the email, closed the folder and returned it to the filing cabinet.

He sculled the rest of the tea, then shut down Clack's computer. He looked around the office, checking to make sure he hadn't forgotten anything, then switched the light off on the way out, and locked up the office.

The woman looked up. He set the cup on her desk.

'All done?' she said.

'Yep. I've sent him an email to explain what was wrong. I've taken all the viruses off, so provided he stops looking at porn, he should be okay for a while.'

The woman laughed. 'You must be a real whiz – I should get you to take a look at mine while you're here.'

Harry pulled out his phone. 'Sorry, I would but I've got to get over the other side of the city by midday.'

'Do you have a card?'

Harry made a show of patting down his pockets. 'No, sorry. If you give me your email address, I'll follow up.'

She wrote down her details on a piece of paper and handed it to him.

'Thanks. See ya.'

CHAPTER 31

Harry knelt naked in front of Mistress Hel's throne, eyes staring at the floor. The edges of his vision were blurry, his head felt muddled, and he couldn't quite recall how he found himself in this position.

He could remember pulling up outside, his body once again wracked by a desire that he wouldn't have thought possible. On the drive here he'd still believed it likely he would tell her it was over. But when he turned the ignition off it was like a switch had been flicked. His brain had flooded with visions of Mistress Hel dressed in fishnet stockings and corset.

'How was your week, Harry?' she purred. She smiled at him, idly tapping her riding crop against her leg. Her legs were crossed, the pointed toe of one patent leather boot bobbing up and down.

'Good, thank you, Mistress.'

Whack! Harry's head snapped to one side. His cheek was on fire.

She laughed. 'Don't lie to me, Harry. How was your week?'

'Terrible. Because I wasn't with you. Mistress.'

She chuckled. 'That's better. Look at me, Harry.'

He looked up but not into her eyes.

'It's okay. I give you permission.'

He stared into her beautiful green eyes. 'Thank you, Mistress.'

'You are suffering because you're fighting it, Harry. Give in, and you life will be pure bliss. All you need to worry about is serving me. Your relationship, your work – all of these things, they're standing in the way of your peace. Give them up.'

'Yes, Mistress.'

'Now, as a reward, you may kiss the tip of my boot.'

'Thank you, Mistress.'

Harry leant forwards, already anticipating the taste of the leather. But at the last moment she moved her foot away, down onto the base of the throne. He leant over, trying to kiss her boot, and she moved it again. Onto the floor. She was half standing now, laughing as he desperately tried to kiss her boot. He leant over further, and the laughter died.

'Get up!' she said, almost a scream. He cowered away from her then climbed to his feet. 'Turn around.'

He complied. She sucked in breath.

'Come here,' she said. She grabbed him by the ear and dragged him to the centre of the room. There was none of the languid movements of the first time. She hurried, almost as though afraid, pulling his hands together and snapping the cuffs around his wrists. He winced as the steel bit into his flesh, but didn't try to fight her. She clipped the rope onto the cuffs and strung him up onto the balls of his feet. He remembered last time, how stiff he'd been. But this time he was flaccid.

Her gloved hand caressed his shoulders. Burning pain

exploded across his back as she pressed a finger into one of his cuts. She let out a deep breath.

'What's this?' She thrust the finger in his face and the awful stench assailed his nostrils.

Anger flared. 'You should know. You cut me.'

She grabbed a fistful of his hair and pulled his head back so hard and fast his neck cracked. 'DO. NOT. SPEAK. TO. ME. LIKE. THAT!'

Something pressed against his throat, and blood trickled down his body. He closed his eyes, then flexed his hands, thinking of the swallows. Thinking of the swallows led to thoughts of Bec. Harry focused on Bec's eyes, sucked in a deep breath, and exhaled the pain and fear.

She won't kill me.

'You won't kill me,' Harry rasped.

There was a noticeable pause, like the world was holding its breath. But maybe that was just Mistress Hel. The scalpel dropped from his neck.

'What did you say to me?' She grabbed his chin.

He squeezed his eyes shut, gritted his teeth to stop himself speaking. Failed.

'You won't kill me.'

Mistress Hel let his chin go. 'Maybe so, but there are worse things.'

She walked to her bench and returned with a flogger. *Smack! Smack! Smack! Smack! Smack!*

Harry cried out.

'It's to do with this, isn't it?' she spat, pinching the skin at the nape of his neck. 'What is it. What is this thing?'

'I don't know.'

Smack! Smack! Smack! Smack! Smack!

'I told you. I got drunk.'

Smack! Smack! Smack! Smack! Smack!

Harry hissed through gritted teeth. His back and arse tingled. She brushed against his burning skin. Her breath ticked his ear. In spite of himself, he grew hard.

'Harry. I've seen a lot of tattoos in my time.' She traced a finger down his back, between his legs. She grabbed him and pulled.

'Argh!'

'I know a bit about dark magic. Enough to know that isn't some random design. What. Is. It?' she asked, punctuating each word with a yank on his balls. 'Do you think your girlfriend would like a eunuch to play with? WHAT. IS. IT?'

Harry panted. Sweat dripped off his face. He didn't hear his phone ringing until she let go of him to get it.

'No!'

She returned with the phone in one hand. The other still clutched the scalpel. She held the phone up in front of his eyes.

'Who is Sandy?'

It took every ounce of willpower for Harry to choke back a reply.

Mistress Hel stared at him, eyes hard. 'You will break. They always break.'

She put the phone down on her throne and picked up a piece of chalk. She drew a circle around him. When the circle was complete, Harry felt the atmosphere in the room change. It was harder to draw breath. He felt cocooned by a warm, pulsing glow. His cock grew harder, throbbing. But there was something else; a bass note of pain in his back.

Mistress Hel muttered under her breath. Harry couldn't make out the words but he could hear her perfectly.

Every syllable was in his head. The desire grew.

'Please...' he said.

She looked up at him, smiling. Then she continued around the circle, marking the symbols at regular intervals. With each sigil, the air thickened further and the feelings of desire multiplied. The pain in his back grew. It felt as though spindly fingers had slithered into each of his wounds and were trying to drag him away.

'Who is Sandy?'

No-one. A friend. A contact for a story I'm working on.

'No... one... important.'

'Hmm...' She cut him. But unlike his first visit, the pleasure was doubled up with a lightning bolt to the brain.

It would be okay, he told himself. He could tell her. What could she do? Sandy lived all the way up the Sunshine Coast. Harry could warn her before anything bad happened. Harry could drive up there himself. Get himself away from Mistress Hel. And sort himself out. It would be okay.

'Harry. If she's not important, why do you have her saved as a contact?'

'She's a psychic. A spirit guide.'

Fuck! Harry couldn't believe that he'd spoken the words until he saw the smile on her face.

'Interesting.'

Mistress Hel disappeared from Harry's sight. He was salivating, waiting for it. Anticipating it.

Cut. Harry cried out. His mind split in two. One half revelling in an oily mess of pleasure. The other half watching in revulsion as he capitulated.

'So she's the one. Sniffing around in my business. It's not right, is it, Harry?'

'N-no, Mistress.'

'No, and you're going to help me, aren't you, Harry?'

Harry groaned. Tried to clench his mouth shut. His resistance crumbled. Walls fell and dark oily smoke engulfed him, shrouding his body. It was terrifying and it felt fantastic. Harry was no longer thinking about how to resist, he was thinking about how to give Mistress Hel what she wanted.

'Y-yes, Mistress.'

'Okay, good. Here's what you're going to do. Tomorrow, you're going to pay Sandy a visit.'

'Okay...'

The scalpel trailed across Harry's back, not hard enough to cut.

'You're going to close your fists with their pretty tattoos, and you are going to beat her...'

'No!'

'Yes. You're going to beat her. Every time you hit her, you will feel the most incredible sensation you've ever felt.'

'No!'

Mistress Hel grabbed Harry's hair and pulled his head back. 'Yes. And when she's on the floor, you're going to choke her, and you're going to come back to me and tell me the job is done, and I'm going to reward you.'

'NO!'

Mistress Hel walked in front of him again. She laid a hand against his cheek. 'It's okay. I won't make you do anything you don't want to do, Harry,' she whispered. Her hand trailed down his body. His chest, his abs. She grabbed him, her hand sliding up and down. Harry whimpered. The pleasure surged through his whole body, through the cuts in his back, through every nerve cell. Through every memory. Up and down, up and down.

Cut. Stockings, panties, silk, lust. Dust, blood, pain, guilt.

'Please…' Harry said. He swallowed. His mouth was dry.

'Well, if you won't do it, I'll have to find someone else. Where does she live, Harry?'

Fight it, Harry. Fight her! He was too exhausted to look up, but he closed his eyes and pictured the swallows. He concentrated on the details, the shading that had caused him so much pain. He thought of the tattooist, with her purple t-shirt and ratty jeans.

'I… I…'

Cut. Harry felt the orgasm rising in him. He started crying. 'Please… please don't make me…'

'Where does she live, Harry?'

Up and down, up and down. The pleasure, so intense now it was pain.

She leant her head against his shoulder. 'There was this one guy,' she said. 'I left him with four cuts instead of five. You know where he is now?'

Harry shook his head. His body quivered.

'Wolston Park. The psychiatric hospital. As far as I know, he's still humping anything he can get his cock near, still can't get himself off. I literally drove him insane with desire. No more fucking around. Where does this bitch live?'

Harry closed his eyes again. Flexed his hands. Felt the pain there, a million miles away. Saw the triangle. A symbol of strength. *I won't tell her. I'd rather die.* He opened his eyes.

'I forget,' he said.

Mistress Hel stared at him. She knew he was lying. But there was no rage this time. No threats. Just an inscrutable expression on her face.

'My, my. You're the stubborn one, aren't you? No matter. I'm sure I can find her from what you've told me.'

'No!'

'Hold still now.'

Cut.

'Argh!'

Harry blacked out. When he opened his eyes he was hanging by the wrists, staring at the mess he'd made. Mistress Hel was on her throne, legs crossed, gazing at him. Thoughtful. She rose and walked to him, grabbed his hair and pulled his head back. She stared into his eyes.

'Hmm. We still have some work to do, I fear,' she said. 'But that will have to suffice for today.'

'Yes, Mistress. Thank you, Mistress.'

'Harry. Look into my eyes.'

Harry looked. She gently rocked his head from side to side. Her pupils had dilated, to the point where the irises had swallowed all but a thin sliver of green. Harry had the feeling there was something moving back there, in the darkness. Mistress Hel's lips were puffy and red, engorged with blood.

'Harry, when you have your shower, you won't just wash away the blood and the come, you'll wash away the memories, okay? Everything that happened at our session. All you'll remember is the pleasure. All you'll hold onto is the realisation that I am the only one who can bring you that pleasure. Do you understand?'

'Yes, Mistress.'

She went to the wall and released the rope. Harry fell to the ground, legs tingling. The pins and needles were so bad he crawled to the shower. *Sandy. I have to warn her.* He saw his phone as he passed it, but knew Mistress Hel wouldn't let him use it. *I have to get out of here and warn her.*

He stepped into the shower. The water felt fantastic, the temperature perfect, the jets pounding his aching muscles, and suddenly warning Sandy didn't seem so important. The bathroom steamed up. Harry closed his eyes and let the water run down his body. *That was amazing.* He didn't understand how she did it. It wasn't fair that he'd missed out on this for so long. Harry turned off the taps and enjoyed the sensation of the slightly cooler air caressing his wet body. He got out and towelled himself off.

Harry cleared the mist off the mirror and assessed himself. He looked tired.

'I'm holding on to too much,' he said. 'I need to let go.'

CHAPTER 32

Harry jerked awake, terrified without knowing why. Momentarily mistook the dressing gown hanging off the bedroom door for an intruder in his panic.

Wincing, he sat up. His back pulsated in time with the pounding in his head. Sweat cooled on his body. Through the gap in the curtains he saw a slice of suburbia lit by streetlamp. Wind whistled through the eaves. He shifted his legs under the covers and the room spun. Nausea washed over him.

He climbed out of bed. He hated the sensation of the cold floorboards against his feet, but he couldn't be bothered scrounging around for his slippers. He pulled on his dressing gown and shuffled down the hallway to the kitchen. He pawed for the light switch, then almost cried out when the fluorescent tube on. He stood there, hands over his face, until his eyes adjusted.

Medicine box. Panadeine. Water. He stood by the kitchen window for a few minutes, cool air on his face. He finished his water. He sniffed and grimaced. It smelt like something had died outside. Then he realised it was him.

'Urgh.'

He carried himself to the shower, wondering what was wrong with him. He'd showered just a few hours ago, after his magnificent session with Mistress Hel. He removed his pyjamas and turned on the taps. Maybe he'd caught a bug. He hadn't really been looking after himself lately.

As the air steamed up, he saw the black stains on the back of his pyjama top. Blood? He picked it up and sniffed it.

'Urgh!'

Harry dropped it, horrified. It stank like rotten seafood. He turned, looking at his back in the mirror as it started to fog up. Five angry cuts. They'd been healing up, but now it looked as though they were fresh. And there was bruising around them.

Something clawed at him, some memory. He pushed it away and got into the shower, letting the hot water wash away all the confusion. The flogger. Had she used the flogger? He tried to think. Water ran down his face. He couldn't remember. Whatever she'd done, it was sensational. Just thinking about it now was getting him hard again.

He stepped out of the shower and dried off. He felt good now. Sleepy. Maybe it was just the nightmare that had made him feel a bit off-colour.

Harry went back to his bedroom and pulled on some fresh pyjamas. Saw his phone sitting by the bed. Again, a flash of memory tried to grab him. He picked up the phone. A stab of pain hit him in the back of the head. He winced. Closed his eyes for a few moments then opened them again. Clicked the button, checked recent notifications. Nothing. Shook his head.

'I'm suffering for no reason,' he said.

He got into bed, and was asleep before his head hit the pillow.

Harry lay in bed, unwilling to move. Despite the bad sleep and the headache, he felt curiously refreshed. The midnight shower had helped. He listened to the wind. Through the gap in the curtains he could see big white clouds skating across a deep blue sky. Harry didn't feel like doing anything.

He reached for his phone, intending to download a movie. Something brainless. There was a message on his lock screen. His mood darkened.

Yo Harry. What's happening? Grapevine says you didn't sort things out with Bec.

Harry took a deep breath. Fucking Dave. Of course, Dave would assume Harry would want to sort things out with Bec. Because Dave assumed that everyone was like him, everyone wanted to get a decent job and get married and have kids. Maybe Harry didn't want that. Harry was starting to feel as though Bec was something that had to be removed from his life. His work too. He wanted to be with Mistress Hel. Just be with her and…

Harry sat up, slid his feet over the side of the bed. Put on his slippers. Him and Mistress Hel? He tried to imagine it. It didn't make sense. Not in any way. But still, maybe it would all make sense if he could just get rid of all these distractions and devote himself to her.

He mulled the thought over, climbed out of bed and shuffled into the kitchen. He saw his laptop open on the dining room table on the way past, but the thought of work just made him feel cold inside. Gloom and doom. Why did he put himself through it?

Harry stopped, looked around. Something about his phone. Something he was meant to do. His neck tattoo flared. He rubbed it. He should get rid of the tattoo, get it burnt off once and for all. He didn't understand why he hadn't done that already, after everything he went through. And where was the thanks for it?

He put the kettle on to boil, got out a cup and put a teabag in it. Stared out the window. It was sunny outside, but cold. He flexed his hands. He'd basically saved the country from electing a highly unstable sociopath. And what had happened? He'd got a bit of attention, and then the world went on about its business.

Harry slopped water into the cup, laced it with milk and sugar, and took it outside. It was nice, just sitting in the sun, drinking tea, not worrying about anything. Not worrying about Bec, or his work, or (*Sandy*) his friends. It would be good to be able to leave all the decisions to someone else for a while. He thought again about Mistress Hel.

As the tea warmed his stomach, memories of his night with Mistress Hel warmed the rest of him. God, she was perfect. Perfect body, perfect face. She was smart, funny. And she gave him pleasure like no-one else ever had, ever could. And she wanted to be with him. That was the bizarre thing.

Harry found himself in a trance, thinking about her. The closest he could remember to this kind of feeling was when he first started going out with Bec. But even that didn't compare. When he first started going out with Bec, there was a lot of fear, anxiety, worry that she wouldn't like him. With this, he knew exactly what was going on and exactly what he had to do.

And for the moment that was just letting go and giving

in to it. It was nice here, out of the wind. It was an apt metaphor for how his life would be, if he could just let go of everything else. A nice warm place, in the sun. He thought of Mistress Hel's milky white skin, her green eyes. Stockings. Knee-high boots. Riding crop. He thought of her long black hair, imagined what it would be like if she ever gave him the privilege of being able to run his fingers through it.

The sun crept higher in the sky. Harry shuffled inside, back to the kitchen. He pulled some bread out of the freezer and ate it cold, then dragged himself to the couch and laid down. His phone rang. There was something annoying about that phone, so he left it, shoved his hands over his ears so he could barely hear it. He switched on the TV, and cranked the volume.

He spent the afternoon watching kids' shows on TV, not really seeing them, just zoning out and thinking about Mistress Hel. Everything he watched seemed to relate to her. A few times his tattoo flared up. He wished he had some beer to drink, to dull the pain.

On a whim, he decided to walk to the pub. He got out of his pyjamas and pulled on some jeans and a t-shirt, then carried himself out the door, barely remembering to pull it closed behind him. He worried that he'd be too tired to walk, but once he was outside he felt good. To be away from his computer, to be away from his home. He realised at the end of the street that he'd left his phone behind, but he didn't care. It felt good to leave it all behind.

Harry woke to ringing. His head seemed to thump in time with the rings. He opened his bleary eyes and saw his phone on the floor. He answered it, just to shut it up.

'Harry?'

For a sickening moment he thought it was Bec, and then he realised this was an older woman.

'It's Lee-Anne. Got a moment?'

Harry's stomach did a slow roll, but he managed to breathe through the nausea. He sat up in bed and rubbed his face.

'Yeah. What's up?'

'I figured it out!'

She sounded extremely pleased with herself. Harry couldn't remember anything from the day before, just apathy and the need to blot it all out with alcohol. And now all he wanted to do was go back to sleep.

'Yeah, me too.'

'What?'

'I went over to the union's HQ the other day. Did a bit of snooping around.' He didn't mention the lock picks.

'Oh.' She sounded disappointed.

'Well, I know they were planning a fundraiser, with the police union. Do you have any more info?'

'Yeah, they're holding it at the Ekka.'

'Yeah, I know.'

'Oh. It's going to be a really fancy do. So they're putting the hard word on everyone they know to contribute. They've even got that hero cop. You know, the flood guy? What was his name?'

Harry's heart pounded in his chest. He had to hold onto the edge of the bed to steady himself. 'Marcus Wilson?'

'That's him. He's going to do a speech or something. The stupid thing is, I'd heard Don talking about this fundraiser. Just didn't realise that it was linked to his...

uh… mistress. Have you found anything out about her?'

Yeah, she's wonderful.

'No… not really.'

'Huh…'

Harry felt bone tired. This was utter bullshit. 'Listen, Lee-Anne. I have to say, there's not really much of a story here. I mean, yeah, he's been seeing this woman, and yeah, he's been using union money… but I think that might be for this fundraiser…'

'It's still fishy. He's still a cheating bastard. He…'

'Sorry, Lee-Anne. I've got to go. I need to have a think about this.'

Harry put down the phone, went to the kitchen and got himself some water and headache tablets. He returned to the kitchen table, put the heater on and sat. He took his tablets and waited for the headache to subside. He was finding it hard to think of anything but Mistress Hel, but he tried anyway.

Mistress Hel gets Constable Brad Brooks to contact Don Clack about setting up a charity fundraiser. Marcus Wilson is involved, the cop who abused Johnny. Harry stared at the wall. What was the connection? He thought back to Zak Godwin, lying dead in a bathtub, guts torn to shreds. Godwin, there was something about Godwin, but Harry couldn't concentrate enough to remember what it was.

Harry yawned. He couldn't handle this right now. He closed his laptop and dragged himself back to bed.

Harry awoke to the sound of his phone again. This time he could open his eyes without spasms of pain, but it was still annoying. He looked at the screen: Dave.

Harry slid the bar across, struggling to control the anger. 'What?' he said.

There was a brief pause. 'And a very good day to you, too, Mr Hendrick.' There was no cheer in this voice.

'Sorry, things have been a bit full-on lately.'

'I gathered. But does that mean you can't return a phone call?'

'Apparently, yes. What do you want?'

'Harry, pull your head in. Have you spoken to Sandy?'

Harry was momentarily thrown off. The room spun slightly. It was as though he dropped into a nightmare, then popped out of it again. He felt the odd sensation of giant fingers digging themselves into the wounds in his back. There was something...

'Yes. I did,' Harry said.

'You did?'

'Yeah, last week. Wednesday, I think it was. I told her to leave me alone.'

'Harry!'

'She's living in a fantasy land.'

'Look, she phoned me on Friday night. She sounded scared shitless. Says she tried to call you, but you didn't answer. Said for me to try and get a hold of you and get you to phone her.'

'Dave, she needs help. Professional help. I've got enough on my plate.'

'Harry, she probably saved your life last year. I don't get you.'

Harry didn't say anything. He heard Dave making a clucking noise with his teeth.

'Harry, I don't know exactly what's going on, but Sandy seems to know how to help you.'

Harry felt rage exploding inside him. A red mist descended over his eyes. 'Maybe I don't want to be helped,' he whispered.

Harry hung up, switched off his phone. He paced the room, barely restraining himself. How dare he? How *dare* he? He pictured himself picking up a gun, blowing Dave's head off. All of them, lined in a row. Dave, Sandy, Bec. *Bang! Bang! Bang!* Problem solved.

He stripped off and got into the shower. He turned up the water as hot as he could bear it. He calmed himself, focusing on the sensation of Mistress Hel kissing his neck. Biting his neck. Her leather gloves on his sweaty skin.

His hand dropped to his cock, and he rubbed himself, harder and harder. He groaned, turning his face to the water. Harder, faster. But he couldn't gain release.

He dropped to the floor of the bath, held his head in his hands, and cried.

CHAPTER 33

Harry barely had the energy to drag himself into his clothes and out to the car, but he felt better once he was moving. He put some Counting Crows on the stereo and zoned out. It occurred to him that they could very easily have done this over the phone, but Johnny was still wary of the police tapping him, and so wanted to do it in the carpark where they'd originally met.

Westerly winds rattled the car and scooped pieces of rubbish into the air. Leaves danced along the pavement, waltzing with ghostly dust devils. An old woman struggled with her umbrella, before a particularly strong gust snatched it from her hands and tossed it under a bus.

Johnny was waiting beside his ute. Despite the cold he wasn't wearing his jumper, just a dusty t-shirt and King Gee shorts, big arms folded across his chest.

Harry got out of his car.

'Hey,' Johnny said. He looked at his feet and thrust his hands in his pockets. The muscles of his arms flexed. Jesus, he was well built.

'What's up?'

'Um… you're probably not going to like this, but I want to pull out.'

Harry looked skywards and ran his fingers through his hair. He cursed under his breath but felt as though he was playing a role, acting how Johnny would expect him to act.

Johnny shuffled his feet on the gravel, looking like an overgrown school kid. 'I just want to let it all go,' he said. 'Do you know what I mean?'

Harry felt torn. Part of him knew exactly what Johnny meant. It was almost as though they were kindred spirits. Part of him felt immense release. He hadn't realised how much this story had weighed on him, the thought of having to see this through and then deal with all the repercussions.

'Yeah, I do, Johnny. I totally do,' he said. 'But...' But part of him felt angry, that Johnny had gone this far just to give up, when Harry had stuck his neck out. Harry had put a lot of work into this story, and he felt if he could stand it up, publish it and not get sued, maybe he'd get a little justice in the world.

'If you don't go through with it, those bastards win. And then that sends a message to the paedophiles who are out there right now, victimising kids just like you were victimised.'

Johnny slow-clapped. 'Oh, bravo, Mr Toughguy. Do you know how hard I've worked to bury this? To make sure no-one else knew about it? Do you think I want my shame all over the newspaper, the TV? People telling me I'm full of shit?'

'It's not your shame, Johnny. You aren't the one who did anything wrong.'

'I could have fought harder!'

'You were just a kid.'

Johnny shrugged. Harry saw himself in that gesture and wanted to shake it out of him.

'It's just a newspaper article,' Johnny said.

Harry snorted. 'I brought down a fucking government with a newspaper article. The bad guy is dead. A whole heap of other bad guys are in jail.'

Johnny looked up the hill. 'Yeah, I'm just saying...'

Harry looked at Johnny, but Johnny still wouldn't meet his eye. 'What?'

He was hiding something. And despite the cold sapping his sense of purpose, that piqued Harry's interest.

'How about that friend of yours you mentioned?' Harry said.

'She's not a friend...'

'Well. whatever.'

'No... she's not interested.'

Harry let out a breath. A cloud covered the sun and the temperature dropped.

'Look,' he said. 'I can't force you to do anything you don't want to. I've got a story. Most of a story. I'll leave it with you. If you change your mind, let me know and I'll try and pick up the threads.'

Johnny briefly looked at Harry. 'Thanks.'

Harry watched the cars pass on Gympie Road. Looked into the empty tray of Johnny's ute.

'You still working for that concreter?'

'Nah. Got jack of it. Too stressful having to live by his schedule.'

'But you've got something going on?'

'Yeah. Doing a few odd jobs.'

'Keeping your head above water?'

Johnny nodded. 'Yeah something like that.'

They shook hands. Harry felt the vice-like grip enclose his hand. It was clear Johnny was aware of his own strength, and knew how to use it.

'Take care, Johnny,' Harry said.

'You too.'

Harry's anger had completely dissipated now. Another distraction had been removed from his life, and now he had more time to focus on Mistress Hel.

Johnny started his ute and backed out of the car park. Harry climbed into his car and sat for a while, remembering their first meeting out here. The dad and the kid playing with the kite. He felt a brief stab of guilt. It would have been great to nail those bastards. But if Johnny could make peace with what happened, then who was Harry to disturb that?

Harry started the car, backed out of the car park, and headed for home. When he stopped at the lights, he looked over at the building he used to work in. He longed for those early days at the *Chronicle*. Everything was so simple back then. He yearned for a life without complications.

Harry sat on the lounge, staring at the TV. He knew what he needed to do. On the way back it had all become so obvious. It was time to clear the decks. But something inside him didn't want to let go. He rubbed the back of his neck, sighed, and picked up his phone. He dialled Phil.

'Hey, Phil.'

'Harry. How are you? Feeling better?'

'Huh?'

'Last time I spoke to you, you sounded pretty crook.'

Harry couldn't really remember the last time they'd spoke. 'Oh. Yeah, fine thanks. It was just a bug I think.'

'Lots of them going around at this time of year. Hey, I looked into that Mistress Hel you told me about...'

Harry felt a spike of panic. He had a flashback to lying on the floor, the world spinning around him.

'...tried to at least. Can't find a thing on her. But then I figured she sounds like a sex worker, so she's probably going under a couple of working names.'

Harry realised he was sweating. He wiped his brow.

'Harry?'

'Yeah, you're right. She is a sex worker. But it turned out to be a dead end. I was climbing the wrong tree,' Harry said. He pictured himself clambering up the mango tree, the first time at Mistress Hel's.

'Barking,' Phil said.

'What?'

'Barking up the wrong tree. You said climbing.'

'Oh, did I? Sorry. But yeah, like you say, nothing on her. And she was my last lead.'

On TV there were images of the sideshow alley at the Ekka. The Ferris wheel. Ghost train. Hall of mirrors. Those freaky clowns you shove balls into.

'I need to drop the story,' Harry said.

'Oh,' Phil said. 'Harry. I thought we had a deal?'

'Yeah, I know. I've really tried. I've worked my arse off. But I'm not getting anywhere. There is something weird about it. But I can't get to the bottom of it. So you can bring me in and frame me with that attempted assassination if that will make you happy.'

'Harry! Come on! That wasn't what I...'

'Well, that's what it sounded like. It sounded like black-mail. And I've had enough of doing things for other people!'

'Hey! Settle down. I've told you, there was never any

intention to threaten you.' A pause. A sigh. 'If the boys thought you were behind that Cardinal business, they would have taken you down long ago. It's just... we were really hoping you'd be able to blow this one wide open for us. Harry, just set everything else to one side for a minute. Are you feeling okay?'

Harry stopped to consider. 'Yeah, I mean, no. I've been doing a lot of thinking about my life. This whole journalism thing, I dunno...'

'But Harry, you're a legend. You saved us all from Cardinal. Who knows what would've happened if he'd been elected?'

'The world would have kept turning, Phil. There are bigger things out there.'

'Are you sick?'

Harry laughed. 'No. I've... I've met someone.'

'Bec?'

Harry laughed again. 'Oh no, God, no. No... this is... different.'

'Harry, you're not making any sense.'

Harry swallowed. He felt hot, just talking about Mistress Hel.

'I guess not. But I'm going to make a difference, just not in the way I once thought I would.'

'Okay. Well... that's good. Maybe we can catch up for a beer soon.'

'Yeah, sure,' Harry said, knowing full well that would never happen. 'See you round, Phil.'

'See you, Harry.'

Harry hung up. He suddenly felt tired, and aroused. He went to his bedroom and slid under the covers. He masturbated until he fell asleep, still hard.

CHAPTER 34

Harry and Dave got out of Dave's car. Around them, the car park was filling up, as other fighters and spectators gathered. Harry zipped his coat.

Dave slammed the door and eyed Harry. 'You okay?'

'I dunno,' Harry said. 'I feel…' Harry shook his head, then slammed his door.

'You're probably just tired,' Dave said.

'Yeah, probably,' Harry replied.

'Are you sure you're right to fight?'

Harry felt the tattoo on the back of his neck flare. 'Dave, just leave it. Okay?'

He had considered giving it a miss. He had broached the subject with Jim at training, but his instructor talked him out of it. *We need you, buddy.* For some reason it was harder to let down Jim than it was Phil or Johnny. But this was it. One fight and then he was giving up karate.

Hard rock was pounding out of the stadium. Someone was addressing the crowd over the tannoy. Harry couldn't make out the words, but it was clear he was getting the crowd fired up. A guy and a girl in red t-shirts were manning a ticket booth. There was a queue, but the woman saw Harry's gear and beckoned him.

'Fighters through there,' she said, gesturing to a side door.

'Catch ya later,' Harry said.

'I have to buy a ticket for this?' Dave said, rolling his eyes.

Harry left Dave standing at the ticket box. He followed the instructions Jim had given him through the labyrinth of cinderblock hallways, past other dressing rooms where fighters were getting strapped up, meditating, practising moves. Finally he came to a room with HENDRICK written on a piece of paper taped to the door.

'Hey, Harry,' Jim said.

'Jim.'

They nodded to each other, then shook hands. It felt strangely formal.

'Nervous?'

Harry considered. *No.* 'Yeah, a little,' he said.

'You'll be right. Once you get out there.'

Harry got changed, then Jim taped his hands. 'You're up against a guy from the southside, Corey Sparks. This is his first MMA bout too. He's got more experience than you but, given how quickly you've taken to this, you can take him. Okay?'

Harry nodded. 'Okay.'

Someone tapped on the door. 'Ten minutes!'

Harry waited behind double doors, jogging on the spot. Heavy metal blared from the speakers in the auditorium, but it was barely audible over the noise of the crowd. Harry's heart hammered in his chest, and he took a couple of deep breaths. Under the aroma of liniment, he could smell the hoppy tang of beer and the reek of sweat.

'Ladies and gentlemeeeen,' a voice boomed. 'Making his Nitro MMA debut tonight... Haaaaarry Hendriiiiiick!'

Jim slapped his shoulder, and the doors opened. Harry jogged down the aisle. The crowd had sounded louder, more fearsome, from the other side of the doors. In fact, given his was the first fight on the card, many of the seats were vacant. Spotlights lit up the cage where the MC stood and a bikini-clad ring girl strutted. It was too dark to make out many of the faces in the crowd, but Harry could sense their ambivalence. Harry's eyes caught on the profile of a woman sitting next to the aisle. Long black hair, slender legs clad in stockings.

'Hey, Harry,' she said. She blew him a kiss.

Mistress Hel? Harry stopped. He had so much he wanted to tell her. But she had already turned away from him and was talking to someone sitting next to her.

Jim grabbed his arm. 'Harry?'

He continued to the ring. He climbed onto the fighting mat and looked back over his shoulder, but the lights were too bright and he couldn't see shit. Still, he could feel her, a tidal pull towards her.

The MC wore a white suit and black shirt. He was talking to someone dressed in black shirt, shorts and latex gloves, who Harry assumed was the referee. Harry danced back and forth and threw some punches, keeping warm.

The MC put his microphone to his mouth. 'I've just been told that Corey Sparks unfortunately has been injured, and cannot fight,' he said.

The crowd erupted, yelling abuse. A cup sailed through the air and slapped against the wire, spraying the mat with beer. The MC held up his hand.

'But we have a very special treat for you. Ladies and gentlemen, a man you all know and love. Returning to the ring just one month after his spectacular Queensland title fight…'

The crowd was already screaming in anticipation, and this cranked up a notch when the opening riff of AC/DC's 'Back in Black' pulsed from the sound system.

'…Janeeeeeeek Murphyyyyyyyy!'

The spotlights swung to the other side of the arena. Janek Murphy ran down the aisle, high-fiving members of the crowd. He wore red shorts, a matching silk robe and a big, bushy beard.

Harry turned and Jim was in the ring, in the face of the MC and the referee. Harry danced over as Murphy climbed into the cage.

'What the hell is going on?' Jim said. 'This is Harry's first fight! This guy is a Queensland champion.'

The referee held his hands out. 'Yeah I know. I just found out about it myself. Calm down!'

'Calm down? This is a farce.'

Harry thought of Mistress Hel out there. She had blown him a kiss. He couldn't disappoint her.

'I can take him,' Harry said.

All three of them looked at him, shocked.

'Harry…' Jim started.

'I mean it,' he said. And he did. He could feel power surging through the ground into his feet. Nothing could stop him. Not when he had Mistress Hel on his side.

The MC considered it a done deal, and left the ring. The referee shrugged. 'If he wants to fight…'

Jim backed Harry into his corner. 'You sure about this?'

Harry nodded.

'Right. Listen. His background is Muay Thai kick-boxing.'

Harry stared through the cage, into the darkness. She was out there somewhere. Harry jerked back as Jim slapped him on the cheek.

'Harry! Stay with me. This guy's built like a brick shithouse. But he's slow. Well, relatively slow. So if you can get in under his guard you can do some damage. Okay?'

'Under his guard. Got it.'

'But Harry,' Jim said, 'watch his elbows. He'll try and get in close and use his elbows and knees. Keep him at a distance. Be patient.'

Jim had one final word with the referee. 'Keep this under control, okay? If it looks like…'

'Yeah, yeah. I got it.'

Jim passed Harry on his way out of the cage. 'Good luck.'

The referee gestured to Harry and Murphy. Murphy removed his gown. A dragon tattoo wound around his torso.

'Fight when I say fight, break when I say break. Got it?'

Harry nodded. Murphy shuffled from foot to foot, staring at Harry.

'Murphy – take it down a couple of pegs, okay? This is his first fight. We want to put on a good show, but don't kill him.'

Murphy said nothing.

'Murph?'

The bearded fighter inclined his head

'Good deal,' the referee said. 'Touch gloves, return to your corners and come out fighting with the bell.'

They touched gloves. Harry turned for his corner, but

something caught his eye. Five red marks, on Murphy's back.

Oh shit.

The bell rang. Murphy lumbered in, fists up – guarding his body. The crowd roared. It reminded Harry of the sound the surf makes, crashing on a beach. Harry danced away. The cuts on his back throbbed with his heartbeat. His ears started ringing, to the point where he could only hear the ringing and the air rushing in and out of his lungs.

Murphy leapt forwards, grabbing Harry in a bear hug and driving his knee into his ribcage. Pain flared. Harry felt as though he was trapped in a nightmare, too slow and weak to break out of the grip. Then suddenly he was free, ducking his head back.

Wham! Harry saw the elbow out of the corner of his eye but too late to avoid it. White sparks flared across his vision and pain flashed along his spine and into his arms and legs, which collapsed under him. When his vision cleared, the referee had pushed Murphy back and was yelling at him, but Harry couldn't hear anything. He opened and closed his mouth, checking for damage. His head was on fire, blood ran down his throat. He swallowed, trying to clear his ears. He blinked. Red darkness bloomed behind his eyes. He took a couple of deep breaths, looked up and saw the referee standing over him. Talking to him.

Harry couldn't hear what he was saying, but he could guess. Harry nodded.

'Yeah, I'm okay.'

The referee held onto his fists and Harry pushed up, to show him he was still with it. He followed the referee back into the centre of the mat.

There was no response from Murphy. No anger,

no laughter. He just stood there like a robot. Not even shuffling from foot to foot.

'Ready! Fight!'

Murphy steamed forwards, this time with a flurry of punches and kicks designed to do nothing more than push Harry into a corner. Harry, still stunned, ducked to one side and drove a kick at Murphy's head, but he parried it away and lunged. Harry skipped out of his grasp, gave himself some room then launched a step-front kick, which Murphy blocked with his beefy forearms.

Murphy grabbed Harry and delivered another blow to his ribs. Harry retaliated with his own knee, then a flurry of punches. Murphy staggered back, dropped his arms. Harry saw his opportunity and launched himself in the air, spinning, aiming to plant his foot on Murphy's jaw.

But Murphy anticipated the move and grabbed Harry's ankle. It slipped out of his grasp almost straight away, but not before Harry tumbled from the air. A fist caught him on the way down. He looked up and saw Murphy above him, driving a heel towards his face. Harry rolled.

Air exploded out of his lungs as Murphy stomped him. Harry squinted up and saw Murphy about to smash a foot down on his arm. The referee rushed up beside Murphy, trying to get between them, but the Muay Thai expert batted him away.

Bam! Another kick to the stomach. Harry tried to get to his feet. Even over the ringing in his ears he could hear the crowd, but the cheering had turned to screaming. Harry regained one knee. He saw Murphy's foot flying at his face in time to bat it away. It glanced off the side of his head, filling his vision with black spots. He went down on all fours.

Murphy launched himself into the air, landing on Harry's back. Harry screamed, felt pain spasm through his whole body. He collapsed on the mat with Murphy on top of him. Harry felt fingers entwined in his hair, pulling his head back. Then the hair tore from his head and his jaw smacked against the floor. He rolled over onto his back, sending another blast of pain through his torso.

Murphy sat astride Harry, panting, holding his head in his hands. Harry's arms were pinned by his sides. A referee grabbed Murphy, who let go of Harry and lashed out with an elbow. He looked at Harry and grinned through bloodstained teeth. He grabbed Harry's chin in one hand and the back of his head with the other. Harry tried to buck him off but barely moved him, and his chest screamed in pain.

Murphy leant over Harry. 'I offer this sacrifice to the Goddess.' He looked up, as though scanning the crowd for her. His brow furrowed.

Then Murphy's head snapped back and he collapsed backwards as two referees surged over him.

Harry's vision doubled, then came back together. Murphy twisted like an eel, out of the grip of the referees. Harry saw the blood on Murphy's back. Five red lines, mixing with his sweat and trickling down to his shorts.

If I don't get to my feet I'm dead. Harry realised he couldn't feel his feet, or his legs. The world dropped into slow motion. Murphy ran for him. The referees chased him. Murphy drew his leg back, like a soccer player getting ready to boot in a ball from the penalty spot.

In his last moments of consciousness, Harry realised it wasn't just ringing he could hear. He could hear something else now. A woman laughing. Mistress Hel.

CHAPTER 35

Harry opened his eyes, then closed them again as pain flooded his system. He tried to move his head, couldn't. Pins and needles stabbed through his legs. He fell into the darkness, and let himself go. He wasn't really thinking, wasn't really dreaming. There was just nothing.

Harry felt a hand slip into his. He squeezed, and pain flared up his arm. A cool hand touched his forehead. He opened his eyes, then closed them again, because clearly he was dreaming. He opened them again. Three Becs looked at him. He blinked again and they merged into one. She looked worried and tired. Her eyes were puffy.

'Harry?'

'Are you real?'

Bec laughed and cried at the same time. She squeezed his hand. She looked up and Harry was aware of other people in the room. He felt a brief spasm of panic, and tried turning his head. He was rewarded with a blast of pain so powerful he greyed out for a few moments.

'It's okay, Harry. It's me and Dave.'

He looked into Bec's eyes.

All of a sudden he was aware of how dry his throat was.

His eyes darted to the glass of water on the bedside table. 'Can you...'

'Of course.'

She picked up the cup and guided the straw into Harry's mouth. He took a sip, which seemed to soak into his dry mouth without any of it making it down his throat. He took another sip. It was heavenly cool.

Bec put the cup back down, took Harry's hand again. 'There are no permanent injuries,' she said. 'The doctor said you were lucky he didn't break your spine. There's some swelling. A cracked rib. Whiplash. Murphy gave your head a good stomping...'

'I always knew you had a bony head, mate,' Dave said.

Harry tried to smile but it hurt his lips. He looked from one to the other.

'What's wrong?'

Dave looked to Bec. 'It's Sandy,' she said.

Harry's heart went into overdrive. Splotches blossomed across his vision. His fingers tingled. He sucked in a deep breath and forced himself to hold onto it, in spite of the pain in his ribs.

'What about her?' But he knew. Somewhere deep inside of him, he knew.

'She was attacked. While you were fighting.'

'Is she...'

'She'll be okay. A neighbour came over, to drop off a carrot cake,' Dave said. 'Damned lucky timing.'

'It was her,' Harry said.

'Who?'

'Her. Mistress Hel. She was at the fight.'

The door opened and a doctor in a white coat entered the room. She looked surprised, peering from Harry to the others, then back to Harry. 'Visiting hours are over,' she said. 'Mr Hendrick needs his rest.'

Dave turned to her. 'It's okay, doctor, I'm a nurse here.'

She looked him up and down like he was some kind of alien race. Harry smiled, in spite of the pain.

'Oh, well if the *nurse* says it's okay to disturb my patient...'

'We'd best be going,' Dave muttered.

'Yes,' the doctor said. 'Good idea.'

Bec leant over and gave Harry a kiss on the forehead.

Dave tipped him a salute, then ushered Bec out the door.

The doctor approached the bed. 'How are you feeling?'

'Like shit.'

'Uh huh, that's to be expected.'

She took a small light out of her pocket, flashed it in each of Harry's eyes. It felt as though she'd stabbed him in the brain. She tested his vision, asked him to follow her finger without turning his head.

'I can't turn my head,' he said.

'Should make things easier for you then.'

She felt his neck, got him to squeeze each of her hands with his. Went to the foot of the bed, pulled the covers clear of his feet, then ran some sort of implement along the base of each foot. Harry felt intense relief that he could feel the scratching sensation on both. She wrote some notes on his chart. Then she reached behind him and pulled out a small button on a plastic thread.

'Painkillers on demand,' she said. 'Push it when you need it. It will stop when you've reached the maximum dose, unfortunately.' She gave him a chilly smile. 'We'll try and get you onto Panadol tomorrow. You were lucky.

You were close to literally being unable to walk out of here.'

'You should have seen the other guy,' Harry said. He was going for a laugh, but it had the opposite effect on the doctor, who went still.

'I did,' she said.

'What?'

She stared at him. 'Did your friends not…' She looked towards the door. 'Sorry, doesn't matter, you try and…'

'What?'

The doctor looked away.

'What? Come on, doc. You can't…'

'The other fighter. I saw him earlier, because he's in the morgue.'

'What!'

'After they pulled him off you, he settled right down. Said he'd had a bad day, said his wife had split up with him, said he lost control but that now he was okay. They escorted him outside, said that the police would want to talk to him. Said it depended on you whether or not they charged him. He said he wanted to go back to his car and get his smokes.

'They found him on the road fifteen minutes later. He'd thrown himself in front of a truck.'

The hospital seemed too bright, smelt too clean. Harry squinted, disorientated, as Dave led him through the warren of corridors. He had no idea where he was going, but was aware of Dave's firm hand at his elbow, guiding him. With each step, a stab of pain shot up his spine. Dave had offered to fetch a wheelchair, but Harry refused. Partly because he deserved the pain, partly because this way it would be slightly longer before he faced Sandy.

They went up in a lift. It was visiting hours, and a few people were coming with flowers or leaving with worried looks. Harry saw a man with two children who were obviously his kids. He looked drawn, the kids oblivious. Dave was frequently nodding to doctors, nurses and orderlies.

They stopped outside the door. Harry felt fevered. His hands were shaking, his vision narrowing. It had only been a couple of days since the fight and yet Harry had had a lot of time to think. As the pain subsided, Harry had been drawn more and more to Mistress Hel. She'd tried to have him killed. He knew that, and yet... and yet, Harry thought if Mistress Hel had wanted him dead, he'd be dead. He'd thought maybe she was just trying to teach him a lesson. And as the pain from the beating subsided, Harry started to believe he'd deserved that lesson. Maybe now he could be a better servant to her.

'Dave. I don't feel so good. Maybe you could go in for me and find out what she wants,' he said.

Dave's hand clamped around Harry's arm. 'You'll be right.' He pushed him through the door.

At first, Harry thought they were in the wrong room. The woman in the bed bore no resemblance to the tanned, lively Sandy Harry knew, with the friendly eyes and full smile. Instead, there was a bloated, bruised face, half covered with bandages. One eye swollen shut, lips cracked and brown with dried blood. The arms, sitting on top of the covers, were black and blue. Her right hand was wrapped in bandages, fingers splinted.

She looked at him. Harry thought he could take it, the waves of guilt washing over him. Then she tried to smile. Her good eye crinkled shut, her lip split again and blood trickled down her chin. Harry felt his knees give out, but Dave was there, holding him up, propelling him forwards. Harry thought he was going to vomit.

Dave eased Harry into a seat.

'I'm sorry, Sandy – I'm so, so sorry. I knew, but…' Harry found tears were streaming down his face.

Sandy placed a hand on his, looked at him until he stopped crying. 'I thought she was trying to take you,' she croaked. Harry had to lean forwards to hear her. He smelt blood and antiseptic. 'But I didn't realise how far she'd gone.'

Harry put his head in his hands, resting his elbows on the bed. He felt Dave's solid presence behind him, guarding the door.

'What's happening to me, Sandy? Please, please tell me you know.'

'Of course I do, you stupid boy. I've been trying to tell you for weeks, but she's got her hooks in you bad.'

Harry looked up.

'She's a witch. A sorceress. A harpy. She controls men like puppets. Not such a difficult thing to do, maybe, given her, ah, charms,' she said.

Harry felt Sandy's stare boring into him. He took her hand. It was cold and clammy. He felt concern vying with anger and disgust.

'Could you pass me the water, love?'

Harry looked around, but Dave was already leaning past him, picking up the cup and putting the straw between Sandy's lips. She took a couple of sips, wincing each time.

'She wanted me,' Harry said. 'She went to all the trouble of ensnaring me. Why would she try and kill me?'

'You're a threat to her. As am I.'

'You? Because you can sense what she's doing?'

'More than that. I know how to break the spell she has over you. I've been busy, these past few weeks. Deciphering the talisman she's left at every sacrifice site. Working out exactly which of the hundreds of demons she's been trying to summon. The key to her power is her identity. Her true identity. Harry, do you remember that name I was sent?'

Harry tried to think. He vaguely remembered something, but couldn't put his finger on it.

'Elizabeth Tawny,' Sandy said.

'Like the port,' Harry said.

'That's right. Like the owl.'

'She and a friend were in a suicide pact,' Harry said. 'Except the friend didn't die.'

'For Lily Sweeney it was a ritual. The first step in becoming... whatever it is she is now.'

Harry felt like he'd been sucker punched. His head spun. 'Lily Sweeney? Mistress Hel? Murdered her friend. Why? Why would she do that?'

'Why do people seek power?'

He thought of everything he knew. Constable Brad Brooks had reached out to the union via Don Clack. But why was paedophile cop Marcus Wilson involved? The hairs on Harry's neck stood on end.

'Sometimes... sometimes it's because they've been victimised.'

Sandy went to speak but Harry held up his hand. 'What if... what if she'd been raped by Marcus Wilson?'

'Who?'

'He's a cop... was a cop... what if he raped her and she went to the cops and they buried it...'

'You're reaching, Harry,' Sandy said.

'I don't think so.'

'Why sacrifice her friend?'

'I don't know.' He rubbed his face. The clarity he'd had was fading fast.

'Revenge. It's a motive as old as time. But that's not all of it,' Sandy said.

'What do you mean?' Harry felt weak as fatigue rolled back through his body. He wanted this to end. Then he looked at Sandy, really looked at her. Under the bruises he could see the fear. And frustration.

'When I close my eyes, I see something stalking through the darkness. It's looking for a way in.'

Outside, wind rattled the window. A siren blared through the night before being carried off. Harry lifted his head. He felt like he was at an AA meeting, about to say those words for the first time. about to start his journey on the Twelve Steps. Part of him wanted to just go back to Mistress Hel, if she'd take him. Give himself over properly, completely. His mouth salivated at the thought. But part of him wanted to fight. The tattoo on the back of his neck thudded in time with the swallows on the backs of his hands, which were bunched into fists on his knees.

'You said you could free me?' Harry said.

'Maybe,' Sandy said.

Harry took a deep breath. 'What do we have to do?'

'Elizabeth Tawny is buried at Toowong Cemetery. If you want your life back, Harry, you need to dig her up.'

CHAPTER 36

Harry parked the car and turned off the engine, looking around at Dave and Sandy then out at the dark cemetery.

'Sandy, will you please just wait in the car?' Harry said. She shook her head.

'You've been out of hospital, what?' He checked his watch. 'Twelve hours?'

'I told you before, Harry,' she said, 'you need me.'

It was true. Even after everything she had told him, he felt sick and fevered. He felt as though he was doing something desperately wrong, something that was going to ruin his life, even though he knew on one level that Sandy was trying to get his life back on track. He hated her for keeping him away from Mistress Hel. And he hated Dave, who had insisted that he sleep at his place. Harry suspected Dave had slipped something into the cup of tea he'd made him the night before, because after drinking it, he'd dropped into a deep, dreamless sleep.

The cemetery was deserted. Wednesday night. No ghost tours tonight. Dave had phoned to double-check. That only left wannabe Satanists and drunk uni students, but they'd have to take their chances with those.

He got out of the car and tentatively stretched his back. The doctor had let him discharge himself, but he was pretty sure graverobbing wouldn't fit her definition of 'rest'. Dave and Sandy climbed out and looked at him across the roof of the car. Dave shook his head. A light was on in the living room of the house across the road. Harry stood and watched for a few moments, contenting himself that it was left on for security rather than because someone was up. It would be hard to explain the three of them, with torch, shovel and pickaxe, in the cemetery.

He checked up and down the road. There were no headlights coming. He let his eyes adjust to the darkness, then checked again, this time for people out walking, or sitting outside their houses. Nothing.

He popped the boot, grabbed the shovel and his backpack with his torch and water bottle in it. Dave reached in and grabbed the pickaxe.

'Ready?' Harry said.

'No.'

Harry gently closed the boot, and they made their way into the cemetery. A silvery moon sat low on the horizon, casting long shadows. Every grave marker became a tower, every stone angel transformed into a giant. They could get by without using the torch, as long as they watched where they were walking.

Sandy led the way through the rows of graves, stopping every now and then to catch her breath and peer around. She was operating on instinct. She set off again, and Harry and Dave followed. Watching her hobbling along, Harry felt waves of guilt washing over him. He welcomed it – at the moment it was the only thing keeping him from running away. They walked in silence, cutting between the tombstones, following the ashen grass further into the cemetery.

'Here,' Sandy said.

Harry looked up and saw the three angels staring down at him. Two were in shadow, but the one up on the plinth caught the moonlight, her white face shining.

The plot was a relatively simple one. A headstone. Her name, birth and death dates: *Taken from us too soon*. A big stone slab, cracked in the middle, covered in lichen.

They stared at it for a couple of minutes. Wind propelled leaves between the graves. Above them, red lights twinkled on the TV towers on Mt Coot-tha. Below them, late-night traffic droned along Milton Road onto Centenary Highway.

'Come on, then,' Harry said.

He wedged the tip of the shovel under the edge of the slab. The base had fallen away an inch or so, giving him a little bit of purchase. He lifted it experimentally, feeling the weight and also the strength of the shovel.

Dave moved in beside him, wedging the pickaxe into the gap as well. 'I'll lift and you push,' he said. 'On three. One… two… three…'

Harry took the weight in his legs, the end of the shovel on his shoulder. When his legs were at full extension, he pressed up with his arms. He felt a twinge in his back. The heavy stone slab scraped against the base, the noise deafening in the deathly quiet.

'How's your back?' Dave said.

'Yeah, okay.' He wondered what exactly was in the tablets Dave had given him before they'd headed out. 'I bet I'll feel it tomorrow.'

They paused, catching their breath, listening for any

sign that someone had heard them. Satisfied that they hadn't been discovered, Harry slotted the shovel in and repeated the manoeuvre. The slab tottered on the edge of the base. Dave moved around to the other side, grabbing it by the edges.

'Watch your fingers,' Harry said. 'On three again. One… two… three…'

The slab scraped the rest of the way off the base and fell to the ground. In the distance a flying fox crashed through leaves in a tree. Other than that, they were in the clear. So far, so good.

Under the slab was a patch of dirt, spider webs, a couple of weeds that had found enough light and moisture to grow. Harry grabbed the shovel and drove it into the ground. He pressed down with his foot, then threw the earth on the grass to the side of the grave.

Are you being a naughty boy, Harry?

He shivered and stopped digging. Did she know what he was doing? Dave stepped in and slammed the pickaxe into the ground, loosening the soil. They developed a steady rhythm, swapping tools every once in a while, pausing to stretch their backs and have a drink of water. Sweat was pouring off both of them, despite the cold night.

As the moon rose, the hole grew, until Harry was standing up to his waist.

'Wait!' Sandy said. 'Someone's coming.' She dropped to her haunches, then climbed into the hole with Harry and Dave.

They listened. Wind rustled through the leaves but, under that, they could hear footsteps, then laughter.

'Shit!' Harry sat in the hole, resting, trying not to think about Mistress Hel. He had this weird feeling that thinking about her was like letting her see through his eyes. He focused on the steady thrumming sensation coming from his ribs and his back. It was getting worse.

The rasping footsteps came nearer. Sandy looked into the night sky. Muffled voices. A man and a woman.

'Hang on,' the guy said.

The sound of zipper opening, then the trickle of water against stone.

'You're going to hell, Muzz. You're going to hell.'

'Not fast enough.'

They laughed. More footsteps, then a squeal of surprise from her.

'Not here, you sicko.'

In the darkness, Harry saw Dave's mouth curl in a grin. Harry smiled back. He wasn't happy exactly, but it was nice seeing something replace the angry frown that had resided on Dave's face for the past twenty-four hours.

The footsteps faded into the darkness. Harry and Dave waited a few moments more before moving. Dave helped Sandy out of the grave. Harry had more water then settled back to digging. He and Dave swapped tools again. The hole grew. Up to his chest, then over his head.

He stepped on the shovel, but this time it only went down halfway before clunking against something solid. A jolt ran up his arm, into his spine. He raised his eyebrows. The moon was overhead now, lighting the ground they stood on so they still didn't need the torch.

Harry scraped the layer of dirt off the top of the casket with the shovel, then got on his hands and knees and brushed away more dirt. Sweat dripped off his forehead onto the dark casket lid. Dave stood at one end, watching him.

'Now what?' he said.

'You climb out. Keep watch with Sandy.'

Dave reached over the edge of the grave. Harry helped boost him out. From here, the gravestone looked very high. If it fell he would have nowhere to go. Dave looked around, then peered at Harry.

'All clear.'

Using the pickaxe, Harry cut a foothold into the dirt wall on either side of the casket. He stepped into them, taking his weight off the casket lid, then reached down to steady himself. He shuffled his hand over to the side of the casket, and tried to lift it. His back and ribs screamed in protest. His calf muscles threatened to cramp. He tried again.

This time the lid lifted slightly, hinges groaning, then dropped back. Harry got off his footholds and stood on the edges of the casket lid. Stretched his back. It wasn't heavy, just awkward.

He stepped back onto the footholds, reached down, and pulled. For a moment he thought he'd lose his grip, then the hinges screamed and the lid opened. He couldn't open it all the way, because they hadn't dug the hole wide enough, but he got it open enough to get his feet into the casket. He was expecting a god-awful smell, but it was a dry odour, not unlike compost.

He pulled the lid open further. Moonlight fell on the dead girl's face. Or what was left of it – some dried skin, remnants of hair sticking up, teeth sticking out, desiccated lips drawn back in a rictus smile. She was buried in a summer dress. Seeing that flowery pattern was the worst part. Her arms were clutching a ratty teddy bear and a CD – The Killers' *Hot Fuss*.

Harry felt a wave of grief wash over him. He flashed on her and Lily Sweeney, holding hands. Suiciding together. Did this girl realise she'd been duped, right before the end?

STOP!

Harry jumped, stumbled, his foot slipped into the grave and he fell backwards, smashing against the casket lid. His ribcage screamed and the world greyed out.

'Harry! Harry!'

Harry opened his eyes, looking around frantically, heart pounding in his chest, half expecting to see Mistress Hel standing behind him in the grave, as ridiculous as that was.

'You okay down there?' Sandy said.

'No,' Harry said. 'She knows we're here.'

'She can't know we're here, Harry,' Sandy said.

'We need to get out of here.'

'Harry. You're safe. If you're hearing her, it's probably triggered by proximity. You're safe with me. If she knew, I would know.'

Harry stared at the dark outline of her head. 'Really?'

'Really. Harry, you're safe. You need to keep going.'

Harry felt sick. 'I'm sorry, but I'm gonna need your assistance,' he said.

Sandy didn't ask questions, she just climbed down with Dave's help. Harry stood up one end, over the girl's head. Sandy stood down the other, using her legs to keep the lid open. Harry pivoted so that he was kneeling in the casket, straddling the body. His ribs pulsed, each breath sending a red flash through his vision. He could feel the girl's bony hands through his jeans.

'Fuck this,' he muttered.

Sandy reached out, touched his hand. 'You're doing well, Harry. Once we find it, we can go.'

'Can you remind me what we're looking for?'

'In West Africa it's called a juju but other…'

Harry rubbed his face. 'I don't need a fucking anthropology lesson, Sandy. Just tell me what I'm looking for,' he said. Then added a 'Sorry' under his breath.

'A small bag, probably cotton or hemp. It will have some things inside it. A bone. Both of their blood. Some other stuff.'

Harry pushed the CD and the teddy bear off the body. He leant forwards, feeling underneath with his hands. His head was now barely a foot away from the girl's face. So close he could see the fillings in the teeth at the back of her mouth.

I AM GOING TO SKIN YOU ALIVE! AND THEN BURN YOU!

Harry jumped back, causing another burst of pain from his ribs. He started to climb out of the grave, then saw Sandy staring at him, concern in her eyes. Even in the gloom he could make out the bruises on her face. That was what got him back down there.

He checked the lining of the casket, felt for something hidden behind the rotting silk. Nothing. He slid his hand along the dress, checked the pockets. Nothing.

'Shit.'

He turned, shuffled down, pulled off her shoes. Checked each one before dropping them in the bottom of the coffin.

'I'm going to have to lift her up,' Harry said. 'There might be something underneath.'

He grabbed the girl by the shoulders and lifted. There

was nothing to her, but her body was stiff and awkward. Harry put her back down.

'Did you hear that?' Dave said.

Harry listened. The wind had picked up, making it hard to hear anything over the rasping of leaves. Cars still droned by on the road below the cemetery.

There. Footsteps. Someone walking through the grass.

'Better hurry up, guys,' Dave said.

He picked up the body again, and this time managed to get it on its side. The lining under the body was stained with something black and thick. Harry wished he'd thought to bring gloves. He ran his fingers along the bottom of the casket, thanking the gods that she had been dead long enough for whatever this was to have dried. But he couldn't find any secret compartments. Couldn't see any unusual seams in the lining that might have suggested something was hidden there.

Harry stopped. Stared. 'I'm an idiot,' he said.

He wrestled the body back into the casket. The old teddy bear was wedged between the casket and the dirt. He picked it up. Flipped it over. The stitching on the back was uneven. He showed it to Sandy.

'Guys,' Dave said, 'someone's coming. I'm coming down.'

He lowered his sizeable bulk into the grave, stepping on the girl's stomach. There was a cracking noise. He looked down and grimaced. 'Sorry.'

Harry's heart pounded in his chest. He looked up, hoping for a shadow or something, but there was nothing.

Crunch, crunch, crunch. It sounded close. Very close. But there was no way to tell for sure; sounds travelled further in the depth of night. And the adrenaline coursing through his body made his hearing super-sensitive.

They waited. Part of Harry wanted to end it, jump out of the grave and tell whoever was out there to fuck off.

Crunch, crunch, crunch.

THEY'RE GOING TO FIND YOU! MY ACOLYTES ARE GOING TO KNOCK OUT YOUR TEETH AND USE YOUR MOUTH LIKE A CUNT!

Harry cried out. Dave hissed at him.

The footsteps paused, then resumed. *Crunch, crunch, crunch, crunch, crunch...*

Did that sound as though the footsteps were moving away? Harry thought so. He looked at Sandy, and she shrugged.

Harry stood and risked a peek over the top of the grave. He saw a shadowy form in the distance, heading towards the road that ran alongside the cemetery. He could see footprints in the dewy grass. The man – judging by his silhouette and the size of the footprints, Harry was sure it was a man – had stopped about ten metres away. He must've seen the open grave.

And then what? Was he on a drunken walk, got freaked out and lumbered home? The pace of the retreat didn't suggest freaked out. Stoned, maybe. Was someone watching them? Had someone followed them into the cemetery? Why not confront them while they were trapped?

'We've got to get out of here,' Dave said. 'They might come back with someone.'

In the distance, Harry thought he heard an engine start up. He listened, but the wind carried the sound away from him.

'Wait,' Harry said.

He turned the teddy bear over in his hands, tore the back seam open. Inside was a small bag, tied at the top with twine. It was blackened and stiff. Holding it, he felt a strange sensation of power and fear, as though he was being torn in two. He showed it to Sandy. She nodded.

PUT IT BACK! PUT IT BACK, YOU FUCKING THIEF! PUT IT BACK OR I'LL TURN YOU TO MINCE MEAT!

Dave poked his head over the top of the grave. 'Fuck! Fuck, fuck, fuck!'

'What?' But when he looked up, he knew what. The police hadn't bothered with the siren, but he could see the red and blue of their flashers.

'Where?'

'Down the bottom, they've come in from down the bottom.'

'Here,' Harry said. He clasped his hands together and bent over. Dave stepped into them and launched himself out of the grave. Harry felt something tear, and he cried out.

One car door slammed, then another.

'Come on, Sandy, move it.'

She stepped onto his hands. Dave took her weight and lifted her clear.

'Quick!'

Harry threw their tools out of the pit. The shovel, the pickaxe, the torch. He had one last look at the body. It was half naked. He felt awful, leaving her like this. Abused by Lily Sweeney and now desecrated by him.

'Harry!'

'Hang on,' he said.

He knelt and fixed Elizabeth Tawny's clothes, placed the torn teddy bear back under one arm.

'Okay,' he said. He grabbed Dave's and Sandy's hands and clambered out of the grave, kicking the casket shut on his way out. His body hurt. His back, his ribs, his arms. His head. But he had to keep going or all this would be for nothing.

He bundled their tools together, risked a look over his shoulder. The police were still down the hill a little way, but they had their torches out and were scanning the cemetery. Sandy led the way, doubled over. Harry followed.

'Hey!' A woman's voice. 'Hey!'

For one moment, Harry had the bizarre thought that it was the girl, calling out from the grave. Then Sandy and Dave ran for it. Harry followed, tools jangling. He felt heat on his back, imagined one of the cops drawing their Glock, taking aim...

He dived to the right, up the hill. Sandy and Dave headed west, following a row of headstones. Harry cut across now, running parallel to them. His chest burned. A stitch bloomed in his side. He risked another look over his shoulder. Torchlight bobbed across the cemetery. Behind that, the police car's lights bathed the cemetery in blue and red.

Harry surged up the low earth hill at the edge of the cemetery, crashed through bushes on the other side. Lost the pickaxe. Thought about retrieving it, then gave it away as he saw the torch beams, closer now. Sandy and Dave pushed through the bushes a hundred metres down the hill.

The car was just up the hill. He ran for it, pulled the door open and jumped in. He thrust his hand into his pocket. No keys.

'Fuck. Fuck, fuck, fuck.'

Dave pulled the passenger-side door open, got in, slammed it shut. Sandy jumped in the back.

'What?'

Harry had a vision of the cops coming over the rise, one in front of the car, one behind. Guns drawn now, or at the very least, Tasers. Then, a memory. Taking his car keys out of his pocket, putting them into his backpack with his water bottle. He'd been worried about dropping them in the grave.

He pulled open the backpack, reached in and felt the reassuring shape of the Eiffel Tower keyring Bec had bought him when they were in Paris. He shoved the keys into the ignition. The car started first time, for once.

He slammed the gearstick into drive and floored the accelerator. Left the headlights off. Sandy looked behind them.

'Well?'

'All clear, so far.'

Harry willed the tired old Corolla to find some extra speed from somewhere. He could taste blood in the back of his mouth. On the left, they passed the turn-off to Mt Coot-tha.

They rounded the corner, heading towards Bardon, and he flicked on the headlights. Harry let out a breath he didn't realise he'd been holding.

'Thank fuck for unfit cops,' he said.

CHAPTER 37

Harry, Sandy and Dave sat at the dining room table, staring at the little bag. It was cotton or hemp, as Sandy had expected, but black ichor had leaked and dried, so the fabric resembled dead, dessicated skin. The light failed around it, making Harry's dining room look darker than it actually was.

YOUFUCKENPIECEOFSHITYOUPUTITBACK PUTITBACKRIGHTNOW!

Harry flinched.

'You don't look so good, Harry,' Sandy said.

'It's her...' He paused as she delivered another blast of vitriol. Harry felt achy and hot. His neck was on fire. He ran his hand over the tattoo, and it came away bloody.

'It's going to get worse before it gets better, I'm afraid,' Sandy said.

She grabbed the bag. The look on her face suggested she felt the same way about it as Harry did. Using her fingernails, she pried the string loose, and then opened the bag. Gently, she tipped out the contents.

'We need a small bowl, some cold water, a clean tea towel, and a sharp knife.'

'I'll get them,' Dave said.

As he rose from his seat, Sandy grabbed his forearm. 'Sharp,' she said.

Dave nodded and disappeared into the kitchen while Sandy spread out the items.

GETYOURFILTHYHANDSOFFITSLUT!KILL HERHARRY!SMASHHERWRETCHEDHEADOPEN!

Harry groaned. Red mist descended. He pictured himself grabbing the knife off Dave and gutting them both. He squeezed his eyes shut.

'H-hurry. Please,' he whispered.

There was a small bone, a scrap of fabric stained black, some plant matter that disintegrated in Sandy's hands, and a small disc, also stained black. She picked up the bone.

'This is a human bone. A finger bone.'

'From who?'

'Probably mail order, back then,' she said.

'Are you fucking shitting me?'

She shook her head. 'Nope. I mean, they're sold for study, not for witchcraft. Anyway, it symbolises getting, or grasping.' She placed it down. 'If we did a DNA test on this, we'd find the blood of both Lily Sweeney and Eizabeth Tawny. It binds them. When Elizabeth died, it gave Lily some degree of second sight, and the ability to control people.'

Dave returned, placing the bowl, tea towel and knife on the table. He assessed Harry and picked up the knife again.

'Thanks, love,' Sandy said.

She turned her attention to the dried herbs. 'Bark, probably from a borrachero tree, death cap mushrooms, parsley and probably some poison squeezed from a couple of cane toads, which is why I don't want to touch it.'

Harry shuddered.

'Sorry, did you say parsley?' Dave said.

Sandy offered him a wry smile. 'Also known as devil's oatmeal, if you can believe it. It was said to grow seven times in Hell before the devil gave it permission to grow on Earth. The Haitian Voodoo high priests would have used these ingredients to make their so-called "zombie powder". Mistress Hel would have something similar in her lair, but this here,' she gestured at the bag, 'this connection with the spirit realm, amplifies her powers on Earth.'

Sandy picked up the final item, the amulet. She wet an edge of the tea towel and wiped it. As the black came away, the silver underneath shone through.

'Sterling silver. Another powerful magical substance.'

She wiped both sides and handed it to Harry. He shook his head.

'I... I can't touch it.' He palmed the sweat off his brow.

Sandy stared at him hard, then looked to Dave.

'Can you do the honours?'

Dave took the disc off Sandy. 'A St Christopher's medallion?'

Sandy smiled. 'Ironic, isn't it. Check out the back.'

Dave turned it over, frowned. Showed it to Harry. 'Mean anything to you?'

Harry nodded. It was a miniature version of the design he'd found under the doormat at Godwin's house, and behind the first aid kit in the cherry picker storage case. And he'd seen it chalked on the floor at Mistress Hel's place.

'Now what?' Harry said. 'You've figured all this out, but how does that help me?'

Sandy took the amulet from Dave and sighed. 'We need to inoculate you, Harry.'

She took all the items and put them in the bowl of water. Almost instantly, the water turned black. The surface seemed to shimmer, then smoke, although the water was clearly still cold.

'If we directly apply this to you, it will sort of short out the magic. You'll be free.'

Harry felt chills running through him.

GETOUTGETOUTGETOUTTHEYRETRYING TOKILLYOU!

Harry leapt from his chair. In his mind he saw himself making it to the car, driving to Mistress Hel's place and waiting it out in the safety of her playroom. He made it halfway across the room before Dave grabbed him.

Harry thrust an elbow back. Dave grunted but held on tight. Harry should have been able to take Dave, easily – Dave's experience of martial arts stretched no further than a bit of biffo on the footy field in high school. But Harry was weak, tired and broken. He felt legs entwining in his own and then he was falling. When they hit the ground, his back and ribs exploded in pain and he passed out for a couple of seconds.

'Get his shirt off!' Sandy said.

'No! No!'

Harry wondered who was yelling out like that, then realised it was him. Dave ripped Harry's shirt off, then rolled him onto his stomach. Harry felt a strong hand at the back of his head, pushing his face into the carpet. He felt rage and fear vying for control. He lashed out, gnashed at the carpet and finally cried in frustration.

'Hello?' a voice called out from behind the front door.

'Yeah?' Dave said, panicked.

'Is everything okay?' a woman's voice. The next-door neighbour.

Harry saw legs pass him as Sandy rushed for the front door.

'Help me! Help...' Dave thrust a hand over Harry's mouth.

Sandy opened the door.

'What's going on in there?'

'Intervention,' Sandy said, her voice perfectly calm. 'My son... heroin...'

'Oh... I'm... I'm sorry.'

'Tough love. It'll be okay. Sorry about the racket.' She closed the door.

Sandy returned, and Harry saw she now had the knife in her hand, dripping with some black liquid.

He groaned. 'Please! *Please*, Sandy. Don't.'

'Harry, I can't lie to you. This is going to hurt.'

'No! *No!*'

'Hold him, Dave. I don't want to hurt him any more than is necessary.'

The knife felt like an electrified brand. Pain lanced through Harry's body, setting alight every nerve ending. He bucked despite his injuries, but Dave was sitting across his back and he couldn't escape. Harry didn't black out again. Blacking out would have been merciful.

'Again.'

The pain was worse the second time, and coupled with horrific visions of Mistress Hel, plunging her scalpel into Harry's body over and over.

'Again.'

Harry saw the pain as lines in his mind. Lines of acidic fire, burning through his sanity. The lines turned themselves inside out and he saw the world, he saw the light die in every eye on earth, he saw a glorious black shape rising into the air.

'I've got to go again, Harry. I'm sorry.'

'Fuck off, fuck off, you cunt. Leave me! I'm fixed now. I'm fixed. PLEASE!'

Cut. Harry rose out of his body. *I'm dying, thank Christ, I'm dying.* He saw Dave lying over his arse, Sandy leaning over him. Black mist spewed from the cuts in his back. Within seconds it had coalesced into a thing with claws and teeth and red eyes. Only he could see it. Sandy was talking to Harry, but he couldn't hear what she was saying. The thing ripped open Sandy's mouth and forced itself into her. She coughed, tried to pull it out. Her eyes bulged. Dave turned, horrified, as Sandy exploded, coating the room in red.

'You're doing well, Harry. Just one more now.'

Harry blinked. *Fuck.*

'No, I can't bear it, I can't...'

Cut. Harry's eyes filled with a light so bright his eyeballs burnt to a crisp. A black tidal wave rose in him, washing the mammoth shape away. Darkness. A moment. An eternity. Harry opened his eyes as his stomach convulsed, sending wave after wave of black bile spewing across the red carpet. He heard Dave cry out in disgust, and felt perverse joy.

And then, finally, merciful unconsciousness embraced him.

CHAPTER 38

Johnny dusted his hands, butterflies dancing in his stomach. He thought he'd done a good job, but what he thought didn't matter – what Mistress Hel thought was everything. He checked his phone, in case he'd missed a message. Yellowing grass stretched away from the shed to the horizon, cut only by rusty barbed-wire fences. Low, dusty hills framed the parched cattle country.

Turning back to the shed, he took the instructions out of his back pocket and checked them over once more. He'd found them on the internet and printed them out. Now they were stained with his sweat and blood and the pages had been folded and unfolded so many times they were falling apart.

Johnny's mind tried to put the pieces together: the police truck, the sacks of ANFO, the wires and the detonators. He felt as though he should have been able to figure out what it all meant. But then he found himself thinking about Mistress Hel. The curve of her thighs, her bright red lips, eyes that saw right through him. All that mattered was that what he had done matched the instructions. Satisfied, he folded the instructions and placed them in his back pocket. On the horizon, dust rose into the sky. She was coming!

Johnny ran to the house, hoping he could get changed and clean before she arrived. Then he stopped, remembering the van was still uncovered, and the doors of the shed were open. He ran back to the shed, then remembered that the gate was closed, and that Mistress Hel hated having to get out of the car to open the gate. He headed for the gate, then stopped. But if it wasn't her, and someone saw the police truck, it might get reported...

Johnny froze, torn in three directions at once, unable to make up his mind. He cursed, wiped tears away, cursing again as the dust stung his eyes. He hobbled back to the shed, pulling the old wooden gates shut on squealing hinges. He yanked a chain through the steel loops but didn't bother locking it.

He sprinted to the gate in time to open it as her black BMW pulled up. Through the dusty windscreen he caught a glimpse of her big sunglasses and red lipstick. He felt a surge of happiness that he'd managed to get to the gate before she pulled up. She would appreciate that. He may not get any thanks for it, but that didn't matter. What mattered was that she was happy. Because when she wasn't happy – he shuddered.

Johnny looked up, cursing himself for zoning out. He was tired. So tired. The car was already edging behind the house. He closed the gate, then ran for the house. He surged through the front door and the bare lounge room. The house was cold. Curtains drawn, dim after the brightness of outside. His eye still stung. He raced into the kitchen. Warped formica benches, a rust-stained porcelain sink, a bar fridge where an old full-sized Kelvinator once stood. This room's window faced away from the road, so he was allowed to keep the curtains open.

The back door opened. He reached for the glass on the draining board, then opened the fridge and pulled out a plastic jug of water. With shaking hands, he filled the glass. Seeing the water made him realise how thirsty he was. How long had he been working out there? *Didn't matter. Didn't matter.* He set the glass on the table and lowered himself to his knees, bowing his head.

Her heels clumped up the back steps, then clacked across the linoleum floor. The sound raised goosebumps along his arms. She stood just out of sight. He knew she was smiling. He could sense it. But that didn't mean she was happy. She knew he wanted to see her, any part of her. She knew that where she was standing was tempting him to disobey a rule. And that would mean punishment.

She stepped forwards so he could see her black patent leather shoes, her stockings. He groaned, then hissed a curse at himself. Then muttered an apology. She ignored him, laying her clutch on the table, ignoring the water he'd set out for her.

'Hello, Johnny,' she purred.

'Hello, Mistress.'

'Are you finished?'

'Almost, Mistress.' Johnny felt a surge of panic. Why hadn't he worked harder? Why hadn't he got up earlier this morning? Or worked though the night? God, it was so selfish of him, to think about his rest when Mistress had done so much for him. 'I'm so sorry... I just...'

'Shh,' she said. She laid a hand on his head. 'You've done well. Go and wait in the lounge room and I'll bring the blade in.'

'Oh! Thank you, thank you, thank you!' Not thinking, he crawled forwards and wrapped his arms around her.

She was wearing a tight black dress. He could smell her perfume.

'Ugh! Get... off... me!'

She kicked him away. All the happiness evaporated. Johnny curled on the floor in the foetal position, panic gripping him. What if she left him? What if she didn't give him relief? It was a week last time, what if...

He risked a look at her. Her face was contorted in disgust as she brushed the dust off her dress.

'I'm sorry, I'm sorry... I'll buy you a new dress.'

'It's Gucci. Where are you going to get two thousand dollars?'

Johnny's mind froze. He couldn't think of anything. He wished he were dead.

'You don't have a job anymore, remember? You work for me now. And I don't pay you – well, not with money.' She pulled a chair out, sat down. Crossed her legs. Tapped her toe. 'How much is an orgasm worth, do you think? To me, I mean?'

She was smiling again. Johnny stopped breathing.

'Answer me! What is it worth to me to give you an orgasm?'

'N-n-not much.'

'That's right. Not much. Maybe five dollars. Maybe. So what if I was to trade that two thousand dollars for your next two hundred or so org...'

'I'll rob someone!' Johnny yelled. 'I'll do over a convenience store.'

Without realising it, he was back on his knees, forehead against the floorboards.

Mistress Hel laughed. 'You would too, you perverted little fuck.'

She placed a heel into the back of Johnny's head.

'Do you remember the first time we met?' she said.

'Yes, Mistress.'

'As in, the very first time. In the basement of that fucker's house. And all those men were... urgh!'

Her heel pressed harder into the back of his head. He gritted his teeth.

'Y-yes... M-mistress.' Johnny's mind was reeling. He hated it when she brought this up. She knew he was just a kid. She knew he was powerless to help her, just as he was powerless to help himself. But he also knew trying to justify what happened wouldn't help him; it would only make her angrier.

'All those men. Revolting men. Unable to control themselves. And what did you do to help me?'

'N-nothing... nothing, Mistress.'

She sighed. 'You see what happens when you disappoint me? It takes me to a dark place.'

'I'm sorry, Mistress.'

She pressed her heel harder into his head. His forehead rubbed against the dirty linoleum.

'It makes me want to hurt you.'

Suddenly, the heel was gone, replaced by her hand, playing with his sweaty hair.

'But I'm trying to be a better person, Johnny. And soon all this – all this pathetic need – will be behind you... but for now, I guess I'd better take care of you.

'Get into the lounge room. Now.'

Johnny felt a massive surge of gratitude. He crawled across the floor, hairs rising on the back of his neck as her heels click-clacked after him.

CHAPTER 39

Harry woke up in bed, disorientated. He wasn't sure what time it was, but his room was filled with golden light. He was in his pyjamas, under the doona, and felt weak but well, as though recovering from the flu. The sheets smelt freshly washed.

Harry stretched. Something felt different. Everything felt different. So different that at first he couldn't put his finger on it. His mind felt truly clear for the first time in weeks. He could think. He panicked when Mistress Hel – Lily – came to mind, because he didn't want to let her back in. But gradually he relaxed and saw her clearly. She wasn't perfect. Nobody was perfect. But more importantly she was evil, and he was seeing that for the first time.

The door opened a crack, then fully. Bec poked her head in.

'I thought I heard someone rustling around in here,' she said, smiling. 'How are you feeling?'

At the sight of her, Harry remembered everything. 'I'm sorry. I'm so sorry, Bec.'

She came over to him and held him. She smelt wonderful. 'Shh. Sandy explained.'

Harry didn't know how to respond, so he simply said, 'Thank you.'

'For what?'

'For being here. For believing.'

Bec frowned. 'I'm not sure I'm quite there yet. But I care about you. I can see you need help. Do you want a cup of tea?'

He shook his head. 'No. No, I want you.' He held his arms out to her, noticing how weak he felt. He buried his face in her hair and breathed her in.

'What exactly did Sandy tell you?' Harry said.

'She... she said that that woman, the dominatrix, had drugged you... with some sort of mind-control substance,' Bec said. 'Is that true?'

Harry considered. 'Yeah, pretty much. I'm sorry for everything I've put you through.'

With some effort, she pulled away from him. He wiped the tears away from his cheeks.

Harry dozed for a while, but he found that he soon became restless. He sat up, wincing at the pain in his back and ribs. He was remembering everything he'd fucked up recently. But for the first time in weeks he felt energised.

He got out of bed and pulled on some clothes.

Sandy looked up from her cup of tea when he emerged from his room, her eyes lined with worry. 'Hello, love,' she said.

Harry strode across the room and gave her a hug, so hard that he squeezed the breath out of her and felt his back scream in anguish. The pain made him feel lightheaded, but also pure.

'Thank you,' he said.

She patted his arm. Her eyes were brimming with tears.

'I don't think I'll ever be able to pay you back,' he said.

'Yes, you can,' Sandy said, pulling away from him. 'We saved you, but she's still out there, spinning her web. Harry...'

'I know,' he said. 'I'm going to take her down.'

'You need to be careful.'

He sat next to Sandy. She held his hand. He found it hard to look her in the eye.

'What you did... last night,' Harry said. 'Has that freed the others?'

Sandy shook her head. 'Unfortunately, no,' she said, then reached into the massive shoulder bag by her chair. She pulled out a Dolmio jar filled with brackish water.

'What's that?'

'This is the stuff we cut into your wounds last night,' she said.

Harry shuddered, remembering the intense agony.

'It needs to go into their wounds too, to free them.'

'But wasn't that bag the source of her power?'

Sandy shook her head again. 'No. When Lily Sweeney made the offering, the Goddess conferred certain powers on her. She still has those powers.' Sandy picked up the jar. 'Think of this as a vaccine.'

'So, if I could get Don Clack to...'

'Let's not worry about Don for the moment. Let's worry about her.'

'What do I need to do?'

'We have to find out what her plan is. Even though you're not under her spell anymore, she's still dangerous.'

Harry nodded. 'Okay.'

Bec emerged from the kitchen, drying her hands with a tea towel.

'I want to confront her,' Harry said.

'Absolutely not,' Sandy said.

'But...' Harry saw the set of Sandy's chin and the hard look in her eyes, and realised she was right. For now. Instead, he reached for his laptop. He opened 'Recent Documents'.

'I don't even remember most of this stuff,' he said. 'It could be that I already know what she's planning.'

He pulled up everything he knew about Mistress Hel. He pulled up everything he knew about the victims.

'Oh shit,' Harry said. 'It's the fundraiser. At the Ekka. She's going to...'

Sandy was leaning across the table, staring at him. 'What? Harry? She's going to what?'

'I don't know. She wants revenge. She knows... my source... shit.' Harry reeled. He remembered his last conversation with Johnny. The dead tone in his voice. It didn't seem that unusual at the time.

He snatched up his phone and dialled Johnny.

'Harry, what...' Sandy started, but Harry held up his hand.

Johnny didn't answer. Harry texted: *Hey Johnny. Just checking to see if you're all right. Call me, okay?*

He went to put down his phone, then dialled another number.

'Harry,' Sandy said, her voice a warning tone.

'I need to do this.'

The phone rang six times before Mistress Hel picked up.

'Hello?' she said.

'Lily, it's Harry. Harry Hendrick.'

'That's *Mistress* to you, remember?'

Harry felt his heart flutter at her voice. In spite of everything. And in spite of everything, he had to bite back the urge to correct himself.

'You've been thinking about unimportant things again, Harry,' Mistress Hel said. 'That's only going to end badly.'

'We need to talk.'

'Do we?'

'I know what happened to you.'

A pause. Harry closed his eyes. In his mind he saw the smile fade on her lips.

'You were raped. As a girl. You went to the police, but one of the rapists was a cop. Right?'

She laughed but it sounded forced. 'Oh, Harry. You really need to stop playing detective.'

'Whatever you're planning – don't.'

'And what's the alternative, Mr Hendrick?'

'I know about Marcus Wilson. I think I can take him down, just like I took down Andrew Cardinal last year.'

Mistress Hel sighed. 'I'll see you next week, Harry.'

'Wait! I'm going to interview him, tonight.' It was a lie. Marcus Wilson had pencilled him in for next week. 'He thinks it's about his work on the flood recovery and the fundraiser, but it's not. It's about what he did. I'm going to confront him.'

'Okay, Harry. You go do that.' She laughed again, and this time it sounded real. The line went dead.

Harry shivered. He stared at the phone for a few moments, mostly so he didn't have to meet Sandy's eyes. When he did look up, she was frowning at him.

'Well?' Harry said. 'It's true. Whatever sort of monster

she is, Marcus Wilson and other sickos like him made her.'

'Is it true?' Bec asked. 'Can you take Wilson down?'

'Look, before… before Lily fucked me over, I was on Wilson's trail. The only reason he hasn't gone down before now is because he was a cop.'

'That's not a trivial reason,' Bec said.

'No, right? Who would dare try to take out a bent cop? But that's also his weakness. He'll be complacent. And all it takes is one small crack, and the dam he's built will collapse.'

'And then?' Sandy said. She still looked angry.

'Maybe she won't go through with it.'

'That's a big maybe, Harry. And yes, maybe Lily Sweeney is what she is because of those men, but that doesn't change what she is. And it doesn't change what she's done.'

Bec sat at the table. 'Can't we just go to the police?'

Harry nodded. 'About Wilson, or Lily?'

'Both?'

'I don't want to go to the cops about Wilson until I've got something solid on him. I'm worried he has mates in the force who will protect him if they can. As for Lily – Mistress Hel – I don't know.' Harry thought about his two most recent conversations with Phil. He'd likely be highly skeptical of anything Harry had to tell him, and with good reason. 'I'm worried that if they take her in before we know what she's up to, maybe it will happen anyway.'

CHAPTER 40

Harry drove through suburbs, out onto the highway then back into more suburbs. The further he got from the highway, the bigger the blocks, the higher the fences. He wondered if he was driving into a trap. He hadn't told Dave or Sandy or Bec that he suspected Wilson knew Harry was writing a story about his alleged involvement in the paedophile ring that had abused Lily Sweeney and Johnny and countless other kids. He knew they would freak out and interfere, and he knew that their interference would likely put them in danger. And Harry had put too many people in danger. It was enough that they knew he was going to interview Marcus Wilson. In the late afternoon light, kids played in sprinklers, even though it should have been too cold for such games.

He pulled up outside an eighties-style high-set surrounded by a high brick wall. Night was settling now. There were lights on in the house. The curtains were drawn. A guy walked past with his dog. He didn't pay Harry any attention.

Harry climbed out of the car and walked through the front gate, and up the stairs to Wilson's open front door. Someone was whistling. He tapped on the screen.

'Hello? Marcus?'

A man rounded the corner, dressed in a tuxedo. Wilson had aged since Harry had seen him on TV during the flood recovery, deep lines gouged into the corners of his eyes and around his mouth. But he looked fit and tanned.

'Hello?' He squinted.

'It's Harry. Harry Hendrick. I emailed you a while back...'

'About the flood recovery article you're working on. Yeah, but that's not until next week and, as you can see...' He gestured to his tux. 'I'm a little busy this evening.'

'Yeah, I know. I'm so sorry. I lost track of time. I'm actually going away with my girlfriend next week. I was driving past and I thought...'

'You thought I wouldn't turn you down if you rocked up on my doorstep? Right?'

Harry tried his best to look sheepish. 'I'll be quick.'

Wilson checked his watch. 'All right. Fifteen minutes?'

Harry grinned. 'Perfect.'

Marcus Wilson pushed open the screen door and grabbed Harry's hand, pumping it up and down. Judging by his iron grip and the way he filled out his tuxedo, he had been working out.

He led Harry into a neat but old lounge room. There was a large TV cabinet against one wall, the shelves around the TV filled with books and framed photographs of Wilson with various politicians, sporting identities and a couple of B-grade celebrities. The top of the cabinet was lined with trophies, each one topped with a statue of a man shooting.

'Take a seat,' Wilson said. 'I'd offer you a drink but...' He checked the time again.

Harry sat on the black leather sofa and opened his notebook. 'That's okay. I really appreciate this.'

Wilson perched on the adjacent armchair. 'No worries. So, just passing, huh? Had a desperate a need to quiz me about the flood recovery?' The smile dropped off Wilson's face. 'Cut the bullshit, Harry,' he said. 'We both know exactly why you're here.'

Harry held his stare, but it was hard work. He could see why Wilson had been such a good cop.

He cleared his throat. 'Well, this certainly makes things easier. You said I had fifteen minutes. Now we can spend fifteen minutes talking about child abuse and paedophiles. Do you mind if I record this?'

Wilson set his jaw. 'What do you fucking think? Get to the point and then get out of my house.'

'I had someone come to me with a story of abuse,' Harry said.

'Oh really?' Wilson said, his brows knitting with feigned concern.

'A former student of St Therese. Abused for years by staff.'

'Jesus,' Wilson said, shaking his head. 'That's terrible.'

'Yeah. On campus and off.'

Harry stared at Marcus Wilson. Wilson held his gaze. Harry felt the anger building. He wanted to slam the former cop's head into the coffee table. Instead, he took a deep breath.

'And he says you were the ringleader, and that the paedophile ring you run is still operating.'

'Care to tell me this joker's name?'

'What do you fucking think?'

Wilson's face hardened. Harry relished the sight.

'I think you're a naïve idiot,' Wilson said. 'I was a cop for more than forty years. In forty years of policing, you make a lot of enemies. They think if they throw enough mud, some of it will stick.'

Harry nodded. 'And you're happy for me to publish that?'

'You publish that,' Wilson said, his voice barely a whisper, 'and you will wish you were dead.'

'Well, I was hoping for a standard denial but that will do just as nicely.' He got up and headed for the door.

'Hang on a minute! Hang on a fucking minute!'

Harry felt a hand on his shoulder. He shrugged it off. 'Don't touch me.'

'You come in here, accuse me of all this shit, and expect to just walk out?'

Harry reached for the screen door. He saw Wilson moving, felt his arm on his shoulder again.

'Wait, Harry, wait,' he said, breath almost in Harry's ear. Then Wilson grabbed Harry's wrist and jerked it up behind his back, other arm cinched tight around his neck. 'No, you don't.'

Harry sucked in a huge breath and lowered his chin to keep Wilson's wiry forearm away from his windpipe. Ignoring the pain in the arm behind his back, he lifted a leg and pushed off against the wall beside the front door. Wilson staggered back, but only a couple of steps. He was strong.

Using the momentum, Harry twisted, eyes wide, looking for something that could help him. The wall unit was too far away. The coffee table just had a couple of magazines on it. The dining room may as well have been the surface of the moon, for all the good it would do him.

He reached up with his free hand and grabbed at Wilson's head, tearing at his hair. Wilson grunted, but held on. His forearm pressed against Harry's windpipe. Wilson was trying to bury his face against Harry's neck, to protect it, but Harry found his ear, grabbed hold, and pulled as hard as he could.

'Son of a bitch!'

Harry was ready when the arm across his neck loosened. He dropped, twisted out of the armlock and pushed Wilson away from him. Wilson stumbled and fell backwards into the armchair, then rolled to one side and ran down the hall.

Harry chased him. Two bedrooms to the left. Bathroom to the right. Wilson went through a door at the end of the hallway and slammed it shut. Harry heard the lock slide across seconds before his shoulder hit, rattling the door in its frame.

'I'm calling the cops,' Wilson said.

'Fine,' Harry said. 'Call an ambulance, too.'

Harry took a step back and lifted his leg, slamming his foot into the door next to the lock. And again. And again. On the fourth kick, the door burst open.

Wilson was on his hands and knees, head in the built-in wardrobe.

'Get out of there!'

Wilson slumped back against the wall. That was when Harry noticed the pistol pointing at him.

CHAPTER 41

Johnny assessed himself in the mirror. Everything had to be just right. He shivered, thinking about how she would be if everything wasn't just right, and then how she would be if it was. They were nearing the end of the road.

He ran a hand down the front of his crisp, short-sleeved, blue shirt. He'd tucked it into his dark blue pants. The name tag was real, but the name was fake. He picked up the utility belt off the chair and strapped it on. It was real too, had everything except the gun. Johnny had asked her, wouldn't he need a gun? She'd just smiled and said no. He'd asked her where she got all the gear from. A shadow had passed across her face, and he'd been suddenly terrified. Then it was gone. She'd patted the side of his face, told him not to worry about such things.

He cinched the belt tight around his waist, picked up the hat off the bed and set it on his head. A perfect fit. Everything was perfect where she was concerned.

Somewhere deep down, he felt a quiver of doubt. He thought for a moment about Harry, the first man who'd actually believed him, and wanted to do something about it. But then he remembered how easily Harry had dropped it, how relieved he'd seemed, when Johnny expected him to be angry. As though he'd realised at the same time as Johnny had that there was no point trying to use the law to fight these people, that the law would never really serve justice upon its own. Johnny needed something more primitive, a blunt instrument, to set things right again. Get things back on track.

Mistress Hel said that completing his task would be worth far more than simple revenge. Far more than sending a message. She said he would be erasing his past. Johnny had tried to argue and for once she'd been willing to accept his doubts. He asked her how it was possible. Ask and the Goddess will deliver to the faithful, she'd replied.

'But aren't you the Goddess?'

At this she had laughed. 'No, just a humble disciple.'

It made no sense. You couldn't erase the past. That's what the counsellor told him. You could deal with it and move on, but you couldn't erase it. Yet Johnny felt himself believing Mistress Hel anyway. Maybe that's what faith was.

Johnny picked up his shoes. Unlike the rest of his outfit, these weren't brand new. Again, Mistress hadn't explained where they had come from, just told him to clean them until they shone. Johnny admired the near-mirror finish. He was proud of his work. It had taken him three days, but he figured it out in the end. He breathed on them, then gave them one last shine with his cleaning cloth. He slid them on and tied the laces.

The sun was down by the time he got outside, but that was okay. He checked his watch and made sure he was leaving at the right time. Everything had to be just so. He walked across the dry grass, frowning as the dust coated his newly cleaned shoes. It didn't matter. Soon none of this would matter.

He opened the shed. The police van was there, as it should be. He went around to the rear and opened it. Johnny had checked it at least a dozen times, but once more wouldn't hurt. All the internal fittings had been stripped out, and sacks of ANFO stacked on either side. He squeezed between the sacks, taking care not to get his uniform dusty, and checked the detonators were in place and wired together correctly. He switched on the relay and made sure the light was green, then turned it off again. Finally, he checked the old phone. All he had to do was call a certain number, and it would be over. But he had to wait until the perfect moment. And the perfect moment was when Mistress Hel told him it was. Johnny dropped back to the ground and closed the back of the van, locking the door.

He went to the front, got in, and drove the van out. He left the shed's doors open. He wouldn't be coming back here. When he was outside, he checked the glovebox for the piece of paper she had given him. He unfolded it. It was full of symbols he didn't understand. There was so much he didn't understand. So much he couldn't understand. Looking at those symbols, he felt shivers of pleasure and pain. He thought of Marcus Wilson, and those dark days at high school, and felt wracked by guilt. Johnny had enjoyed some of it.

Then a wave of calm washed in, and washed out again, taking all the negativity with it. He could almost see Mistress Hel sitting there next to him, smiling, telling him it wasn't his fault. He was just a kid. It was another example of the terrible things men did, and why their time on Earth was about to come to an end.

He followed the wheel ruts from the shed to the front gates, put the van in neutral and got out. The air was cooler now, and his breath puffed in front of his face like a dragon's. He opened the gate, letting it swing on its hinges. Above the sound of the van he heard cattle lowing somewhere in the distance. He breathed in the crisp, clean air, looked at the heavens and took a moment to enjoy the stars. It made him feel insignificant, then he remembered what Mistress Hel told him, about making a difference: anyone could do it.

Johnny went back to the truck, climbed in, slammed the door and pulled out onto the dirt road.

'Time to make a difference,' he said, and switched the radio on.

CHAPTER 42

'**G**et on your knees,' Wilson said.

Harry took a step into the room and Wilson raised an eyebrow in warning.

'Now, shitbag. On your knees.'

Harry dropped to his knees. He scanned the room, looking for any way of escape. There was nothing. Wilson pushed himself to his feet, never once taking his eyes off Harry, who guessed he'd done enough of this sort of thing during his law enforcement career.

'Hands behind your head,' Wilson said. 'Fingers laced.'

Harry complied, even as his mind reeled. People knew where he was. He couldn't just disappear. But this was a former cop. A corrupt cop who had managed to keep his nose clean for many years, despite his predilection for young flesh. Besides, even if Wilson didn't blow Harry's head off, Harry was going to have a hard time explaining what had gone on here.

Wilson circled around behind him, climbing over the bed to get around him without getting in reach.

'Cross your feet,' Wilson snarled.

'What?'

'Your feet, cross them.'

Harry crossed one foot over the other, then winced as Wilson stepped on them, holding him in place. He held Harry's thumbs together with one hand and snapped cuffs on with the other. Harry knew what was coming next. He felt Wilson's foot against his back, and then he was falling forwards, unable to protect his face. He twisted his head just before it hit the carpet. The taste of blood filled his mouth. Then he felt the barrel of the gun against the back of his neck.

Wilson was breathing heavily. Harry looked under the bed. He could just make out a clear box filled with Lego, and a blue teddy bear. He shuddered.

'Do you really think you're going to get away with it?' Harry said.

'With what?'

'Abusing kids? Killing me?'

Wilson sighed. 'Well, as for the kiddy fiddling, lots of people do. My dad sure did. Eight years of that shit, until I left him cradling a broken jaw when I was sixteen. And killing you? Now, there's a thought.'

'Forget I mentioned it.'

'Smartarse,' Wilson said. He slammed his foot into Harry's side. Harry screamed. 'Let's see, you came over to interview me…'

Slam! 'Argh!' Harry tried to roll away, but that sent another burst of pain firing through his ribcage and back.

'… you got aggressive, we fought, I managed to get away and ran to my room…'

Wilson stomped on Harry's back. Harry screamed again.

'… you were kicking the door, so I retrieved my pistol from my safe. That sound about right?'

Harry opened his mouth to speak, but someone beat him to it.

'If you're going with that story, I'd roll him over first,' a woman's voice said. 'So you can shoot him in the face.'

Mistress Hel stood in the doorway, her gun aimed at Wilson. Harry took a few deep breaths – as deep as he could manage – and pushed himself backwards, until he was resting against the wall. Wilson's gun hand twitched.

'I wouldn't, if I were you,' Mistress Hel said. 'I've got you cold. You know the drill.'

Wilson didn't move. 'Put the gun down, young lady,' he said. 'Police are on their way right now.'

Mistress Hel laughed. 'I'm hardly young, and I'm certainly no lady. And no, no police are en route, I'm afraid to say.'

She walked into the room and placed the gun against his head.

'You see that, Harry?' she said. 'He doesn't even remember me.'

Harry took her point but, to be fair, he doubted many people who had known her at high school would recognise her now. Black leather coat and matching gloves, tight black jeans, boots. Flawless hair and make-up. Even though he was no longer under her spell, she looked like a goddess. Her eyes were full of confidence and purpose.

Then, to Wilson: 'Drop. The. Gun.'

The gun clunked against the floor.

'On your knees.'

'Do you really think this is a good idea?' Wilson said, but sighed and got to his knees, lowering one hand to ease himself down.

'Hands behind your head,' she said.

Wilson complied. Mistress Hel looked at Harry and gestured with the gun. 'It's not as fancy as magic, but it does the trick.'

Wilson sneered. 'Do you really think…'

Harry flinched as Mistress Hel kicked Wilson in the face. He cried out and fell backwards against the bed, blood spraying from his broken nose. As he slid down the bed, she pressed her foot against the side of his head, then when he was on the floor, against his neck.

'Get your fucking keys out! Move it!'

'Okay! Okay!' Wilson thrust a hand into his jacket, coming out with handcuff keys. He coughed, blood spraying over his crisp white shirt.

'Do you know what to do next, or do I have to kick you again?' Mistress Hel spat.

Wilson fumbled the keys as Mistress Hel kicked the gun away from him. Harry turned so Wilson could unlock the handcuffs.

'They're all cowards at their heart,' Mistress Hel said. 'These beasts. That's why they do what they do.'

The handcuffs came loose. Harry pushed himself away from Wilson, who now looked genuinely scared. 'Please,' he whispered.

Mistress Hel kicked him between the legs and he collapsed on the floor, screaming, and curled into a ball. She knelt by his head, and pressed the gun into the back of his neck.

'You speak another word and I pull the trigger.'

Wilson closed his mouth.

She turned the gun on Harry. 'Cuff him,' she said.

Harry yanked Wilson's arms behind him and snapped the cuffs over his wrists, closing them tight. He reached for the keys, which Wilson had dropped on the floor.

'Don't bother,' she said. 'We won't be needing those.'

Wilson whimpered, until Mistress Hel pressed the gun into the side of his head.

She walked across the room, to the walk-in wardrobe. 'Oh, you left your safe open, Marcus.'

'Stay out of there,' Wilson said.

Mistress Hel ignored him. She reached into the safe and retrieved a thick folder. She stood over him.

'What could this be, I wonder?'

'You have no right!' Wilson moaned.

She stomped on his back with her heel. Wilson yelped.

'I have no right? Let's have a look-see, shall we?'

She opened the folder and took out a small, battered, black book. 'Lots of names in here,' she said. 'Dates, and sums of money.' She flicked through the pages. 'This goes back years, Marcus. Whatever could it mean?' She drove her heel into his back again, so hard it tore through his tuxedo jacket.

'I recognise some of these names. Zak Godwin. Don Clack. I think Harry might too. Isn't that right, Harry?'

'Yeah. I do.'

'I wonder what they could have been paying you money for, Marcus? What else is in this folder?'

She slid the book into her back pocket and took an A4 envelope from the folder. It was stuffed full. Mistress Hel pulled out something and showed it to Harry. It was a black and white photograph. She turned it back to herself before Harry had much of a look at it, but he saw enough to know what it was.

'This girl looks about eleven, Marcus.' She dropped the photo onto his back, then stabbed her stiletto through it, into his flesh. Blood bubbled up and Wilson cried out. Mistress Hel pulled another photo out of the envelope. She got onto her haunches and thrust it in Wilson's face.

'What about this one? The one being raped? How old was he?'

Wilson tried to spit at her. She held the photo against his face, then pistol-whipped him through it.

'Argh!'

'Lily... stop.'

She pointed the gun at Harry and trod on Wilson's face. She upended the envelope and photos, maybe a hundred of them, fluttered over Wilson. She dropped the envelope, then turned out the folder. Two USB sticks fell to the floor.

'Do you want to defend this man, Harry?'

'No, of course not! But... this is evidence. We've got him! We've fucking got him!'

Mistress Hel smiled at Harry, but it was a sad smile. 'You really believe that, don't you, Harry?'

'You haven't got shit!' Wilson spat. The photo fell away from his face. Blood streamed from a cut on his temple into his eyes. 'You fucking idiots. You just gave me a Get Out of Jail Free card. None of this will be admissible in a court. Fucking amateurs.'

'He's right, Harry. It's funny that he should speak truth with his final words.'

Mistress Hel pulled a stocking from her back pocket and threw it to Harry. 'Gag him.'

'No, Harry! No!'

Harry took the stocking and pulled it around Wilson's face. As the former cop spoke, it slotted neatly between his teeth. Harry tied it tight at the back of his head. While

Harry was busy, Mistress Hel backed up to the bedroom doorway, picked up Wilson's revolver and put it into her jacket pocket.

'Good boy.' She pulled out her phone and dialled. 'A slight detour,' she said into the phone. She gave Wilson's address, then put her phone away. She gestured at Harry with the gun.

'Get him downstairs,' she said.

'Lily... you don't need to do this,' Harry said. 'Whatever you've got planned. You don't need to do it. Please, just talk to me for one second.'

Harry gestured to the doorway. Mistress Hel looked at Wilson. He wasn't going anywhere. She nodded.

They stood just outside the room.

'I know what Wilson did was wrong,' Harry said. 'Obviously. But killing him isn't the answer. Think about it... can you imagine what life will be like for him in prison? Far worse than dying.'

Mistress Hel stared at Harry. 'Finished?' She turned back to the room. Harry grabbed her arm but she pulled away from him.

'Jesus, you like it, don't you?' he said. 'Having the control. Killing people. You got a taste for it with Elizabeth Tawny and you've never looked back!'

Mistress Hel surged at Harry, slamming him against the hallway wall. The back of his head smacked the plasterboard hard enough to dent it. The force of the impact caught him by surprise and he shook his head to clear it.

'You know nothing about Liz!' Mistress Hel spat. She pressed her forearm against Harry's throat.

'I know you entered a suicide pact with her, and then conveniently didn't die. And then used your little bag of tricks to get in good with this goddess of yours.'

Mistress Hel snorted a bitter laugh, then pressed the gun under Harry's chin. 'This is what you think of me? Did you know that the reason Liz and I got to know each other was because of that fucker in there?'

Harry tried to speak, but couldn't with the gun in his face. He shook his head.

'No, didn't think so. The suicide pact was real. It wasn't a cry for help. I...' Mistress Hel blinked back tears. 'I wanted to die. I still want to die. Every day. Liz and I both offered ourselves to the Goddess. I was left behind. To do this.'

'I'm sorry,' Harry said. 'But... what? Were all of them paedophiles? Brad Brooks – the young cop? Christopher Lawrence – the mine worker? How about the farmer? John Moncrieff? Jeff Stafford? Janek Murphy? Well? Were they?'

'No, they weren't. But they were useful.'

'Did they deserve to die?'

She stopped him with a look. 'You still don't get it, do you? Man's time on Earth is coming to an end. Tonight. Now MOVE!'

CHAPTER 43

When Harry saw the police van waiting out front, for a few seconds he thought Wilson had somehow managed to get word out. But the flashers were off and there weren't a dozen cops breaking down the front door. Harry remembered Constable Brad Brooks, who had decided to aerate his own head after hanging out with Mistress Hel for a while. Phil had said something about Brooks being suspended shortly before his suicide, for 'erratic behaviour', although he'd never been forthcoming on details of what that behaviour had been.

'Brad Brooks stole this thing for you?'

'For the Goddess, yes. But then… he wavered. He was under a lot of pressure.'

'So you killed him?'

'Come on, Harry, move it,' Mistress Hel said.

Harry dragged Wilson by the scruff of his tux, wincing in pain whenever Wilson tried to jerk out of his grip. By the time Harry had pulled Wilson across the lawn, he was dripping with sweat. Ms Hel opened the gate for him. A cop got out of the van and walked towards them. Crisp, pressed uniform. Cap perched on his head. Harry was so distracted by the uniform he didn't immediately notice who it was.

'Johnny?'

Johnny ignored him and looked to Mistress Hel for instruction.

'Get this one in the back of the van,' she said, gesturing to Wilson. 'Oh wait,' she said, pulling the spare gun from her pocket. 'Here.'

Johnny took Wilson's gun and slotted it into his holster.

'Johnny, what are you doing?' Harry said. 'We've got him. We've got the evidence. Photos. Names. Everything.'

Johnny grabbed Wilson, who was looking wildly around him, as though hoping to see someone he recognised. Harry looked up and down the street. It was deserted. He followed Johnny around the side of the van. Johnny dropped Wilson on his knees and opened the rear doors.

'Holy shit,' Harry said.

The pungent reek of ammonia hit him so hard he staggered back a step. The rear of the van had been stripped and packed with large white sacks. Between the sacks were blocks of something wrapped in brown paper. These were strung together with yellow cable. Wilson's eyes went wide and he yelled through his gag. He fell on the ground and tried to roll away. Mistress Hel put a foot on him. Wilson started crying.

'Put him in,' Mistress Hel said.

Johnny grabbed Wilson by the back of his jacket and his belt and hefted him into the back of the van, in the narrow aisle between the sacks of ANFO.

'Marcus?' Mistress Hel said.

Wilson lay in the back of the van.

'Marcus? Answer me or I'll shoot your nuts off.' She thrust the gun between his trussed legs. Wilson whimpered in response and tried to shuffle away from the gun.

'You may have been a piece of shit in life, but in death, you're going to become the portal that allows Her to come into this world.'

Marcus groaned.

'I know, I know,' Mistress Hel said. 'I know you don't understand. All you need to know is this...' She climbed into the back of the van and lowered her voice. 'It's going to be painful. Imagine all the pain you put me through, and Johnny here, and all those other poor kids. Now multiply that a thousandfold, and then coat it in flaming shards of razor wire, and you're starting to get an idea of how bad it's going to be for you. It will only last a moment, but it's going to feel like an eternity.'

She got out of the van and Johnny slammed the doors. Harry considered bolting.

'You can run,' Mistress Hel said, as though reading his mind. 'Go on. Give me your phone and run away. Try and foil my plans. Go back to your girlfriend. Enjoy the last moments of life as you know it.'

She stood there, gun lowered. She meant it. He could go. Harry's mind reeled. He tried to calculate the odds of him getting onto the police, convincing them there was a massive truck bomb headed for the Ekka. Harry cursed.

'Didn't think so,' she said. 'You can ride up front with us.'

Harry registered the glow of the lights before he saw any of the actual rides, and his heartbeat quickened. Johnny hadn't said a word, despite Harry's attempts to engage him in conversation. From time to time Mistress Hel would jab the pistol into Harry's ribs, to warn him against pushing too hard. He could feel his phone in his pocket, but couldn't see him getting an opportunity to use it. When they exited the freeway, Harry saw the top of the Ferris wheel.

'So, this goddess, does she have a name?' Harry said.

'Not one that can be pronounced by humans.'

'Must make it awkward at dinner parties.'

Traffic was snarled around the exhibition ground, Ekka traffic and the people who didn't realise the Ekka was on, or who had forgotten, and found themselves trapped. On top of that, they were in a police van so everyone was driving extra safe, which was making matters worse.

'Mistress, should I flick on the lights and sirens?' Johnny said.

She checked her watch. 'No need.'

Eventually they cleared the gridlock. Johnny pulled into the RNA Showgrounds and stopped at the gate. He wound down his window as a young constable approached his side of the truck. Harry felt the gun in his ribs again.

'Smile,' Mistress Hel said. 'Say nothing. Or I'll shoot her in the face.'

'Hey,' the cop said.

'Hey.'

'What's this all about?'

'Got the special guests for the fundraising thing. Lilith Sweeney and Harry Hendrick.'

The constable checked her clipboard, folded back a couple of pages, ticked off their names with a pen.

'They needed an Incident Response van?' She looked from Harry to Mistress Hel. Harry tried to send a warning to her through force of will alone.

'Dunno. Someone probably screwed up. You know how it is.'

The constable gave Johnny a wry smile. 'Yep, same shit,

different day, am I right? You need someone to clear the way?'

'Nah. I can handle it.'

The constable waved them on and Johnny flicked on the hazard lights and crawled through the crowd.

CHAPTER 44

Don Clack felt like he was going to vomit. All around him, men in tuxedos paraded their trophy wives. The grog flowed freely. It was turning out to be a hell of a successful night, despite his initial reservations. But there were far too many familiar faces from a scene Clack had left behind years ago. Many of them recognised him and he could see in their eyes that they were freaked out too. It wasn't helping that Marcus Wilson was nowhere to be found. Had Marcus been caught and turned? He'd certainly have plenty of motivation to blow the lid off the whole ring. Clack had thought about leaving, but every time he did, the cuts on his back flared and his body was filled with this strange calming sensation. It was that kinky bitch. She'd done something to him.

His phone buzzed in his pocket: *Showtime.*

Clack had no idea what 'Showtime' meant, and didn't recognise the number, but at the same time he felt compelled to walk up to the low stage at the front of the room. He felt sweaty. The hairs on the back of his neck stood on end. The cuts on his back pounded in time with a throbbing in his genitals. He salivated in anticipation.

Clack climbed the stairs to the stage and stood in front

of the microphone. 'Ladies and gentlemen, if you could just take your seats,' he said. He had no idea where these words were coming from. He tried to walk off stage. He imagined himself walking off stage, but then found himself still in front of the mic, the crowd looking expectantly at him. Clack wiped the sweat out of his eyes, and grinned. He wanted to scream. He wanted to run. But he was rooted to the spot.

'Thank you so much for joining us and thank you so much for your support of the Lilith Foundation. For those who don't know me, I'm Don Clack, the secretary of Australian United Workers. Does anyone here like magic?'

A few rowdy voices called out.

'Great. Because we've got a magic show for you. Can you fellas at the back get the doors?'

At the back of the room, two guys pulled the huge hangar-style doors open. Headlights flooded the room. Guests had their phones out, and were chattering excitedly. Clack now realised why the room had been laid out with a wide corridor down the middle, leading to what he'd assumed was a dance floor in front of the stage. As the police van entered the room, it put its flashers on and issued a short blast from the sirens. A woman barked a short scream, and people laughed. Clack wanted to scream too but instead he grinned.

The van pulled to a stop in front of the stage. The headlights turned off, and Clack caught a glimpse of Mistress Hel through the glass. His legs felt weak.

'Ladies and gentlemen, it's my great pleasure to introduce to you – Mistress Hel!'

As they pulled into the pavilion, Harry saw Don Clack on the small stage at the front of the room. A couple of hundred of people sat at tables around the room, smiling and clapping. He rubbed his face.

'What is wrong with these people?' Harry said.

'I told you,' Mistress Hel said, 'most of the time you don't need magic to get people to do what you want. In this case all it took was a few crates of wine.' She placed a gloved hand on Harry's and whispered in his ear, 'It's not even very good wine.'

Johnny gave the siren a quick whoop. The people closest to the van let out cries of surprise, then cheered.

'Park right in the middle of the pentagram, sweets,' Mistress Hel said.

Harry quickly surveyed the scene. Multiple bottles of wine on pretty much every table, and wait staff making sure the tables stayed well stocked.

'Do all these people deserve to die, Lily? The waiters? The kitchen hands? The people outside? You're going to kill hundreds, maybe thousands.'

'Didn't you hear, Harry?' she said. 'We all die. What's important is using our lives to make a difference.'

Outside the van, the crowd applauded and cheered. Mistress Hel slid her gun into her pocket. She climbed over Harry, giving him a peck on the forehead before she opened the door and got out of the van. Johnny pulled out a phone, an old Nokia. It chimed as he powered it up. His thumb rested on the 'Send' button.

Clack felt light-headed as Mistress Hel ascended to the stage and gave him a kiss on the cheek. Someone wolf-whistled.

'You've done well,' she whispered. 'Not long now.'

'I have sinned,' Clack said. 'I give my life for the Goddess.'

'All in good time.'

Clack took a step back as Mistress Hel grabbed the microphone. 'Good evening, ladies and gentlemen. How are we?'

Drunken cheers.

'That's great. Could we get the doors closed, please? A bit of privacy?'

Wait staff around the room moved to the doors and closed them. Mistress Hel pulled the gun from her pocket. There was some nervous laughter.

'Now, I'm going to give this gun to Don here,' she said, and handed it over. 'And he's going to shoot anyone who gets out of their seat.'

More nervous laughter. Near the front of the room, a ruddy-faced man pushed up out of his seat. Clack moved. It felt as though he was floating above himself, able only to watch as he strode off the stage, gun out.

'What if I need to...'

Bang. Real screams now, as blood and gore jetted from the back of the man's head. Clack felt a surge of adrenaline and a burst of almost orgasmic pleasure, as he watched the dead man stumble back over his chair.

One table over, a woman made for the door. Clack twisted and fired. Bang. The round caught her in the back, coming out her chest and severing her string of pearls. They bounced across the linen tablecloth, landing alongside spots of her blood. Again, Clack felt a surge of pleasure flow through him, from his groin to his fingertips.

'STAY. IN. YOUR. SEATS,' Mistress Hel bellowed.

Clack spun, looking for someone else to stand up so

he could shoot them. He knew it was wrong. He knew he would go to prison, if he lived that long, but it felt so good. A man towards the back of the room made to stand up, then saw Clack's gun trained on him. Clack's finger tightened on the trigger and the man dropped back into his seat.

'Let that one live. For now. Give me the gun,' Mistress Hel said. Clack handed it to her. 'Drag those two onto the platform. Quickly, while the blood is still warm.'

A silence descended on the room. People were crying. Outside there were sirens, and screams. Clack made his way between the tables to grab the bodies.

'When we came in, I noticed a few of you taking photos with your phones. Please feel free to keep doing so. Take photos. Video. Stream it. Don't forget the hashtag. It's important people know what happened here. That they understand. Call your loved ones and say goodbye. Jesus, call the cops if you like – I mean, the ones who aren't already sitting in this room. And make sure you tell them that I have a massive truck bomb,' she gestured to the van, 'which I'll detonate if they get within five hundred metres of me.'

'Give me the phone, Johnny,' Harry said.

Outside the van, Clack dragged the bodies through the crowd. Johnny stared through the windscreen. His finger remained poised over the green button.

'Johnny? I know what you're feeling. For once I can say that and know it to be true. But she doesn't control you. You are in control of you. I know it seems hard to believe right now, but it's true.'

Harry stared at the swallows on the back of his hands.

'Do you really want all these people to die? That woman out there. Did she deserve to die?'

Clack dumped the woman's body in front of the truck. Harry wondered if Johnny could even hear him. A tear leaked from the corner of Johnny's eye and ran down his cheek, dropping onto his shirt.

'Just give the phone to me, Johnny, and I swear, I'll take responsibility. She'll never hurt you again.'

Johnny looked at Harry. It seemed as though it took all of his strength to perform that simple action. Johnny's hands were shaking badly, his thumb lightly brushing the Send button. Harry reached for the phone.

Then the door opened behind him and Clack yanked him out of the van. Harry fell to the ground, landing in a pool of blood.

'Come up here, Harry,' Mistress Hel said.

Harry pushed himself up, but remained sitting, blood soaking into his pants.

Mistress Hel pouted. 'Come on,' she said. 'You're not going to make me beg, are you?'

Clack dragged Harry along the ground until he found his feet and walked up on stage.

'Ladies and gentlemen, ace reporter Harry Hendrick,' she said. Clack clapped as though he was at the football. The only other sound was hysterical laughter somewhere in the room.

'Now, I'm going to need some volunteers from the audience, to add to these two,' Mistress Hel said, gesturing to the bodies. Blood spouted from each – as well as the pools near the wounds, it was running in rivulets, marking out a shape around the van.

'Any volunteers?' Mistress Hel said. 'No takers? Okay then,' she said, and pulled from her back pocket the notebook she'd taken from Wilson's safe. She held it up for everyone to see. 'This belongs to Marcus Wilson, who is trussed up in the back of the van.'

Shocked cries greeted the announcement.

'Yes, the great Marcus Wilson. Hero of Brisbane. And paedophile. He raped me. He raped my colleague in the van there. And many others. And he took photos. And he sold those photos. He was very particular about record-keeping.' She threw the book to Harry, who caught it.

'Choose two names,' Mistress Hel said. 'I've highlighted the ones who are here tonight.'

'No.'

Mistress Hel sighed. 'Come on, Harry! These men, if you can call them men, these monsters, don't deserve your sympathy.'

Harry stared at the ground, mind racing. He had nothing. No way out. No cavalry rushing to save him.

'And you know what's worse,' Mistress Hel said. 'It's not just them. It's not just those who are raping the kids, looking at photos and videos of monsters raping kids, it's the people around them. Those who turn a blind eye. Those who facilitate their sick needs.'

Harry gritted his teeth and threw the book on the floor.

'Fine. Spoilsport. Don, bring me someone. Anyone.'

Clack grabbed the man next to him, dragging him away from his screaming partner.

'Please… please!' he cried.

Clack dragged him to the back of the van, and pressed his face against the floor. Mistress Hel got down from the stage and sauntered over to the man. She pressed her boot against his neck and aimed at his head.

'All right!' Harry screamed. He dropped to his knees, frantically pored through the book, stopping on the first highlighted name he came to. 'Rick. Rick Tay.'

'Would Rick Tay like to come forward and take this man's place?'

Johnny watched in the side mirror as a man rose from his seat and moved slowly to where Mistress Hel was waiting for him. Rick Tay. Thick head of silver hair. Sharp tailored charcoal suit. Tanned. He begged, he cried, he apologised. Johnny couldn't hear all the words but he could see it in the man's face and in his gestures. Mistress Hel nodded as though she understood. Johnny shivered in anticipation. He'd seen that false understanding before, many times during his training.

'Kneel,' Mistress Hel said. 'Kneel and kiss my boot, and I'll forgive you.'

Rick Tay dropped to his knees, holding his hands together in prayer. Mistress Hel held her boot out. Rick dropped his head. At the last moment, Mistress Hel pulled her foot back, lowered her gun and shot him in the back of the head. Harry jerked at the gunshot and ran his fingers through his hair.

The ritual was repeated. A man chosen from the book. This time he tried to run. Clack shot at him and hit him in the shoulder, then the back. Clack dragged him to the front of the room and laid him on a point of the pentagram, where Mistress Hel finished him off.

Mistress Hel stared at the body, muttering incantations under her breath. As she spoke, she walked around the truck. Johnny heard every word. He thought again of Marcus Wilson staring up at him. He thought of that horrible afternoon at Wilson's house, the day his world collapsed. Tears streamed down his face.

Get ready, my love.

Johnny jumped. He looked out the window and Mistress Hel was smiling at him. He checked the phone, and nodded.

CHAPTER 45

Harry clutched his head. For the first time since he was freed, the cuts on his back ached, as did the tattoos on his hands. Whatever Mistress Hel was doing, it was working. Across the room, a woman in a shimmering sequined dress slumped off her chair and hit the ground, spasming on the floor. Two tables over, a man vomited red across the white tablecloth; Harry wasn't sure if it was blood or wine or both. The screaming had stopped, and most of the crying. Around the room, hundreds of pairs of eyes stared at Mistress Hel as she completed her circuit of the van. The bloody pentagram on the floor was almost complete. The symbols around the edge pulsed with darkness. The van itself seemed to shudder in and out of existence. The air felt heavy and oppressive, as though a thunderstorm was about to hit.

'Fight it,' Harry muttered to himself, and flexed his hands into fists.

Over the buzzing in his ears, he could just make out the drone of a chopper overhead. Through the windows, he saw a spotlight light up the bitumen.

'Tell those fuckers to back off or I'll blow the truck!'

No-one seemed to do anything, but next minute the chopper moved away.

'Can you feel it, Harry?' she said.

He could. The oppressive feeling was growing. The ground vibrated with blackness. More flowed from the dead. It pressed in at the edges of Harry's vision.

'She's on her way. Don, your time has come.'

Clack walked over and knelt on the pentagram's fifth point. Harry waited for Mistress Hel to level the gun at him, but it stayed by her side.

'Don! Run for it!' Harry called.

Don Clack pulled his jacket open, gving no sign he'd heard. In the top pocket was a scalpel. He took it out and removed it from its packaging. Contemplated it. At the doorway, Lee-Anne appeared, eyes red, mascara running.

'Donny! Wait! You silly bastard!'

Clack looked at her and smiled. 'It'll be okay, honey.'

He screamed as he drove the blade into his guts, but the expression on his face was one of pure ecstasy. Lee-Anne ran for him and Mistress Hel made no move to stop her. Harry ran for him too, but by the time they reached him, Clack had stabbed himself half-a-dozen times, the scalpel wedged between his ribs. Harry cradled Clack as Lee-Anne held her hands to his belly. Blood gushed between her fingers, spilling across the ground and following the path Mistress Hel had made for it, until the pentagram was complete.

'See you in the next life, Harry Hendrick,' said Mistress Hel. She nodded at Johnny.

Johnny had thought he would feel happiness when this moment arrived. He pictured Wilson in the back of the van, hearing the gunshots and the screams, probably pissing his pants. It's what he had wanted. He'd wanted Wilson to understand what real fear was. But now, he felt nothing more than a growing sense of dread. Making someone else scared hadn't done anything to allay his own fears. He'd wanted closure. This… this felt like the birth of something.

Then Mistress Hel looked into Johnny's eyes, and all doubt evaporated. She was beautiful. Radiant. She nodded once. The signal.

He looked at the phone. The compulsion to obey was so powerful he didn't even consider the fact that this was the end of his life. He thumbed the green button.

Nothing.

Johnny blinked. Tried again. Nothing.

He stared at the phone for a moment, trying to figure out what was going on. Sweat trickled down the nape of his neck. He was close to panic. He scanned the small screen. There was something different. At the top of the screen, where he should have seen at least four dots, there were none.

No signal. *No signal?*

He looked up. Mistress Hel was staring at him, furious. 'Do it!'

'It won't…' Then he realised she wouldn't be able to hear him through the glass. He got out of the truck, heart hammering in his chest. In his panic he dropped the phone, and fumbled before scooping it up. He looked up, for the first time seeing the swirling mass of darkness over their heads.

'N-no signal,' he said.

'What?'

'No signal.'

He showed her the phone. She took it from him, stared at the screen.

'You told the world you had a bloody big bomb,' Harry said. 'Did you think the cops would let you detonate it?'

CHAPTER 46

Mistress Hel screamed in frustration and threw the phone to the floor, then went for Harry.

'Come on,' she said, jabbing the gun at him. She dragged him to his feet, and pushed him towards a set of double doors at the back of the room.

'Go!' she screamed. 'Move it!'

Harry felt Mistress Hel's hand entwined in his collar, and the hard steel of the gun barrel at the back of his head. She pushed Harry through the double doors into a deserted kitchen. The bright fluorescents dimmed, then exploded in a shower of sparks. Mistress Hel cried out. Harry shielded his head against the falling glass, then risked a look over his shoulder.

Mistress Hel was deathly pale, except for dark circles under her eyes. A shroud of dark, smoky cloud trailed her. Just looking at it made Harry feel nauseous. The pain in his ribs and back intensified. He dragged his eyes away as they reached the fire exit.

The door opened onto an alleyway. Sirens blared from seemingly every direction, and the helicopter droned above them. Harry could hear someone screaming and someone else talking through a loudhailer, but they both sounded a long way off.

'This way,' Mistress Hel said.

'Just give it up,' Harry said. 'The police are going to be...'

'MOVE!'

The alley opened into a thoroughfare, the ground littered with abandoned showbags and chip packets. A can of Coke rolled across the bitumen, spilling its contents. Wind rustled through trees bordering a litter-strewn picnic area. Someone's day pack was lying on the ground next to a bruised apple and a pair of kids' shoes. The thoroughfare was blocked by two police cars, nose to nose, lights flashing. Harry could just make out heads peering over the bonnet. He scanned the top of the grandstand, looking for snipers.

Mistress Hel dragged Harry away from the police cars towards a tunnel under the railway line. Their footsteps reverberated on the tiled walls. The swirling black cloud followed in their wake, as though tethered to the crown of Mistress Hel's head. The lights flickered.

A body lay on the ground. A man, maybe thirty, face down. His white shirt was covered in blood and footprints. Trampled to death, in the panic that must've followed those first gunshots. Harry peered over his shoulder. There were police everywhere. Mistress Hel pressed the gun into his neck.

'Oh Jesus,' Harry said. He looked down as they passed the body. Black mist flowed from his eyes and mouth, drifting towards Mistress Hel. There were more bodies ahead, at least two, each trailing filmy black mist from their mouths and eyes. The lights flickered, then died. In the darkness someone... something... took a shallow breath.

And then another. Darkness pressed in on Harry's vision. He wanted to scream, but he was too scared.

'Are you beginning to understand now?' Mistress Hel asked, then pushed him forwards again.

As they emerged from the tunnel, cops in riot gear advanced across the oval to their right. Mistress Hel pushed Harry in the opposite direction, parallel to the train line, up Sideshow Alley. The bloated, cancerous cloud of darkness hovered behind them.

'Stay back!' Mistress Hel roared, and fired in the direction of the riot police, even though they were clearly out of range. She pushed Harry past a rickety rollercoaster, the carts still trundling along the tracks with nobody on them. As Mistress Hel changed direction, the cloud of darkness swung over the tracks. A cart pitched off the rails, slamming into the ground.

Harry blinked. Had he really seen that? Mistress Hel may not have completed the ritual back at the venue, but she'd done something. She still muttered under her breath, words that had no meaning to him.

A green skeleton laughed and jiggled back and forth outside the Ghost Train. Mistress Hel waved a hand at it and the lights running across the top of the ride shattered. The skeleton burst into flames. Mistress Hel panted in Harry's ear, her incantations punctuated by sobs.

Up on the train line, Harry saw a flash of blue. Cops swarmed along the platform, staring at them. There was another exit ahead, but it too would most likely be blocked by police. Behind him, the cops he'd seen streaming across the oval were now halfway up Sideshow Alley. Mistress Hel was running out of options.

Cops converged from the train tracks, the exit on

Harry's right, and behind them on Sideshow Alley. The closest were about fifty metres away, screaming at Mistress Hel to put down the gun, *put down the fucking gun*. Mistress Hel spun around, backing Harry towards the last ride on the alley – the House of Mirrors. Darkness swirled over their heads.

'There's no way out, Lily,' Harry said. 'Is it worth dying for?'

Mistress Hel smiled, and dragged Harry into the House of Mirrors. *The Amazing Mesmerising Mirror Maze! Don't get lost!*

The door at the back of the ticket booth was open. Tickets cascaded across the floor. The entrance to the mirror maze was grimy with the passage of time, but there was a big, red handprint in the middle.

She dragged Harry inside and he saw himself a thousand times over: gaunt face, red eyes, crazy hair. Blood stained his chin. Mistress Hel didn't look much better. Every ragged gasp of breath was agony. His legs throbbed.

Mistress Hel pushed him deeper into the maze, the passageway so narrow it touched both his shoulders. He remembered coming in here as a kid with his dad. They'd gotten separated. He was at an age when he should have known better, but part of him still believed the stories tacked up on the hoarding outside, about kids being lost forever. He made it out eventually, frantically wiping away the tears when he saw his dad waiting for him, hands on hips. His dad was a patient man. Over a dagwood dog and a Coke he'd explained the mystery of the mirror maze, a hidden doorway that let you out from what was basically one pathway that followed a loop.

A gunshot rang out. Glass shattered. Harry flinched.

Mistress Hel laughed, the laughter morphing into sobs. Harry's ears rang.

'You know, we could have some fun in here, Mr Hendrick. One last fling. On the house.'

'You failed, Lily,' Harry said, sounding more confident than he felt. She pushed him on. The lights flickered. Harry and Mistress Hel were bloated pigs. They were rake thin. Short. Tall. With each twist and turn, Mistress Hel looked paler, less substantial. The dark cloud darker, more real. The tattoo on Harry's neck warmed.

'Oh, Harry.'

The lights flickered, only came back on at half strength. Mistress Hel stopped pushing him. The gun barrel rested against his neck. She panted in his ear. Outside, the cops were calling out, telling Lily Sweeney they just wanted to talk to her. Mistress Hel muttered incantations under her breath. Harry reached into his pocket, fingering the handle of the scalpel he'd pulled from Don Clack's ribs. He took a deep breath.

'How many did I kill?' she said. 'At the van, I mean?'

Harry was caught off guard. His mind reeled, replaying the scene. 'F-five,' he said.

'That's right. How many points does a pentagram have?'

'Five.' He let his weight drop slowly against her. They were squeezed in tight between the mirrors. In their reflection he could see her eyes peering out from behind his head, darkness swirling around her in the confined space. It was almost intimate. 'What's your point?'

'I only need one more. A special one. Like you.'

He jerked away from her as she fired. Heat bloomed in his chest. The stench of cordite filled the cramped passageway. He forced himself to his feet. Blood splattered the front of his shirt, ran down his pants, shoes and onto the careworn floor. The world spun, lost contrast, but Harry bit into his cheek, forcing himself to stay conscious. He kicked back at where he guessed she was and heard a satisfying grunt, then stumbled forwards, trailing bloody smears across the mirrors.

The lights flared. In the reflection he saw Mistress Hel, grinning and pointing the gun at him. Behind her, swirling darkness and then – there! The goddess, the demon, whatever the fuck it was. And if he'd thought Mistress Hel was beautiful and terrible, she paled into insignificance in comparison. It was like staring into the abyss, staring into calamity, staring into a tsunami or category five cyclone. Harry felt his bladder go, and warmth flooded his legs.

The lights dropped out, then flickered on again. Harry tried to run, but his legs gave way. He collapsed and clawed his way around the next corner.

Gunfire boomed again, and the mirror above Harry shattered. The pieces fell all around him. He dragged his body over them, not feeling much more pain. The chest wound drowned everything else out.

C'mon, Harry! C'mon!

Mistress Hel laughed. She muttered under her breath. Harry heard every word as though she were whispering in his ear. The words were... they were *wrong*. Harry couldn't think of any other way to describe it.

He looked up, his sweat-soaked hair clinging to his face. Ahead, the maze doubled back on itself. The lights flickered and he saw himself crawling along the floor, Mistress Hel barely a couple of metres behind him, still trailing the terrifying blackness. He was never going to escape. He thought of Dave. And Sandy. Most of all Bec. No trip to London for him. No more exclusives.

The lights failed completely. And yet as his eyes adjusted to the darkness, he realised there was light coming from somewhere. Probably gaps in the roof.

Mistress Hel shuffled around the corner. The thing, the dark thing, was wrapped around her like a shawl. Its face swam over Mistress Hel's. When the eyes converged, Harry had never seen anything so beautiful or terrifying. And still she hissed those horrible, insane words. Harry thrust his hands over his ears to block it out. It made no difference.

Fight her, Harry! Or you're fucking dead meat!

Harry blinked the sweat out of his eyes.

'Now or never.'

Harry grabbed the scalpel by the handle, pulled his legs underneath him, ignoring the pulsing pain in his chest, and launched himself at Mistress Hel, scalpel thrust in front of him like a sword.

Mistress Hel's eyes widened and she fired again, the sound deafening in the confined space. Harry felt his leg go numb. The impact threw him off balance and he tumbled towards Mistress Hel. The scalpel buried itself between her ribs and he let go of it to embrace her. She pressed the gun into Harry's guts. *Click, click, click.* Mistress Hel's eyes widened. Her lips parted as though for one last kiss.

He wanted to hold onto her, to make sure, but his strength was draining faster than the blood pouring out of his wounds. With his last ounce of strength he pushed up on the scalpel blade, ripping her open on one side. She screamed.

Harry's legs buckled and gave way. He fell backwards into a broken mirror. The shadow grew darker, more defined, and swirled faster. Harry thought he was going to pass out.

Mistress Hel shook, eyes wide. She pressed her hands to her wound. Blood pumped thickly between her fingers, pooling underneath her.

I only need one more. A special one.

'Oh fuck,' Harry whispered. 'I've helped it find a way into this world.'

Harry's eyes drooped. He forced them open. Had to see.

Mistress Hel staggered, hands slapping against the broken mirrors, painting them with her blood. There was a sound. A deep vibration. The world began to spin. Mistress Hel looked truly scared for the first time.

'I almost…'

Another vibration. Harry gagged. Mistress Hel shook her head.

'I can't…' she cried. Despite everything, Harry wanted to hold her. He could barely move, let alone do anything to save her. He looked at the bloody scalpel in his hand.

'Please…'

Please.

Another intense vibration, so strong, Harry thought his head would explode. He heard thunder, but he knew it wasn't thunder, it was something he couldn't comprehend. This was the only way his brain could process it.

'Okay,' Mistress Hel whispered. She dropped onto all fours, grabbing shards of broken mirror and shoving them into her mouth, one after the other. She cried, then screamed. Blood poured from her mouth. She crawled along the passageway, collecting all the pieces she could find and swallowing them.

'Please,' Harry said. 'No.'

Please. No.

Mistress Hel stopped, and dropped back onto her haunches. Her mouth was shredded. She was struggling to breathe. When she thrust her head back, shards of glass pressed through her throat. How could she even be alive?

A final, terrifying vibration, carrying a million screams. Mistress Hel opened her mouth. The air crackled. Her jaw strained. The shadow pulsated. Mistress Hel's eyes rolled up into her head. The shadowy mist surged down her throat, into her gut. Her throat swelled and Mistress Hel gagged. She slapped the broken mirrors so hard she tore her arms open.

The room quieted. Mistress Hel staggered against the broken glass. She looked at Harry. Smiled. Blinked.

Blood oozed from the corner of her eyes. From her forehead, like sweat. Blood seeped from every pore. She looked at Harry, eyes black.

'Please…'

Then the world turned red.

EPILOGUE

'Do you ever get sick of hurting yourself?'

Dave stood at the door, Bec by his side. She looked pale and drawn, but her face lit up with a smile when she saw Harry was awake.

'Hey guys,' Harry croaked. He reached for the glass of water by the bed.

Bec took a seat beside him and gripped his hand. They kissed.

'Well, I'd love to hang around but,' Dave said, gesturing to his uniform, 'you may have noticed that I'm working. I'll catch you later.'

'Thanks, Dave,' Bec said.

He waved and disappeared back through the doorway.

'How are you doing?'

'A bit better. The doctor says I was extremely lucky. Anyone would think getting shot twice and surviving was rare.'

She squeezed his hand. 'And you got blown up too, remember?'

Harry nodded. He had told Bec what had happened. And Sandy too. Sandy said it sounded as though the demon or goddess or whatever it was had tried to occupy

Mistress Hel's body, but the body couldn't take the strain. The police said that Mistress Hel must've had a suicide vest on. They'd found her severed head at the scene, and had helpfully informed Harry that's what happens to suicide bombers. Harry wondered what they would think when they discovered there were no traces of explosives at the scene. Probably that there was some new type of untraceable explosive on the market. He would worry about that if it happened.

'Has Johnny tried to contact me?' Harry said.

Bec shook her head. 'Not that I know of.'

Johnny had been taken away by police, charged with conspiracy to commit a terrorist act and possession of a weapon of mass destruction. Harry wasn't sure when fertiliser bombs had gotten placed in that category, but in this case it was probably fair enough. The terrorism expert on the TV had said it was up there in size with the Oklahoma bombing, and would probably have brought down the function venue, resulting in the loss of hundreds of lives. Phil said there was some hope Johnny could claim to have been manipulated by Mistress Hel. Harry considered what it had been like being under her spell. Manipulation didn't really cover it. He wanted a happy ending for them all, but in this case it wasn't likely. It could so easily have been him.

'How is Sandy going?'

One of the first things Harry had done after regaining consciousness was to call her and apologise again. She accepted it graciously.

Bec watched Harry, and understood what he really wanted to know. 'When Lily Sweeney's body couldn't accommodate the Goddess, it sort of catapulted back to wherever it came from. The door is shut. As far as Sandy can tell.'

Harry nodded and looked out the window. At times, he thought he could feel that terrible darkness descending on him, could feel it lurking in his peripheral vision. But maybe that was just the comedown, or some kind of psychic hangover. He rubbed the back of his neck.

On the TV bolted to the wall he saw a picture of Marcus Wilson flash up.

'... retired police officer Marcus Wilson survived the terrorist attack at the Brisbane Exhibition...'

Harry muted the sound.

'Some unfinished business there,' Bec said.

'Yeah, well, Phil called. He said police were swarming all over Wilson's place, so...'

'Good. It's the least I can do for Johnny.'

Harry looked out the window again. Blue sky. Light clouds. A beautiful winter's day. But something was wrong.

'There's something you're not telling me,' he said. He looked at Bec.

She smiled. 'My boss called just before. He says the London job is mine.'

Harry forced a smile. 'That's... that's great news. When do you leave?'

She gripped his hand. 'As soon as you're ready to come with me.'

ACKNOWLEDGEMENTS

Publishing a book is a team effort, and I have some fantastic people in my corner.

Thank you to:

The irrepressible Angela Meyer and the Echo team, along with editor Kylie Mason.

Alex Adsett – agent extraordinaire.

Tom Dullemond for another insightful beta read, and everyone who helped answer my weird and sometimes creepy research questions.

My parents for always believing in me.

My wife Amelia – you are my hero, now and always – and to Eamon and Aurora, who I find more amazing with each passing day.

And special thanks to you, dear reader, for coming on this ride with me. I hope you enjoyed it as much as I did.

A GUIDE FOR READING GROUPS

1. Did you learn anything new by reading *Bad Blood*? Has it changed your ideas about anything, or confirmed them?
2. *Bad Blood* has some confronting moments, in terms of violence and sex. Do you feel as though the author crossed the line at any point and, if so, when?
3. Do you feel that Harry has changed by the end of the novel? If so, in what way? Has he learned anything about himself or the other people in his life?
4. Harry becomes ensnared by Mistress Hel. How much of this is his doing, and how much hers? Could Harry have achieved his goals without becoming entrapped?
5. Mirrors play an important part in the beginning and ending of *Bad Blood*. Do you think this is just a useful plot device, or do the mirrors have a deeper, symbolic meaning?

Also by Gary Kemble

Shortlisted for the Ned Kelly Award for Best First Fiction

When washed-up journalist Harry Hendrick wakes with a hangover and a strange symbol tattooed on his neck, he shrugs it off as a bad night out.

When more tattoos appear — accompanied by visions of war-torn Afghanistan, bikies, boat people, murder, bar fights and a mysterious woman — he begins to dig a little deeper.

There's a federal election looming, with pundits tipping a landslide win for opposition leader Andrew Cardinal. Harry knows there's a link between these disturbing visions and Cardinal's shadowy past, and is compelled to right wrongs, one way or another.

Skin Deep is the thrilling, layered, genre-bending debut novel of Brisbane author and journalist Gary Kemble.

> With an intense and immediate sense of place, a cracking pace and a great everyman hero, *Skin Deep* is by turns thrilling and haunting, and will keep readers glued to the page – ANGELA SLATTER

> Not many ghost stories have this kind of immediacy, or tactility. No strange frissons or fleeting shadows here! It's all blood, drained batteries and murderous rage, stinking of bourbon in the subtropical humidity – TABULA RASA

> *Skin Deep* is a fine debut for both Kemble and Echo, which offers more than a passing nod to John Birmingham and Stephen King – BOOKS + PUBLISHING

Paperback	9781760406950
Epub	9781760069018
Kindle	9781760069025